MOHAMME

Тне
SECRET
of тне
MORISCO

A NOVEL

TRANSLATED BY CHRISTIAAN JAMES

Mohammed AlAjmi

The Secret of The Morisco (Novel)

Translated by: Christiaan James

© 2022 Dar Arab For Publishing and Translation LTD.

United Kingdom
60 Blakes Quay
Gas Works Road
RG3 1EN
Reading
United Kingdom
info@dararab.co.uk
www.dararab.co.uk

First Edition 2022
ISBN 978-1-78871-086-2

Copyrights © dararab 2022

دار عرب للنشر والترجمة
DAR ARAB FOR PUBLISHING & TRANSLATION

Text Edited by: Marcia Lynx Qualey
Cover & Text Design by: Nasser Al Badri
Cover Photo Source: AdobeStock_320869615, By Krafla

Table of Contents

Dedicated to

Robert G. Febin

You trail after the mapping of the stars

and traverse the waves of eastern mists,

where roots sprout without scent...

alike only to balms embedded since history's dawn.

Is the sunset logged in your ledgers?

Processions and punches and the acts of preachers...

are in the last drop of the ink.

From Margherita Viviani's poem *The Dice of the Bird* [1]

---

1. Poem translation courtesy of Dr. John Peate.

Historical Timeline

1609 (April): Philippe III issues edict expelling the Moriscos from Spain.

1610: Maronite fathers bring the first printing press from Rome to the Levant. It is housed at the Monastery of Saint Anthony of Qozhaya in northern Lebanon. It was a Syriac printing press and did not last long.

1613: Ahmad bin Qassim Al-Hajari, known as Afoukay, visits Holland on a diplomatic mission on behalf of the Saadian state in Morocco and meets the Dutch Arabist Thomas Erpenius, the first chaired professor of Arabic studies at the University of Leiden.

1618 (May): Beginning of the Thirty Years' War in the Holy Roman Empire.

1624 (November): Erpenius passes away. Professor Jacob Golius replaces him as chair for Arabic studies at the University of Leiden.

1628 (April): Death of Savary de Brèves, former French ambassador to the Ottomans. His Arabic type is transferred to the Imprimerie Royale in Paris.

1630: René Descartes meets Jacob Golius and becomes his student at the University of Leiden. The two become lifelong friends.

1637 (February): The battle of Lizard Point between the Spanish Armada and the armadas of Holland and England.

1641: Descartes publishes his *Meditations on First Philosophy*.

1642 (January): The death of Galileo Galilei.

1642 (August): Outbreak of the first civil war in England.

1642 (December): Death of Cardinal Richelieu, chief minister of Louis XIII.

Part 1

The English Prisoner

Over time, it became clear that the Morisco's secret concerned me and me alone. In any case, secrets, by their very nature, are emotional things that render you incapable of exercising sound judgment. And as my father would often say to my mother, "When one door closes, another window opens!"

Chapter 1

The ship made its way out to sea, slowly giving those standing on the dock one last chance to say their final goodbyes to loved ones as they departed Holland. Wearing his tall black hat, Mr. Jos barked at the stevedores, commanding them to bring back the carts they had used to haul the printing-press crates onto the ship. I had failed in my attempts to chip away at Mr. Jos' stubbornness, to convince him to sell us only the punches and matrices, but he insisted we purchase the entire press itself. He wasn't one to leave things to chance. And though I tried to tell him that the taxes would be exorbitant if I bought the entire apparatus, he simply responded that there were numerous ways to lower the burden (and even get around it altogether), but who would buy half a press from him?!

At least that's how he justified himself as he pushed away a homeless man clinging to his coat as he begged to be hired. I was about to give up entirely when he made me an offer: take the crates along with the wheeled, leather-bound containers. The deal cost me dearly, leaving me with just enough to cover the customs fees and royal taxes imposed by the king who—worrying he might be the last—was always trying to stay one step ahead of both merchants and Parliament.

Tulip mania was still the talk of the town, following the shocking price collapse of the rare bulbs just two weeks prior. On the port docks, I could see some of the men who had lost their minds after betting everything they owned in hopes of turning a quick profit. They stumbled and fumbled around aimlessly in their tattered clothing, conversing nonsensically with the fish wriggling out of the fishermen's nets and into baskets below, oblivious to the frigid cold that chilled even the most hardened of crewmen. Unlike these flowers, fishing had never betrayed the Dutch, not even for a day.

As the port of Amsterdam faded from view, I looked on excitedly while the faint weeping of women filled the air, attracting the attention of seagulls who gradually realized ours was just a merchant vessel and not a fisherman's boat. I looked around for the warmest spot I could find on the ship, thinking of my father. This printing press would turn his dream of becoming the first publisher of Arabic books in England into a reality. And while Cambridge University had beaten us to procuring Arabic typeset, they had been unable to put it to use. As for Oxford, they were still awaiting the return of Edward Pococke from Constantinople, which would make our press indispensable for printing their works in Arabic.

I began to think about just how long this journey would take. I glanced down at the Italian pocket watch that my mother had planned to give me on my 18th birthday, still two months away, but I told her I couldn't wait that long. A woman from the countryside—a wool worker—warned me to not flash my watch in sight of the sailors while on this journey. I picked a spot near this lady and her adolescent son, who was clutching a collection of sacks of lambswool that they had picked up in Amsterdam. She kept nattering on about "opportunities" and the "right moment" to seize them. "A stitch in time saves nine," she told him, noticing the gold watch I had just pulled out.

Ours is a prosperous family. Beyond the printing press, my father also owned the most important paper-making factory in southern England. And while our income from the press had dwindled over the last few years, due to the strict censorship imposed by Parliament, the demand for paper was up, especially overseas.

The ship set sail shortly after noon. My father advised me to hire a couple of dockworkers to protect the goods, but I thought that unnecessary. After all, the ship would be joining a large fleet of commercial vessels guarded by several warships. And it was a printing press after all. Who would think of stealing that?

On the fourth day after setting sail, cannon fire boomed. On the horizon, the sails of the Spanish Armada suddenly hove into view, and everyone began to fear the worst. Panic gripped us as the Dutch ships began to launch distress signals toward the English coastline. To this day, I still don't understand why England held back from sending any help to our fleet, which only emboldened the Spaniards to begin their attack shortly after dusk. Asking nothing in return, England delivered the entire convoy of ships to the Spanish. Was it because the king wanted to pass the new tax on ships?

Some ships sank during the night-long battle, while every single Dutch vessel was rendered incapacitated. Victorious, the Spanish towed the plunder back to their base in the Spanish Netherlands.

When it had become clear that our fates were sealed, many started hurling themselves overboard into the ocean, swimming toward the English coast in the distance, hoping to reach it before death reached them first. I too jumped, along with everyone else, but immediately realized I had made an absolute blunder. The English Channel was ice cold, and my body was not going to be able to save me, so I swam back to the ship. Convinced that the printing press was stronger than the Spanish Armada's cannons, I burrowed myself deep inside my father's dream.

Morning dawned on the fluttering of Spanish flags as soldiers rounded up passengers and detained them on the lower deck. It was slavery. In light of this turn of events, I doubt the wool worker's "stitch" had really saved her son—who was now holding on for dear life, despite his mother's attempts to push him overboard—any time at all.

The soldiers began to sweep through the ship. Two or three of them passed by me but took no notice. The container's huge size served me well, and I went undiscovered even when one of them began to rummage around in it a bit. Yet through it all, my hand clenched the hilt of my knife. Surrender was not an option.

For days, I remained hidden away. The only indication I had of the passage of time was sounds and shadows. When the ship finally arrived at the Spanish base, passengers were led down to the prison camp while the plunder was inventoried. With the crew swapped out, we departed again early the next morning. It seemed as if life had come to a standstill. I lived off the food I had on me and then scoured the area for anything edible until it had all run out. I reckoned time by my ability to withstand my hunger pangs. The first hours passed unnoticed, but gradually they grew longer, to the point I could not differentiate an hour from a day.

Time and everything around me began to merge frightfully, heaping me with blame for having rushed to purchase the printing press. A small hole in me quickly began to expand, swallowing up everything below. It was something akin to regret or anger. Or perhaps the end of a beautiful dream. I imagined a thousand Roberts, ganging up on me and saying: "What have you done to us?" And, as time went on, the reproof only grew crueller and the hunger more unbearable, to the point I began arranging the typeset with my hands. Words sprang to life to defend me against this barrage of accusations. Sometimes, nonsensical words that I conjured up myself seemed to empathize with me, saying: "No one could have known." Yet eventually the will to live overtook me, forcing me from my hiding spot so I could find something to eat.

I'm not the sort of person who can ignore hunger for too long. I'm not lean enough for that and, if anything, tend more toward stout. And while exhaustion doesn't show easily on my broad face, my stores of resilience might crumble at any moment, like a boat dashed upon the rocks by a swift-moving wave.

A deadly thirst seeped into my veins as I made my way toward one of the large staterooms. I hadn't even noticed the soldier who fell upon me and knocked me to the ground. He was just about to fire a shot from his musket when he realized that a bullet would have had no more worse effect on me than what terror and hunger had already inflicted. Or maybe he merely softened up once he realized I was just a kid, unable to even sprout a moustache.

He led me upstairs to the captain's quarters. His name was Captain Simon, and he took pity on me, ordering someone to fetch water and dried fruits along with some salted fish. After eating a few morsels, I told him, "I'm not Dutch." He advised me not to eat too much on an empty stomach, and I added, "My name is Robert. I'm an Englishman and my family works in printing and paper making. We bought printing equipment from a Dutch merchant." Taking a sip of water, I continued, "I wasn't able to have my horoscope read before this journey or else I would have happily spent a night or two more in the brothels of De Wallen!" The captain reminded me that the Church prohibited fortune telling, falling silent for a moment, before grumbling something about being unsure, however, of its position on whores.

The captain ordered me to be detained in one of the cabins, saying,

"I'll look into this further with you in the morning. You might be a spy."

"Spies don't starve themselves, Sir."

"We don't know that for sure," he said while gesturing for the soldier who had caught me, Álvaro, to lead me to my confinement.

I remained in detention until we reached the Spanish shores, although they interrogated me multiple times during the journey. I explained everything I knew about printing and Oriental languages: Arabic, Persian, and Turkish. And while they tried to get me to talk about cannons on English ships, Dutch navy rudders, and French firearms, I could only regale them with tales of printing presses, books, writers, ledgers, and what sells best in winter versus summer.

Some of them scoffed when I said, "Religious books don't sell well except in wintertime, and secular books only begin to fly off the shelves at the start of spring. As for calendars and astrology books, they do a brisk business all year long." The captain asked me to read his horoscope. "But I thought the Church prohibited that sort of thing!" I retorted. To which he responded, as he and Álvaro laughed, "Don't worry. I wouldn't have believed you anyhow."

When we sailed into port at San Sebastián, the soldiers handed me over to the authorities. Earlier, I had asked Simon if I could return to my country with the printing press, but he said, "If it were my decision, I would keep you as part of my crew. But we are pirates employed by the Spanish navy, and we're only commissioned to undertake limited naval assignments. I can't personally promise you anything, but I will recommend you to the guards."

"The king has no clue I was on this ship. Who would even know if you hid me among your men?"

He didn't answer. However, as he handed me over to the port guard, Álvaro whispered in my ear, "Royal Navy spies are on every ship."

I was taken to a cell in the harbour master's office where I remained for two weeks. In the beginning, I rehashed my tale and the story of the printing press to anyone who would listen, but despair soon pushed me to embellish more. At the very least, I wanted to entertain myself. At one point, I told the harbour master's aide that I had been searching for the book *The Seven Wise Masters*, spinning a whole yarn about that magical text and how three of King Sulaiman's *afreets* had whisked it away to Spain.

Another aide told me that I would be treated as a captive and consequently returned to the naval base with the rest of the prisoners. However, a few days later, it was relayed to me that my trial would take place in another city. Yet in the end, two members of the Santa Hermandad, known as "the green sleeves," interrogated me for less than a half hour before arriving at the conclusion that I was indeed spying on Spain and sought to harm its interests.

I didn't understand many of their questions, and it seemed to me that these two men, garbed in green robes and wearing strange hats embroidered with the Spanish crown bisected by a cross, were deflated and a bit disappointed. They had come such a long way from Madrid, and all for a young man who had never stepped foot on Spanish soil. For that reason alone—and to give their journey a sense of purpose—I had to have been extremely dangerous. I demanded to meet the prison warden, to complain about the manner of my interrogation. But one of the guards told me that a special council would pay me a visit soon to reinvestigate and pronounce a final judgment.

I waited three months for that council to arrive. Composed of two

Jesuit priests, the council hadn't really come to interrogate me, but rather to confirm my skills and abilities in operating a printing press. They offered to transfer me to a Jesuit monastery where I would remain effectively under house arrest, telling me that the monastery had procured my press from the Spanish navy, and they needed someone to run it. They had come to free me from jail in exchange for my labour.

I absolutely refused, demanding they return the printing press to me and send me on my way home. They retorted that no law on earth obligated a sovereign state to return the spoils of war. England itself wouldn't do such a thing. They tried to entice me in other ways, offering that I might join their college and work in the print house with a stipend, along with all the perquisites of belonging to their fraternal order, not to mention access to the monastery's library and other workshops. But I refused it all, and so they returned whence they had come, reminding me on their way out that, at any moment, I could ask for them again.

My longing to return to England wasn't what caused me to refuse the Jesuits' offer. Rather, it was something seemingly far more important at that moment. The Morisco had promised to divulge his secret to me, conditioned on my willingness to stay in prison and turn down the council's offer. Truth be told, I fully intended to sell his secret to the prison warden in exchange for my freedom and the printing press. That deal would certainly be better than the Jesuits' offer. However, over time it became clear that the Morisco's secret concerned me and me alone. And in any case, secrets, by their very nature, are emotional things that render you incapable of exercising sound judgment. And as my father often said to my mother, "When one door closes, another window opens!"

Chapter 2

Upon the clanging of the bell, which was rung by an aged convict standing at the Gate of Salvation, the prisoners rushed into the large chapel inside the tower. The old man called out for everyone to get inside before the gate was shut. "That gate hasn't saved you after all these ages!" said one, trying to goad him a bit. With a smile as serene as his gaze, he responded, "My salvation is in this bell!"

Though some were late to arrive, a man who looked to be in his early fifties had beaten them all there and was now reposing silently, tucked away in a distant corner as if he had made peace with all the commotion. Two days had passed since I'd been moved into his cell, and, in that time, we hadn't said more than a word to each other. Nor had I talked with any of the other five prisoners, not even a little. I was still indulging a hope that I would soon be released, perhaps in two or three days' time. One of the guards told me to thank the prison warden because he had put me in the dungeon closest to God. I didn't understand what he meant and began to ask myself, "What am I supposed to do here?"

The priest was laying out and arranging his paraphernalia while his acolytes, robed in white cassocks collared in silk and embroidered with yellow thread, lined up next to the altar, waiting for everyone to come in and settle down quietly. One of the acolytes was readying the organ that would accompany the hymns, and this time a sermon would follow the mass. Amidst all this hubbub, a gaggle of priests who had arrived early were offering guidance and other spiritual support to some of the prisoners.

I met with one of them before prayers began and explained my story in detail, telling him how I had ended up there. I thought perhaps he could arrange something on my behalf, but he only responded serenely that "God's wisdom will manifest itself in due time." The days passed quickly, and I still could not believe I was being held captive in Spain. Just a month earlier, I was in my father's printing house typesetting stationery for the English government!

The sermon began with hymns inspired by verses from the Bible. I noticed some of the prisoners weeping, perhaps out of regret or from sorrow, or maybe just yearning for their families back home. I mustered what I could to show my reverence and contrition as I settled into an entirely unfamiliar mass, hoping that someone's heart would take pity on me and help me get out. The nave was filled to the brim, but very few were actually paying attention. Later, I discovered that what drew the prisoners inside was the chapel's atmosphere, its spaciousness, and the pungent incense rising from the wax candles being paraded about by the priests, to make no mention of the majestically mordant dirges.

My cellmate kept his silence, breaking it only when he asked to make confession at the end of the sermon. I grew agitated as the priest leading the mass purposefully disregarded the man who stood amidst the hissing and goading of the other prisoners. "The Arab won't give up trying to confess!" one of them said. "What would he confess in the first place?" asked another.

At the end of the service, I dropped the charade of reverence and piety and walked over to the man they all called "the Arab" and introduced myself. "I'm Robert. I'm in the same cell as you."

He gestured as if to say, "Yes, I know who you are."

"Did the priest ignore you because you're an Arab?"

"But he didn't!" he said, looking into my eyes with a penetrating stare.

As he got up to leave, he saw that I was baffled and added, "I confessed. And the priest listened to my confession with his whole heart and guided me to my salvation."

That night, I went back to him and admitted that I hadn't understood everything he had said in the chapel. Despite having previously advised me against talking to him, one of my cellmates insisted that the Arab knew God better than any priest there.

When I went back to find out more from the Arab, he said, "The priest understands the battle I face. You need to understand what a person lives for."

"And what is your battle?"

"You would need a lifetime to know that. Your heart is still closed."

"Then will you allow me to spend time with you?"

"It's better that you keep your distance."

"I won't. But I'll take care to not be a nuisance."

He continued to avoid me and purposefully kept me at arm's length, sometimes gently, and at other times rather brusquely. I kept trying to get to the bottom of his story but each time I went to talk to him, I found myself telling my own story, though I admit he was the sole person in prison who had piqued my interest. On his forehead, above his right eye, there was an old, jagged scar. He told me it was courtesy of the French—not the Spaniards.

The Arab, Yusuf Al-Mouriski—the Morisco—was not one to talk at length about people and things. In his speech and description of the world around him, he was laconic. Yet he gathered up precise details, acutely observing the world, as if he were composing a *qasida* or arranging a gift to delight a king. Yet in the end, he did not offer up this gift.

Yusuf wasn't tall, though he was slightly taller than me. His body was rather weak—something that went unnoticed, given the ill-fitting clothes that he'd amassed without much thought from the piles of discarded clothing that arrived as new donations to the prison. I asked him about this once and he said, "The prisoners choose what they wear, and my clothes choose me."

His clothes. His medium-length beard, just beginning to be flecked with grey. And the faint wrinkles on his face, criss-crossing his light brown skin. All of these combined to create a certain majesty or splendour that you scarcely saw in all the paintings of the Apostle James. Indeed, you felt yourself before a great soul, one refined through suffering and tribulation, having mastered himself through stringent self-denial.

That afternoon, the prisoners were required to attend an exceptional event: an execution by hanging in the prison courtyard. Normally, executions took place in the main square in front of a large crowd. This time, however, the punishment would be meted out within the confines of the prison. Everyone gathered in the courtyard, around a gallows that had been hastily erected the night before. I was standing next to the Morisco as we awaited the execution.

"Have you ever thought that you were born in the wrong place,

Robert?"

"I don't know. Why do you ask?"

"Spain refuses to accept me as Spanish. Nor do the Spaniards regard me as Christian, and so I'm imprisoned here. I was born during a golden age in Spain, but the situation today remains unbearable for the Moors. The mountains of Alpujarra still fill my memory, even now. I was just a child when we came down from them, returning to Granada. Our family had chosen to make peace. Become Christian. And renounce the fight. But can the Moors ever truly wipe away their history?"

An icy silence descended over everything as the prison warden emerged onto an upper balcony. Everyone assumed he would deliver a speech, but Yusuf was sure that he would not. The prisoners wagered among themselves that the warden had never even opened a door for himself, something his assistants always did for him. Some thought it was because the whip never left his hand, but others saw him as arrogant. Pompous. Unwilling to touch anything that a prisoner's hand had grazed, or even a guard for that matter. Unsurprisingly, many of the guards loathed him. "To speak before a crowd, you have to exhibit at least a modicum of humility," Yusuf said, underscoring his earlier position.

"I am still perplexed by the slow rhythm of this country," he added, before saying, "Why is it that, in Spain, the dead are more alive than the living?"

"Why do you say that? I'm not following."

"Spain has begun to lose. She has made powerful enemies for herself and now wants to reform Catholicism, but Spain is flailing about because of the fanaticism of her kings."

I didn't understand what he was driving at, especially with the loud ruckus vying for my attention. Yet I found myself asking him, "Does it offend you when they call you 'the Arab'"?

He gazed out at the crowd for a moment before replying, "It doesn't bother me. They're not mocking me when they say 'the Arab'".

"What makes you so sure?" I asked, trying to make myself heard over the din.

"Because we're all equals here. Insults lose their value when differences melt away."

He asked me, "What are you accused of? You seem to be a young man. What brought you to Spain?"

I rehashed my story from the moment I left the port in Amsterdam until I ended up in prison, and he listened intently. I finished up just as the condemned man began to dangle from the gallows. As we stood up, Yusuf the Morisco and "the Saltman" made the sign of the cross, and Yusuf asked me, "So, you know Arabic? Would you like to speak it together?"

"I don't know. Whatever you like."

"Does the warden know?"

"I don't know. I haven't met him yet."

"Surely he does, and that's why he threw you in with me, but I don't imagine you'll stay long in prison."

"What makes you say that?"

"Just a hunch. Perhaps you know him more than I do."

From his response, it seemed he was keeping his guard up, so I pushed him a bit more: "Are you suspicious of me?"

He didn't respond right away, but after we returned to our cell, he asked, "How did you learn Arabic?"

I told him about my grandfather, Owen Febin, who had been captured by Arab and Turkish corsairs in the Mediterranean long ago and was enslaved for seven years, finally managing to escape to Spain, where he was welcomed as a hero for commandeering an Ottoman vessel and liberating dozens of Spanish captives. For that feat, the king personally summoned him and bestowed honours upon him before sending him back to England. During that time, he had learned Arabic and Turkish and so had his family.

Likewise, I told him about our family's involvement in printing and paper-making. He started to ask me about it, and about the difference between printed books and texts copied by hand. It was clear that he preferred hand-copied books. In his view, "A printing press churning out hundreds of copies in mere days is incapable of replicating the soul of a book."

"It's just a matter of time and familiarity. Nothing more," I said. Then, trying to change the subject, I asked, "What made you bring up Spain this morning?"

I should say that, in addition to his close attention to his surroundings, the Morisco was equally careful in his speech, as if he were fully aware that his present situation could deteriorate at any moment. His caution was natural, given the disappointments and vagaries of fate that had worn him down along the way and left his options in life quite limited. He had a propensity for using words and expressions layered in meaning, which meant that failing to understand his intentions was better than guessing at something he had not implied. Indeed, prison is a trial of the absolute limits of one's humanity. The prisoner is its raw material, either to be refashioned as human or moulded into beast. And when that prisoner does manage to hold onto his humanity, then poetry, art, and prayer become his last fortresses of strength. I discussed all these thoughts, and the meaning of the Morisco's words, as I spoke with my other cellmates.

I repeated my question to Yusuf, but he didn't respond until I had nearly given up hope he would. All he said was, "Because I love Spain." As we drifted off to sleep, I could hear him say, "When freedom is absent, there is no legitimate way to express one's love for anything."

I didn't fully grasp what he meant, but he added something about the libellous propaganda against Spain churned up by France and the Protestants, and about how the French authorities had encouraged him to write reports exposing the Spaniards' strategic weaknesses and barbarity, which they in turn used to blackmail him later. In fact, he had never considered it too far-fetched that it was the French who double-crossed him, ultimately leading to his arrest. And all just to oppose Spain's serious attempts at reforming its past. Execution behind prison walls (not in public squares, as was normally the case) was just one of these Catholic reforms.

I argued that he didn't need to constantly reaffirm his loyalty to Spain in front of me, as if the warden's watchful eye was always on him. I asked him, "How can you love a people who hunted you relentlessly?" He answered, "When you love the land, you love its people, too." When I asked if that was why he hadn't left Spain, he dove into a long digression about the suffering of his people, the Moors, and what befell them after the fall of Granada. He spoke as if he were Muslim, and in the end I told him I could not tell whether he were Muslim or Christian.

The Morisco repudiated Islam forward and backward, describing it as a fabricated religion. But I still recall one time when we were discussing Arabic dialects, he insisted that classical Arabic was completely separate from the spoken forms. He admonished me to read Arabic poetry and verses from the Qur'an to improve my language. I discovered that he had memorized large portions of the Qur'an, and suddenly his animus toward Islam seemed to fade away.

At the same time, Yusuf had memorized even more parts of the Old and New Testaments and often would compare accounts in the Bible and Qur'an, affirming each time the biblical narrative while refuting the Qur'an's telling. However, all that failed to convince me that he was truly a Christian and not still Muslim. He must have spoken like this only out of fear that I was acting as the eyes and ears of the warden.

As the weeks progressed, I was eager to stick close to the Morisco, and I learned many things from him, including Arabic orthography, manuscript illumination, and even astronomical calculations, all of which he excelled at. He spoke to me about the tables of Maslama Al-Majriti and their use alongside other astronomical instruments. Despite my gratitude for his knowledge, I still harboured suspicions that he only pretended to be Christian and was actually trying to win me over to Islam. His haughtiness and brash self-confidence, however, made me keep my distance—especially as I slowly discovered that he was keeping a secret to himself.

At least that's what he revealed to me before my meeting with the Jesuit delegation, going so far as to suggest I remain in prison with him. "You have come to know part of my story," he said, before the Jesuits' arrival. "I need you in order to finish it." From the very start, he believed I wouldn't remain long in prison, and he needed to recruit me to accomplish something on his behalf once I got out.

Chapter 3

We bunched up behind the Saltman as he tried to peep through the small opening in our cell door. We asked him what was going on. It all started after a scream split the air and woke everyone and everything around us. At that moment, the Saltman was the most nervous of us all. He was also the tallest and the only one whose hand could reach the upper window, where small bundles of herbs were hidden and sometimes prescribed to treat prisoners suffering from upset stomach, headaches, or nausea. He related many stories of how using such herbs had kept the salt revolt going for four years.

All through the night, guards dragged prisoners from their cells. Some came back unscathed while others returned roughed up, bloodied, and bruised. We alternated keeping watch each time we heard the clanging of the guards. The only one of us able to sleep was the Morisco, immersed in a strange serenity, as if he were certain that the guards would not come near us. His ability to sleep through it all was somewhat reassuring. In the morning, we found the man from Lombardia, fettered and chained to a stone bench in a corner of the outside courtyard, being kept under surveillance by a handful of guards.

I should mention here that several days prior, one of the warden's men had announced that a leather satchel belonging to a priest who had visited the prison had gone missing. The bag contained blacksmith tools, a few knives, and some blades. It seems that the following night, they discovered that the Lombard was the culprit. I didn't know much about him, except he was ostracized by the others, which was why no one really sympathized with his plight. That is, except for Yusuf, whom I overheard say to the Saltman as we passed by the stone bench, "The warden has things he wants to tell us. This satchel is nothing more than the key for messages to come."

Shortly after noon, the executioners began taking turns on his back. Everyone thought that the Lombard might die during the whipping, and a clamour arose demanding that it stop. It finally did, along with the man's groaning. Suddenly, the Lombard became everyone's friend.

The man remained suspended for two days, hallucinating at times and passing out at others. It became clear that he had endured more than any of us could bear, or even that he himself could. Some swore that they had seen worms eating away at his back, and the assault scandalized the prisoners so much that voices rose in protest, demanding the man be spared such treatment.

The night they unchained the Lombard from the bench, I returned to see Yusuf and asked, "What makes you so sure that the warden made it all up and purposefully inflicted such torture on an innocent man?"

"Your heart is still closed, Robert. The warden wants to hold all the cards in his hand. He outmanoeuvres everyone and prevaricates when it suits his purposes. Our constant need to guess how he runs this place is what makes him feel superior to us. Omnipotent. Do you understand now?"

My heart kept telling me that I was standing beside a painting filled with dark colours and that Yusuf was working assiduously to brighten it. Meanwhile, I searched for something that would clarify and reveal the whole picture before me. So when he asked if I understood, I sensed him saying, "Give me a stronger reason why I should tell you everything I know."

In reality, I couldn't fully understand my feelings toward him, although a voice whispered to me that I had known him for a very long time. When I first entered the cell, his bald pate was the first thing my eyes fell on, though he hadn't raised it nor had anyone tried to make me feel welcome despite my nervous smile. The prison walls, with all their graffiti left by former inmates, spoke more to me than any of the people.

It wasn't until the Morisco finally said hello, several days later, that any of the others began to interact with me. When I asked one why they had suddenly changed toward me, he said that they trusted the Morisco's hunch that the warden had not sent someone to spy on them.

I wasn't convinced, so I asked the Morisco directly, "Why would the warden spy on all of you? None of your crimes are particularly serious. Espousing various Lutheran ideas, perhaps engaging in petty thievery, or money troubles. The crimes were inconsequential. Take for instance the Jewish man accused of falsifying his lineage, claiming to be pure-bred Castilian only later for his lie to be exposed." Among all the cellmates, the most dangerous one (after the Morisco) was the Saltman, who had led a revolt against the salt taxes enacted by Philip IV several years back.

Yusuf's response, however, could not have been further from my expectations: "Livestock have no right to hide anything from their owner."

I needed the Morisco to trust me. He was the key to the other prisoners' good graces. When I brought that up to the warden, after being summoned to his office the first time, he said that the Morisco was tricking the others in some way, and he wanted me to learn more and report back.

My meetings with the warden began the morning after the Lombard had been punished. I was frightened, especially since his torture still rang in my ears. Yet, the gentle and disarming manner of the warden, with his round face that bordered on feline, and his well-appointed office decorated with paintings and sculptures, instilled in me a certain measure of peace.

He informed me that today was a Moorish festival. He asked if I had observed the Arab showing any sign of celebration or joy.

I batted it away, saying, "The Morisco does not profess the Mohammedan   religion."

"We know the Morisco's religion, and I notice that you spend quite a bit of time with him. That does not bode well for you at all. I've also come to learn that you speak with him in Arabic. That certainly complicates the issue of your retrial and release."

"I'm only trying to gain his trust. If you want me to report back to you what he says, I have no issue with that. Nothing connects me to him other than the fact that my family's business and his knowledge are coincidentally related. If you want, I will trap him in his words."

"Don't do that. He is extremely perspicacious and might become suspicious of you. Later, I will tell you what you need to do. For now, you must report back anything he says. You're being tested. No one here can help you except for me. Keep that at the front of your mind."

On my way out, I told the warden that the Morisco had taught me some verses from the Qur'an and a few lines of Arabic poetry, but it was nothing more than to remind me of the rules of Arabic grammar.

When I went back to Yusuf, I divulged to him everything that had taken place between me and the warden. Somehow, I thought that would exorcise the suffocating feeling that I was merely a pawn on the warden's chessboard.

I told him matter-of-factly that the warden wanted me to spy on him. He didn't take it seriously and downplayed my conversations with him, which I had in any case begun to plot out as a test of my ability to manipulate events and circumstances.

On one occasion, I told the warden that the Morisco and the Saltman suspected the Jew was working on the warden's behalf and had been the one who tempted the Lombard to steal the priest's satchel in hopes of making an escape. The following day, the Jewish man disappeared from our cell. Likewise, I went back to the Morisco several days later and told him that the Jewish man had reported him to the warden, saying it was "the Arab" who incited protests against the Lombard's punishment and was running an underground cell inside the prison, and that he should keep watch. But he didn't react at all.

The Morisco really got under my skin by ignoring what I'd said and disregarding the information I brought to him, as when I told him that the Lombard would make an appearance in the next sermon and apologize to all those he had wronged. The warden told me to say it, so that Yusuf would believe I wasn't just making things up. However, the Morisco sternly repeated, "Your heart is still closed, Robert."

When the Lombard appeared during the sermon to apologize, he looked like a broken and defeated man, a shadow of his former self. Torture had stolen away all his senses, maybe even his mind. He stammered out his apology and showed no reaction to any of the profanity hurled at him from some of the other prisoners.

In a low voice, Yusuf whispered, "Unfortunately, by the laws of nature, there is no power that protects those who have lost their ability to inflict harm. You must remain a constant source of fear to everyone around you so that this natural law in turn protects you."

The Saltman added, "Only the strong can join together to be a threat."

I reminded the Morisco of what I'd said earlier, about the Lombard's apology, but he just lowered his head slightly before unleashing on me the most withering scolding I had ever received, warning me that the warden was gradually annihilating my soul and replacing it with his own. In short order, I would be nothing more than a mere copy of the warden, one that he could destroy at any moment without even batting an eyelash.

"You can resort to the warden's techniques to influence and manipulate your environment and circumstances, but you will turn to stone quicker than he ever will. The power he wields now keeps him safe—for the moment—from turning into a senseless, inhumane mass. But it won't be long before you end up like the Lombard. A lump of flesh, devoid of all taste and smell. Nothing more than an illustrative example to show just how far an individual will go in losing their dignity and their soul."

His words cut to the quick, leaving me defenceless under the lashes of his tongue. The fact that it was true made it all the more searing. It was as if I were at my most abject and he was trying to pull me up. I could see now who I truly was. Afterward, for several days, I went into isolation, ensconced in my cell. If a guard managed to pull me out by force, I retreated into a corner of the prison and remained motionless. On several occasions, the warden asked to see me, but I declined each time.

After Yusuf's reprimand, I told myself that, out at sea, a hand must have taken hold of me and dropped me into this man's cell for some specific purpose. His initial influence on me stemmed from the fact that he was the only one who had paper and writing materials in prison. The only Spaniard who ever visited him, a stationer and merchant from San Sebastián, would bring him these accoutrements. Their acquaintance went back years, to when they were both young boys in Zaragoza. And whenever Yusuf would leave the cell, he would wrap his head with a piece of cloth, which may have been the reason why the others called him "the Arab".

Following this scolding, people stopped talking with me, except for the Saltman, who insisted that a loyal friend is a prisoner's greatest hope. Yet that didn't last long. Well after midnight, the guards dragged me from the cell so I could spend a grand evening being beaten and tortured, the horror of which remains etched in my memory. The sun hadn't risen before I was returned bloodied and unconscious to the cell, my face and body covered in bruises. When I finally came to my senses the following evening, I found Yusuf and the other prisoners around me asking, "What happened? Why did they beat you so mercilessly?"

I asked Yusuf, "Is this part of the reforms Spain is undertaking?" He assured me that it was a warning not to betray the warden. I asked him, "Couldn't he have found a better way to warn me?"

"It is nothing but fate and a way to manage his fear. It was the first test to break your will. The warden began to fear you, so he punished you in a way that was commensurate with the fear he felt. That's what

Philip III did with us back when he expelled the Moriscos from Spain."

Yusuf sank into a deep silence, as if recalling his former travails. I asked him to tell me the story of what happened to his family when the edict was issued to expel the Moors. The Saltman had told me that the Morisco's catastrophes began when he turned 15, the day his family departed Zaragoza—one year before the edict was proclaimed.

In the beginning, Yusuf remained reticent, but that evening, as our conversation turned to astrology, astrolabes, and that great astronomer Al-Zarqali, he regaled us with the importance of astronomical calculations in understanding the messages of the stars and in avoiding whatever evil could be lying in wait.

That was how his mother ended up buying a house in the mountains where they spent the sultry summer months. And, in that same way, they had left Zaragoza once bad omens urged them to depart, hiding in the mountains for years and moving from one place to another. If the situation calmed down, they settled. If things became agitated, so too did they. And thus, it continued, until finally they reached the French side of the Pyrenees.

In the mountains, the Morisco lost most of his family. By the time they made it to France, the only ones who remained with him were his wife Najma Al-Hajari and her younger sister, Hind, and their servant named Hasan. Then one night, they were forced to separate after Yusuf consulted the stars and placed his confidence in their message. Early the next morning, he fell into the hands of the French authorities, thus becoming forever separated from the sisters and the servant.

"I left them to face their unknown fate alone. That is what pains me the most. But they are strong. As of today, it has been eighteen years, seven months, and twenty-two days since that event. The great *Saphaea* astrolabe and manuscripts of Al-Majriti remained in Najma's possession. The French baron who hid us in his home for several weeks suggested I call her Madalena Despucci. And Hind became Maria Despucci." These sentences flowed forth from Yusuf's mouth followed by a stifled groan. I could not understand why he was telling me all this.

"So, how was it you came here?"

He swore that he would have been put to death immediately had the stars not sent him a sign to take precautions. And so, when he was captured, he had nothing on him that could damn him.

"Regardless, they sent me to work in one of the mines on the isle of Sardinia. I toiled there for seven long years before they transferred me here, to this prison, after I uncovered a group of Protestants who were secretly working in Spain. Five years on, I am still waiting for them to fulfil their promise of amnesty and let me go."

In spite of his difficulties with the warden and all the guards' provocations, I had not once heard the Morisco complain. He had always shown his love for Spain. But that evening, old wounds resurfaced.

"When you flee from oppression only to fall into something worse—for a sin you don't know when, where, or how you committed—you immediately realize that your roots are a curse upon your children, who can't understand why they are starving. And as that feeling of weakness and helplessness intensifies, you discover that your very existence is a curse. And not just upon your children, but upon every inch of your body. You would rather be crushed under the weight of a gigantic boulder than bear the insufferable agony of being alive. To be a Muslim—a Moor—in a country that considers Catholicism the very stuff of life is to probe your entire being, searching for something to prove that you, too, are infused with that essence. The simplest man, ignorant of religion entirely, can pass judgment on you for all your faults and offences—not against the Church, as you might think—but against your very being. For simply being a Moor. Something you never chose to be.

"You then become the scapegoat for plagues, defeats, and all manner of catastrophes that befall Spain. A long litany of coded words confronts you, on street corners and in alleyways. At the same time, you know that the mere colour of your hair and skin is enough to make one question multiply into dozens. It doesn't matter whether you look Gothic or Galician because in the end it is your birth that determines who you are. Not all Moors have swarthy skin. My wife and her sister were closer in appearance to the Spaniards than they were to the Moors, but that offered them little help. The Inquisition interrogates and investigates everything, even the privies of our homes and our very limbs, believing that they have come with the intention to liberate and cleanse us of this disease."

The Morisco stayed by my side during this period, but not for long. After several days, I was summoned and found myself once again at the warden's mercy. I began to spin yarns to please him (or was it to take revenge on him?) even if it was to the detriment of the Morisco and Saltman. I satisfied myself that it was all justified, because when I asked Yusuf why they had ignored me after he berated me that day, his only response was, "I didn't believe you were English."

Chapter 4

The door opened, and the guard slowly escorted me into a spacious corridor hung with paintings and other works of art. He then led me into a reception room. On the left, at the far end of the room, stood a door that opened into the warden's office, while off to the right, an arcaded portico led to a balcony and watch tower. Like the corridor, the reception was adorned with art and sculpture: books, seashells, and religious handicrafts sent by monasteries and churches on various occasions. Some had been produced in the prison workshop itself.

When I walked in to see the warden, I found him reading, engrossed in verses from the Book of Revelations. It surely was by design that he was reading about Babylon, that mother of harlots and the abomination of the whole earth. At ease and relaxed, he softly mouthed the text as he read, confirming he was doing so on purpose. He knew that I understood what he meant. For, as a Christian believer, one must always flee from Satan and seek refuge in the presence of God.

However, I sensed something paradoxical in the warden. At first blush, his round face made him appear trustworthy. However, a sneaking suspicion that he was up to something quickly upended that feeling, accentuated further by his reading spectacles. The warden never liked the prisoners to see him wear them, which was why he folded them up in a brass case, hung from a delicate chain attached to his undershirt pocket. Out of sight. He went even further, obscuring the case by attaching a whistle to the same chain.

I had paid a call on the warden more than once since that

inauspicious day that brought me here, though he had first visited me in my cell carrying with him a scrap of paper in English for me to translate. Later, he asked if I would teach him English, but I told him it wasn't as practical a language as Italian, Spanish, or Arabic. He claimed he needed the language to understand some English legal texts, the content of which was quite well-articulated. On one of his recent visits, he made it known that the prison of San Sebastián was one of only a few in Spain where the Inquisition worked alongside the Jesuits to put the new reform laws to the test.

Fearing his sly craftiness and knowing full well the punishment he could inflict, I needed to appear trustworthy to the warden. He apologised for the other night and said he had done it because the prisoners had started to become suspicious of me. According to him, his orders to the guards had been crystal clear—a light sting, nothing more. But they had misunderstood and were summarily punished.

He didn't speak immediately as I pushed deeper into the room, giving me the chance to run my eyes over all the boxes of books that had recently made their way to the prison, as well as architectural drawings for an execution platform that required little effort to set up or take down and could be easily folded up and wheeled away. There was also a large, framed painting of *Christ the Redeemer* next to a diagram of Archimedes using a lever to move the world, below which was inscribed his famous dictum, "Give me a place to stand and I will move the earth."

When the warden noticed I was transfixed by the painting, he gestured for me to come closer. Setting the Bible aside, he asked me to read a piece of paper in his hand. "Today, in Spain, Robert, faith and science are united. Here, read this aloud so I can listen." When he noticed that I wanted to inquire about the painting of *Christ the*

Redeemer he added that it was by a Greek painter named Domenikos El Greco who fled from the Turks and was now living in Spain.

I took the slip of paper from the warden. It was clearly an old scrap. It was discoloured, covered in sepia-toned gradations, and pockmarked with holes along its edges. I began to read, "The *Lion de Oro* with twenty-four cannons shipped off from the Bay of Getxo, captained by Alonso Martínez de Leyva on the night of October 14. The ship is carrying food provisions and aid for the people of Sardinia, which has been ravaged by famine." When I went silent, he told me to read the note at the bottom. So I read, "The *Lion* is a warship and departed to crush the fishermen's revolt in Naples." At the top of the scrap was written MDCXXV, perhaps the date it was composed.

It was clear that the two notes were written by two different people. A suspicion overcame me that the first note was in the Morisco's hand. When I told the warden my instinct, he said, "You are very clever, Robert. From this, we can draw the conclusion that the Morisco did not give the French all the information he knew. He was misleading them. But nobody knows why!"

"Perhaps because of his devotion to Spain?"

"Maybe that's why the judges hesitated to condemn him to death."

"Why are you telling me this, Sir?"

"I have a feeling that the Morisco was forced by the circumstances of his expulsion from Spain to work on behalf of the French despite his antipathy toward them. He provided a noble service to Spain several years back when he uncovered a Protestant cell within our borders. He would have been freed then and there, had our spies not suspected he was in communication with the Ottomans or Saadian sultans of Morocco."

I asked what I had to do with all this. He said, "In a week's time, a Jesuit delegation from Bilbao will visit you to make an official inquiry. It would appear that they are interested in you specifically. They have been commissioned by the Fifth Protocol of the Inquisition courts, conferring upon them the authority to transfer you from our prison if they so choose. Given the Morisco's trust in you, he might very well direct you to communicate with people on the outside for some unknown reason. I want to know about that. We want to help the Morisco, since he has helped us. And, in light of the new prison reform laws, we can release prisoners when new evidence surfaces that warrants a retrial, or if it comes to light that someone has provided valuable services to the Spanish crown."

I left the warden after asking his permission to take a handful of sweets. They were on a shelf in his office and had held my rapt attention during our meeting. I also asked if the guard escorting me out could allow me to peruse the works of art in the reception room and on the corridor walls. Art is the sole consolation able to remind a man of his humanity.

Although everyone knew I was meeting regularly with the warden, their trust in the Morisco helped attenuate their doubts about me, and so I gladly distributed the sweets among them. Yusuf caught sight of me as I approached the outer courtyard and gestured toward me. As I walked over, my mind was filled with thoughts of what I would relate to him about my meeting with the warden.

As soon as I reached him, I divulged our discussion and the matter of the old scrap of paper. "The warden thinks that you run an underground cell of Turks on the outside," I said, "and he wants me to find out more before the delegation arrives."

"The warden pours fantastical ideas into your head! They know I'm incapable of something like that. Just so, I wasn't spared execution because I deceived the French. They didn't discover that until years after the trial. I was spared on account of our family's distinguished history in Aragon and the lack of clear-cut evidence that I was spying for the French. The reports that fell into their hands were benign. Rather, they've left me in prison on purpose—hoping I would expose other secret groups for them. But I refuse to rat out other prisoners. The warden wants you to stay in prison, too, but he can't go against the wishes of the Tribunal of the Holy Office of the Inquisition."

On the eve of the delegation's arrival, I told Yusuf, "If the Jesuits pull me out of prison, I won't hesitate. I'll accept."

"Would you still do that if I told you I needed you for an important matter—one that concerned both me and you?"

"Why not tell me now? If it's something I can do once I'm on the outside, then I will be free to do it."

"I'm not yet sure you will be able to handle all I have to say. In any case, if the Jesuits need you now, they will need you later. For God's sake, I don't think they just want to let you go."

The day before the delegation arrived, the warden summoned me one last time. He showed me that the objection I had raised regarding my previous sentencing had been accepted, as had been the recommendation to apply the Catholic qualification law to me, which meant that the delegation was basically coming to transfer me. He revealed, however, that he hoped I would stay. The Jesuits would surely ask me again in the future. And if I agreed to help the warden out, he promised to draft a memorandum in support of returning me to my country along with my printing press.

The situation was exactly as the warden said and as Morisco predicted. After the monks gave up trying to persuade me to leave with them, they pulled out one of the sets of type I had purchased from the Dutch merchant, asking me to lay out the Hebrew equivalent for each Arabic letter. I didn't understand what they were trying to accomplish, but Yusuf later said, "They were reminding you of the printing press so you would change your mind."

I chose to remain in prison despite the enticement of monastic life. Perhaps the Jesuits' reputation for being a secret society intent on controlling everything from behind the curtain factored into my decision. Such secrecy did not appeal to me. Neither did the idea of house arrest. Nor did the fact that the printing press would not be returned induce me in any way to want to leave. To say nothing of the Morisco's secret! In the end, the monks' proposal was the same: Freedom in exchange for labour. And their offer wasn't any better than the one made by the warden.

I didn't fully comprehend the warden's endgame, nor the reason he wanted me to stay. In the days that followed, however, I came to discover that the warden was more than a lowly prison administrator. He was a Jesuit reformer intent on making a success of the Catholic Church's new philosophy, which had developed in the wake of the reforms. And prison reform in particular was high among its priorities. When I told him that the Morisco was going to reveal something important to me, he thanked me for staying and echoed what he had said, "Your reward will be no less than your return to England along with your father's printing press."

After returning to the cell, I pretended to be deflated, hoping to give the impression that the delegation had reaffirmed the previous ruling against me. However, it was clear that I was a terrible actor and the Morisco knew right away that things had gone as expected.

I had known all along that he had left something unsaid, even before he acknowledged it. Once he saw that our bond was stronger than mine with the warden, and that his prediction about the delegation had been correct, he decided to let me in on his secret. I have to say that what he told me surpassed my expectations entirely. I had always assumed it was connected in some way to his plans for escape or related to people on the outside. However, the matter was altogether different.

Chapter 5

As Yusuf began to recount his tale, he asked me right from the start, "Do you remember that priest who feigned to not hear me? He belongs to a creed that spread throughout southern Spain after the failure of the Alpujarras rebellion. They believe it was the Arabs who brought Christianity to Spain even before the Romans themselves had converted. As the story goes, two Arab monks took refuge on the Iberian Peninsula, bringing with them a veil belonging to the Virgin Mary. After a number of putative miracles occurred, thanks to the veil, Christianity began to take root. Later, the veil was hidden deep within a church in Granada that was subsequently repurposed as a mosque after the arrival of the Muslims. During the revolt of Granada, however, the Christians razed the mosque and discovered the veil along with a trove of manuscripts written in Arabic, Castilian, and Latin.

That discovery softened the enmity toward the newly converted Christians, the Moriscos, and the old notion that Arabs could faithfully reembrace their former Christian heritage became prevalent once more. Some priests even spread folktales that Arabs would be the standard-bearers of Christianity during the end times. All this relieved the pressure on the people of Granada, allowing them to speak Arabic again and return to their Andalusian customs. It was during this period that my uncle Afoukay Al-Hajari managed to seek refuge at the Saadi palace in Marrakech, while my father, Ma'mun, set out for Aragon, carrying with him a personal letter from the archbishop of Granada.

We purchased a home and some farmland in Zaragoza and our

family's success there was substantial. Because of my father's many charitable deeds, he enjoyed the respect of the priests, and a large throng even attended his funeral, held just before our good fortune changed for the worse.

That priest who refused to hear my confession knows full well that the strong in spirit neither reveal their secrets nor deceive themselves. Only he who fears being deceived by the devil needs to confess his lost truth and make excuses for himself to be acceptable before God. That priest wants to first see contrition before believing that we are sincere in our Christianity, so that he does not bear false witness to a faith that might be feigned."

I tried to interrupt him, to ensure he would actually tell me a secret. Was the secret his tale? Yet, given his habit of speaking deliberately and carefully, I kept silent.

"When conditions worsened in Aragon, my mother proposed that we buy a home in the mountains not far from France, where we would go from time to time. When we left Zaragoza, we entrusted the farm and most of our hired hands to the Church. On account of being the eldest male, the weight of responsibility gradually fell upon me. At the time, I was perhaps a bit older than you are now. And once my mother, sister, and the two servants were caught, the remaining family came under my charge.

My mother admonished me to marry Najma, the daughter of my uncle Afoukay who lived in Marrakech, which we did in the mountains after things began to grow calmer. We then left our home and moved to a new town. But things began to deteriorate once again. The remaining family members who attempted to return to Zaragoza were captured and I was forced to flee to France with my wife, her sister Hind, and the servant Hasan, after leaving behind the last two children with a family there. We entered France, tracing the switchbacks that pilgrims took as they made their way to the Catedral de Santiago de Compostela. With us was a cart laden with manuscripts. It was the winter before the wars in central Europe had begun, and, along the route, we had to offer bribes just to be able to enter France and flee the hell we had suffered in Spain. I still don't know what became of my mother and the rest of the family."

I tried to interrupt him again, during the pauses that seemed to indicate he had stopped speaking. But he would raise his hand each time, signalling me to wait. By now, I had become used to his manner of speaking: words would become logjammed before finally bursting forth all at once. Anyone who listened would be overcome with the sense that he was piecing together a patchwork of memories, attempting to distil them into specific moments, perhaps as a way to avoid losing control over his emotions or to ensure he did not reveal something he did not yet want you to know. I kept trying to interrupt him, rashly asking, "Do you know someone outside of prison who can help you? Are you thinking of escaping?"

He returned to his story. "Winter hadn't passed before we were welcomed into the home of a French baron, a Calvinist and Huguenot named Despucci. He was hiding out in the south of France and, as bad luck would have it, he was being surveilled by the government. I had tried to get in contact with the University of Leiden after I found out that my uncle Afoukay ended up there, under the auspices of the noted Dutch Arabist Thomas Erpenius, where he taught Arabic for two or three years. However, I hadn't received a response before we were forced to leave the baron's home. Less than a month into our journey northward, I was apprehended.

"From then on, I lost all communication with my wife and her sister. I tried to find out what had become of them after the French let me go, but to no avail. Hundreds of manuscripts, Arabic, Hebrew, and Persian were in Najma and Hind's possession. It seems likely these manuscripts made their way to French universities or to Arabists, given how unlikely it is that my wife would be able to hold onto them for long. I made numerous inquiries, but again with no luck. This was an intellectual treasure of immeasurable value."

At that point, Yusuf stopped talking, but I was still waiting to find out more. Or perhaps I just hadn't heard what I'd wanted to hear. He glanced at me, as if looking to strike a deal. It was as if he were saying, "I've got nothing to lose," but I wasn't completely sure what he was expecting from me, what might induce him to fully reveal his secret. I felt a tinge of shame that I was even trying to find out.

I thought about what I would tell the warden. Surely, he was expecting some grave, dark secret. But it was nothing more than a lost library, and I couldn't fathom how that could be of any use to him at all. Maybe he already knew about it and gave it no import. Nowadays in Spain, books in Hebrew and Arabic were worthless. In any case, the warden must not catch wind of this library. That was what I told myself. But if Yusuf didn't know where it was now, how would I?

I can't deny that being privy to his tale created within me some sort of moral commitment toward him, and he was expecting something in return for what he had said. All along, I had thought he simply wanted to escape prison, but that didn't appear to be the case. Yusuf the Morisco wanted to leave prison, return to Zaragoza, and regain his family's possessions. He wanted to be free to yet remain in Spain. And, in his estimation, these manuscripts could help him cut a deal with the Inquisition if only he could locate them.

I wasn't sure what I could do for him, given the complexity of my own relationship with the warden, my doubts that the Morisco actually knew where the library was, and above all, my disappointment in knowing something of interest to the warden. All this led to things proceeding in a seemingly absurd manner, to the point that I began to regret my decision to remain in prison.

I was once again forced to prevaricate and confabulate to spare myself from making any commitment toward either one of them. All the while, I still hoped Yusuf would confess something substantial to me.

A few days later, I requested a meeting with the warden. I met him at the weaver's workshop, where he thanked me again for my sacrifice, for choosing to remain in prison, saying, "The delegation's visit was quick, and we are on the verge of bringing down the Morisco."

"Although I have his confidence after turning down the Jesuits' offer, the Morisco is still wary of me."

"How so?"

"He has a network on the outside working for him and the Saltman. And they're hatching a plot to spring them both, with help from some of the guards."

"Why don't they do it without you?"

"Because on the day of the escape, I'm supposed to come see you—as a ruse—while the operation is carried out. And because I can leave here at any time, they think I won't hesitate to help them out."

I told the warden that the Morisco hadn't disclosed the names of the guards in cahoots with them, how they would escape, or even the people who were working on the outside. As I was leaving, I told the warden, "Surely, he will reveal all, but he needs more time."

It seemed the warden believed everything I said. Two days later, I found myself repeating it all back to the Morisco, as if it were a plan to help him escape. Although he gathered that I was thinking seriously about it, he commented that my proposed plan would not work, because the boxes brought into the jail filled with donated clothes were far too small to fit an adult. The same was true of the trash receptacles that were emptied and weighed before being loaded back onto the carts.

"Don't think too rashly. If this were easy, I would have made my escape long ago. What I'm thinking about goes far beyond what you can imagine. I don't want to remain on the run, pursued and hounded forever in Spain," he said, hoping I would still think of ways to help him.

Apart from the idea that was rolling around in his mind, and which I could not fully fathom, it later became clear that his interest in me stemmed from his belief that something was bound to happen. And so he gradually filled me in on the details of his story.

He told me that, prior to his capture, he had been corresponding with a French periodical. One of the issues dating from the mid-1620s noted the death of the esteemed intellectual Thomas Erpenius and mentioned a rare Arabic text in his possession on astronomy and horary astrology, in which the author expounded on mathematics and talismans. It was likely the text had been written either by Abu Mu'sher Al-Balkhi's or Maslama Al-Majriti. If the latter, then it had previously been with Najma and subsequently found its way to Erpenius, either through her or a third party. Yusuf thought it most likely via an intermediary, for reasons he mentioned, which I found unconvincing at the time.

Over the next few days, he began to rattle off what he could remember about the manuscripts that had been with the two sisters and asked me to write it all down so I would not forget. Then he began to teach me the unique language of the Moors, called Aljamiado, which he said the two sisters probably used to some degree. This language required knowledge of both Castilian and the Arabic script, although Castilian wasn't the only language the Moors wrote in the Arabic alphabet; they sometimes also used Aragonese and Catalan.

Once, when we were celebrating mass on the occasion of some prisoner's baptism, he told me that, years ago, the stationer had brought him some scraps of paper, an index of the Leiden library that dated back most likely to the late 1620's. These scraps related to Oriental manuscripts and publications and had been excised from a larger catalogue. However, none of the manuscripts the two sisters had held onto were among the entries, which made him nearly certain that they had not reached Holland.

Yusuf didn't think the sisters had made it out of France because, if had they arrived in Holland, their manuscripts would surely have appeared in the index, and Arabists would have certainly written about them. When he was cast into prison, his uncle Afoukay was still alive, but he'd had no success in contacting him to find out what had become of his daughters.

Why not just be straightforward and tell me where this lost library is, I wondered. *Spare me all these boring details*. Fine, he needed to know what happened to his wife and her sister. But I was already daydreaming about how my father would welcome me as I carried back a huge haul of manuscripts. The great scientists and Arabists of the day would blaze a trail to our home in England, and from all over Europe!

He mentioned that he wanted to buy his freedom with these manuscripts. He said, "A single Arabist would need to spend years in the Maghreb, or the Levant, or Egypt and Constantinople just to gather a few dozen manuscripts. What if he knew that he could obtain an entire library in one fell swoop? All without taking any risk traveling to the lands of the East?"

"The matter is entirely impossible in Spain," I said. "Spaniards no longer care at all for Arab or Hebrew heritage."

"What might be impossible in Spain certainly isn't in France, or Holland, or even England. A prisoner exchange deal with these countries could get me out of here."

"But you're Spanish!"

"Can you convince the Spaniards of that?"

"But convincing France or Holland that you're French or Dutch would be an even more difficult feat."

I had several more encounters with the warden during this period, each time embellishing some bit of information on the spot or feeding him what I had agreed to say in advance with the Morisco. Until the time eventually came when I told him that, this very day, those two were going to pull off their escape plan. However, as it drew closer, I went back to tell the warden that the Morisco and Saltman had gotten cold feet at the last moment.

The warden began to grow sceptical of my stories, realising that I was toying with him. When he became absolutely sure of it, he didn't punish me directly, but instead yanked the Morisco and the Saltman out of the cell one night. After beating them severely, he ordered them to be whipped in the courtyard for five straight days. Every day, they got twenty lashes for the charge of trying to escape. That was all it took for me to fall afoul of the other prisoners. Days later, the guards found me hovering between life and death in a corner of the prison. To them, worse than ratting someone out was doing so under false pretense.

The warden didn't lift a finger to help me, besides putting me in a room by myself. Only the prison doctor, who was also a priest, visited me. Was he there to treat me or administer my final rites? I remained in that room for nearly two months. Once or twice, the warden visited me and told me that I had ruined everything he had built up because of my stupidity, and how, if it had not been for Father Gaddis who had asked for me by name, he would have let the prisoners finish me off.

I told him that I wanted to go to the Jesuits. If I was sent back to the cell, the inmates would surely kill me this time. He assured me that was what he hoped that would happen. I waited three weeks until a delegation from the Monastery of the Divine Incarnation arrived to take me with them. As I left prison, I thought about the Morisco. I had done him wrong, but what I had been subjected to and endured was double what I deserved. What else could a young man like myself think? Tossed as I was into the world of criminals, innocent of any wrongdoing, and only guilty of bad luck in finding myself aboard a ship that the King of England had purposefully delivered to the Spaniards!

Part 2

The Jesuits' Monastery

"The sign that you are complete and whole is not that you know all the answers, but that you know all the questions. It's not that you deny yourself everything, but rather that you are in need of it all. It's not that you talk to yourself, but that the universe speaks to you. For the soul expands and contracts to the degree that you offer or shun, reveal or hide."

Chapter 6

Several days passed before I actually met Father Gaddis, abbot of the monastery, but I didn't notice the slow passage of time. Nor did I notice how seemingly mundane things had begun to carry deeper meanings, more than if I had seen them outside the monastery. Such was the case with the mats placed at the entries and exits of the doors, or the small garden fountains that blurred into the background, or the seashells placed in forgotten corners of the monastery. The mats could wipe away your burdens and lighten your spirits, while the neglected fountains poured forth the ancient Greeks' hydrological wisdom, and the shells reminded one of past journeys of knowledge and rebirth.

I imagined that access to the deeper meanings of things was the natural outcome of finding yourself in a place intent on protecting your truth as you, too, endeavoured to protect the truth of everything around you.

It all took me back to the ship as it departed Holland, carrying with it the printing press. That scene, too, had passed by slowly. And because I had been in a light and jovial mood, things long familiar appeared as if I were seeing them for the very first time, as if they had been hidden from view until that moment.

Leaving prison was an altogether different affair. My soul was laden with numberless disturbing images, rendering me unable to notice anything around me at all. Everything I saw vanished without leaving the slightest trace. All I could do was rest my heavy head on the velvet cushion of the carriage that was transporting me to the monastery and close my eyes for a few hours.

I stopped resisting the wind and pulled back my hand. In that moment, all I wanted was the fresh breeze along the trail, to fill my lungs and expel the last of the prison air. All I could think of was protecting what was left of the Robert who had implored his father to send him alone to close the deal for the Dutch printing press.

One of the monks who came to retrieve me from prison (the same one who had come previously) commented, "What have they done to you?!" when he saw me in such a weak and withered state.

"They prepared me for life at the monastery!" I said as I turned my back on the prison and got into the carriage. The younger monk said, piously, "May your heart ever be turned to God. Everything else will diminish before you, and only He will remain." I thanked him as I turned the page on my time in prison and found the finality of closure within myself. Had it been possible, I would have ripped the page out entirely with my own hand.

Several days after my arrival, the Monastery of the Divine Incarnation appeared to me as a place where earth and heaven embraced and where form and content united into one great whole Here, that impermeable confusion over one's existence dissipated, as did the right to speak, or even have a secret. Instead, we spoke with the intimacy of silence, possessing everything while holding nothing, as everything around us protected the secrets that everyone knew.

Outside these walls, the stars were indifferent to us, yet from within, they called out to us by many names, each one a manifestation of our own truths. For the names differed only in word and not in their deeper meanings. It was as if one might grasp eternity yet remain convinced he understood nothing at all. That was what Siraj, the young monk who escorted me from prison to the monastery and who was now serving as my guide, meant when he said repeatedly, "The world will speak to you inasmuch as your heart is pure."

Siraj was somewhat shorter than me, though I couldn't determine his size precisely, since his black cloak never left his body. Its pleats ran from the top of his clerical collar, cascading all the way down to the knee before ending in a tasselled flourish of grassy-green linen the same hue as what the Arabs call "lion's paw," while in English we say "lady's mantle" or "mantle of the dewy lady."

Siraj reminded me of the Morisco. As far as I knew, he, too, was the progeny of Christianized Muslims. Father Gaddis had brought him to the monastery after catching his attention during a pastoral visit to one of the villages along the coast of the Bay of Biscay. His name sounded strange, so I asked him what it meant, but he couldn't answer. And while he was aware that his roots were Moorish, he knew nothing at all of Arabic or Islam. He told me that he had even asked the father to change his name, but he forbade it.

A gnawing voice inside me said that Siraj was enamoured with appearances and had wholly sublimated himself into Father Gaddis' strong personality. Perhaps it was a way to benefit from his influence and power, but it was also why I decided to keep some distance between us. He made it clear that he was awaiting his ordination as a theologian and would then be sent off as a member of the Jesuit mission to China, despite being so young, barely a few years older than I was.

During my first few days, he wandered around with me to the various parts of the monastery. I visited the garden—accessible from several sides—but the western entrance, overlooking the quadrangle beside the chapel of Saint Teresa the Carmelite, was the one closest to the monk's cell where I was staying.

The quadrangle was divided into two halves, which looked out onto the garden and were bisected by a diagonal line that ran between two corners of the square. The western section was connected to the monastery's main buildings while the eastern section led to the classrooms and workshops, as well as to the kitchen, dining hall, and a showroom for handicrafts. It was this eastern side that was normally open to the masses on Sundays, and where I mingled with the people visiting the monastery, most of whom were simple folk living off handouts and the grace of God.

It was apparent that the eastern side was a recent addition to the monastery, appended during an expansion. The walls that were so boisterously decorated and detailed with carvings and bas reliefs suddenly fell silent as you made your way to the eastern end. Artists had offered up their services to paint and beautify the plain walls, but the father was waiting first to annex a clutch of homes located beyond the perimeter at the south-eastern corner of the monastery, where he intended to move the living quarters, now in the main building.

The oldest buildings were located on the western elevation, including the main entrance to the monastery, and housed the office of the abbot, a grand reception hall, and various smaller meeting rooms, as well as the library and archives that could be accessed by a set of stairs in the library. The room for the printing press was also connected to the library, but it had a separate entrance via the abbot's office on the upper floor.

The church, in all its Gothic glory, was just behind the main building. Three bells, each with a specific purpose, dangled from two towers. The large building abutting the quadrangle housed the monk's living quarters (students came from the furthest reaches of

Spain and all its colonies), in addition to rooms for contemplation and study, and a small infirmary.

No one had given me details about the kind of work I would be engaged in or how long I would stay. Each time I tried to raise the issue, the response was the same: You must wait for your meeting with the abbot.

Beyond Brother Siraj, I also made the acquaintance of the librarian, pastor Isaac Loyola, a native priest the Jesuits had brought back from the American colonies. Siraj told me that when he arrived, he was still a pagan and had remained one for some time before wholeheartedly professing his Catholicism and adherence to the Jesuit monastic order. At one time, he had even been a teacher of Christian ethics, but Father Gaddis removed him from the position as soon as he became aware of his religious zealotry and puritanical streak that was out of step with the openness embraced by the Jesuits.

I decided to go see if the library contained any Oriental manuscripts, but pastor Isaac told me that, although the library once held some theological texts from Andalusia, they had all been sent to the Royal Monastery of San Lorenzo de El Escorial, north of Madrid. Intrigued, he asked me, "Why are you looking for those?"

"To see if there is anything among them that would be of interest to my father," I replied.

I also met Father Savila, who would be my teacher during the four weeks of instruction in Ignatian spirituality required of all novices who were to join the Jesuit order. The Jesuits were masters of reading the hearts of their pupils. How they did it, I have no idea. But I surmised that these spiritual teachings were at the heart of it. Yusuf the Morisco once described it as knowing and understanding the battles people are waging in their lives. So, when I met Father Savila, he quickly discovered I was trying to hide my total disinterest in anything related to the Jesuit order. Consequently, the impression of me that he passed to Father Gaddis was quite negative, which I only learned later.

I was also introduced to the science instructor, pastor Juan Andrés. He was a natural scientist and a proponent of the new movement that embraced the knowability of the world through science. Truth be told, I liked this priest more than any of the others I had met and would visit him often in his laboratory while he ran experiments on materials, liquids, and air. On one occasion, he brought up the topic of aether. Was it a question for theology or the natural sciences?

Pastor Andrés proposed that aether was a substance that could be understood through scientific inquiry. He would prattle on about various thought experiments that could help determine its nature—like placing gigantic mirrors on several mountain peaks to reflect the light at the moment of sunrise, under various meteorological conditions, such as humidity and heat. If the light struck the final mirror more slowly under a specific condition compared to others, then it would prove that light does indeed travel through a medium—aether. Naturally, since this experiment was more dream than reality, the question remained unresolved and, consequently, theologians could wade into the debate.

It became clear two weeks after my arrival at the Monastery of the Divine Incarnation that this was more than just a monastery. I hadn't really understood the meaning of "house arrest" until my meeting with the head of the monastery and our heated discussion. Prior to that moment, I hadn't felt any restraint outside of needing to ask permission from Father Gaddis when I wanted to go out. And it wasn't just me. Many others were in the same situation.

The Monastery of the Divine Incarnation was the oldest in the city, dating back more than three centuries. In the beginning, it was Dominican, before being taken over by the Jesuits. Despite its religious and educational mandate, it also played a political role, not only in administering Bilbao, but also the many villages and towns spread throughout the Basque region, including San Sebastián and its prison. The Jesuits themselves seemed to be welcoming of commerce and industry in the city and maintained connections throughout Holland and England as well as with the sultans of Marrakech. Nor did the Jesuits seem to be sticklers regarding the general ban on using Arabic and Hebrew in Spain. Their network of influence was truly extensive. They were fully aware of our impounded Arabic printing press, which they bought and then expressly sought me out to operate. They fully intended to use the press to print Catholic books directed at Christianized Muslims and their children, whether at home in Spain or abroad, where their missionaries were labouring to win new souls for Christ.

Chapter 7

I couldn't quite fathom why Siraj was so enthralled by Father Gaddis' talents at argumentation and rhetoric, mentioning it even before my first encounter with the father. "He is a mix of Socratic entrapment and divine gifts."

"You can talk all day without the father interrupting you with a single word. But you should be aware that, the more you speak, the more you are disclosing about yourself. He listens intently while plumbing the depths of your soul to know just how to catch you off guard, as if to slip in through a backdoor you thought you had locked! Argumentation for him is almost an end in itself. What he finds so appealing about it is that it fully disrobes the person before him, disarming him of any means of self-defence."

Father Gaddis tried tirelessly to introduce argumentation into the foundational principles of the Jesuit order, but the fathers in Rome baulked. Undeterred, he added it as a course in the student curriculum and presented it himself. I studied under him, and I must admit that I learned a great deal from his lessons. However, while I may have been intellectually convinced that argumentation was a powerful tool to expose the soul, emotionally, I found nothing palatable about taking advantage of my opponent's weakness during debate or feigning gentleness toward him in his defeat while still pummelling him with velvet blows. Why not just open his eyes to what he didn't know and then leave him to himself? Must we convince him through anger? Did we really have to force him into paradise?

I remained unconvinced that defeating a person was the key to guiding him toward the right path. What value did the path to God have if the person was vanquished along the way? I raised my concern once to Father Gaddis and asked him, "Shouldn't we help people to protect the truth they have?" He answered, "If that truth is corrupted and false, then we must awaken him to his awful state." My soul was ill at ease with Father Gaddis, and I kept asking myself: Are the godly forged through the laying bare of their internal contradictions or by the opposite? Is the very purpose of our God-given talents really just to find new followers?

This unsettled feeling began the moment Siraj brought me to the abbot, who was in a prayer room next to his office, accessed via a long corridor running alongside the chapel of Saint Teresa, then up one level and to the right before finally opening onto the spacious room. I don't recall its specific name, but it seemed to be used by the fathers for deliberations convened by the abbot.

In that room hung an enormous painting of Saint Ignatius de Loyola receiving a papal bull heralding the birth of the Jesuit order. I was led into a small chamber at the end of the room on the right. It was a simple hermitage, but it had a certain solemnity, perhaps owing to the beautifully crafted statue of the Virgin Mary, mother of Jesus, cradling her child and weeping over him. This small enclosure seemed to be the back entrance to the abbot's office, used primarily by simple folk and other unimportant people. Or perhaps it was a safe place to withdraw for those not wanting to pass through the visitor reception hall.

We waited for about a quarter of an hour. I thumbed through dozens of thick stacks of papers on the small table beside the fireplace, including several guides to living a spiritual life (perhaps the father was reviewing them) when I noticed two identical works of art composed of seashells. Each one was painted with a black cross and placed on either side of the statue. Siraj and I sat alone together in the room until Father Gaddis came in, his face wizened and brow furrowed by time, while his beard (a bit longer than the Morisco's) was snow white, evoking a reverential dignity that befitted his august spiritual stature.

Siraj moved toward him, kissing his hand, and bowing in deference. I followed suit and, when the father permitted me to be seated, Siraj remained standing to take the father's Aragonese cloak and ceremonial ivory-tipped mace. The father welcomed me with a faint smile that quickly disappeared. At first, I was startled. However, the soft, weary sounds he made as he exhaled brought a measure of calm to my heart. This was a calm I later realized was more profound than I had expected.

The father began to speak. "Robert my son, I know your soul is in turmoil, and that you are seeking solace to calm your troubled heart. But what the spirituality of Saint Ignatius teaches us is that we only seek that which is also seeking us. You will not reach the depths of your soul unless you are completely free. And, at this very moment, you yearn to be with your parents in England rather than in a gilded prison operating an Arabic printing press. The Jesuit tradition is concerned first and foremost with the safety of one's being from the things of this world that try to possess the body. And when that safety is provided, then everything else—the diseases and maladies of the soul—can be overcome and borne with patience."

After all the worry that had preceded his appearance, these words filled me with comfort, and, when he allowed me to talk, I quickly began to reveal the things hidden in my soul. "It's just as you said, Father. Father Savila caught me off guard when he said I had to follow a course of Jesuit instruction and the Spiritual Exercises of Saint Ignatius. All I knew was that I was here to operate the Arabic printing press—a press that my family paid a boatload for. How can the monastery allow itself to buy an item it knows full well was stolen?"

As I summed up my argument, I recalled what Siraj had said about the father's talents. "You can imagine, Father, that my heart is not inclined to be here. Even if the printing press were war plunder, it wouldn't be the property of England or Holland. It's private property. We paid dearly for the press and for my passage on that ship. We were even going to pay the customs taxes to bring it into our own country! I languished nine months in prison. God alone knows what I endured there."

I fell silent and lowered my head. He responded while looking past the tears I was pushing back. "We can compensate your father for the press. The true value of such a press transcends its material value. It has a moral value as well because it will be used in the service of the Lord. It can also be used, however, in the service of the Church's enemies, such as the Lutherans and the heretics. I don't think you would raise such an objection knowing that we are not chasing after commerce or profit like your father. Our objective isn't earthly in the slightest. Can you really say that your use of the press is more noble in purpose than ours?"

"Yes, I can, and excuse me, Father. The monastery can achieve its goals without taking what does not belong to it. You can buy another Arabic press. Or hire those who produce Arabic typeset. At the end of the day, the means at your disposal are much greater than those of a simple English print master who lives in the English countryside and must rely entirely on his limited influence. What is the point of making a young man in the prime of his life—who himself committed no wrong—remain among criminals? Perhaps you would take pity on us if I told you how my father suffered trying to procure this press after numerous attempts that all ended in failure. Maybe you would pity us even more if I spoke of the hopes we had hung on that press. We too want to serve the Lord by selling publications that carry the spirit of Christianity to those who have not yet heard the good news and glad tidings."

"It sounds like your experience in prison was more than you could bear. We tried many times to contact you, from the moment you entered prison, but the warden made excuses each time. When we did meet you, you yourself refused to leave."

"The warden influenced my refusal, Father. He had a plan and delayed me by saying that, if it succeeded, he would send me directly back to my homeland with the press."

The father turned to Siraj, asking him to summon his deputy. Then he continued, "We will look into the matter of the warden. He should not have acted in such a way." Then, after noting something down in his papers, he said, "As for the press itself, what you said would be accurate if the monastery had dealt directly with your family. The printing press became ownerless the moment the battle ended. If England and Holland had been victorious, then the roles would have been reversed, and Spanish goods would have consequently fallen into the hands of others. You can also blame your country. Had England maintained good relations with its neighbours, then it would not have caused these losses."

Just as he was saying this, Siraj and the abbot's deputy entered the room. The father kept going, "Are you so sure that the press you bought wasn't stolen from someone else? If you knew that the press was originally French and seized by Dutch Protestants through deceit and trickery when it was on its way from Paris to Antwerp, would you honestly think that you had bought something you had no right to? You can take my word as a promise—with my deputy and Siraj as my witnesses—we will compensate you for your losses on the condition that you remain with us for an entire year. What do you say to that?"

"I kiss the ground beneath your feet, Father. However, there is something else if you will permit me. It's that I have not been able to write to my parents ever since I fell into captivity, and they are surely worried sick about me. May I write to them letting them know where I am and that I'm still alive?"

"Yes, you may. Write what you would like, and we will send it on its way."

"I am at the service of the monastery and its needs, Father."

The father got up from his seat and walked slowly toward the statue of the Virgin and *Christ the Redeemer*, saying, "The four weeks of Spiritual Exercises that you will undertake are not solely for those desiring to join the Jesuits, and they differ according to the readiness of the seeker who comes of his own accord. Since you will work for us at least a full year, you will have dealings with the full membership of the monastery and will experience first-hand life among Jesuit monks. So these lessons will be exceedingly important for you—and us as well, naturally. Perhaps, after passing them, you will find yourself more able to understand your inner self and improve your soul. At its core, it is religious and spiritual training with some modern science, as well as teachings of the saints and Greek philosophers. It isn't four weeks exactly, that's the average. It could be longer, or it could be shorter, depending on the preparedness of each student."

As the father returned to his seat, I said, "If you'll allow me to speak. I met a man in prison. A Moor named José bin Hajari. As I spent a great deal of time with him in prison, I learned he was a Christianized Arab. I also learned that the prison administration knew the charges against him were not entirely accurate. He had sent reports to mislead the French and helped expose a cell of Protestants working against Spain. Afterward, he was promised amnesty in honour of his devotion to Spain and his Catholic faith. And yet he is still in prison. I found him to be a learned man with a high degree of knowledge. An ascetic. His family was renowned for their charity in Zaragoza, so much so that a huge crowd came out for his father's funeral. They even bequeathed all their possessions and farmlands to the Church before departing Zaragoza. Could I beseech our Father to intervene on his behalf, to release him from prison given that he is eligible under the Catholic qualification law, for example, or however my Father sees fit?"

He responded calmly, "What makes you ask for that, Robert?"

"This man trusted me, but I betrayed that trust. If I could, I would atone for my error and help him. My guilt and dereliction toward him nearly kill me."

The father commented determinedly this time, "It's not yours to make such a request, Robert. Don't forget. You are not a Spaniard and will one day return to your country. Cases against Moors, their problems and their conspiracies against Spain are innumerable, and you know nothing about them. Perhaps this Hajari is a devoted Catholic and his family are workers of good deeds, but we can't plumb the depths of his soul to know with certainty he wants the best for Spain. His legal case is political in nature, not criminal. His uncle, Afoukay, conspired with the Dutch and Saadians against Spanish interests."

"But what guilt does he bear for his uncle serving the enemies of Spain?"

"He was corresponding with his uncle. I have no control over this matter, nor do the Jesuits. His sentencing came from the Tribunal of the Holy Office of the Inquisition."

Angrily, the father got up to leave, gesturing to the deputy and Siraj to follow. I was unable to move for several minutes before Siraj returned and told me that I had been insolent in asking such a thing of the father, and that I had to apologize and vow to never raise this subject again with anyone as long as I remained at the monastery. I agreed immediately. I needed the trust of the father as I tried to untangle my new environment. I told Siraj to inform Father Gaddis that I was at his service—heart, mind, and body.

Chapter 8

"To Heaven its wisdom and to the troubled soul its resting place. Is pain simply the outcome of experiencing freedom? A moment of silence, protected from all intrusion and disruption, ought to grant man the courage needed to harmonise his passions with his logical reasoning and thus allow him to begin to notice—not just what he has failed to see before—but what he has directly and unconsciously gained as well. Man's will, derived from both mind and heart, serve as a mirror, reflecting the whole soul as it makes its journey through this life.

"Subsequently, confession is no longer a bargaining or negotiation with life, its purpose, or its justifications. Rather, it becomes akin to a conversation between father and child in which you do not reveal something hidden from everyone, but rather you hide something that everyone knows. Perhaps what you are keeping hidden is a tear, a laugh, or a pearl of wisdom that even lowly cattle know. You did not wish to convince anyone of something, nor for someone to convince you either. You simply dissolve and submerge yourself within the grander meaning of life that lifts you up to the level of wholeness and completeness. For as long as the fences around your heart remain in place, you can never be whole.

"Your many secrets will keep you divided internally. However, the sign that you are complete and whole is not that you know all the answers, but that you know all the questions. It's not that you deny yourself everything, but rather that you are in need of it all. It's not that you talk to yourself, but that the universe speaks to you. For the soul expands and contracts to the degree that you offer or shun, reveal or hide."

That was Father Savila's teaching during the first class I attended, during which he offered commentary on the word of the Lord in the 16th chapter of John the Apostle: "In all truth I tell you, you will be weeping and wailing while the world will rejoice; you will be sorrowful, but your sorrow will turn to joy."

For some reason, though the room was full, I felt he was addressing me directly. Is it truly good and useful for man to confess all the doubts raging inside him? I was trying to completely forget who I was and what I wanted. I had cast from me the Morisco's spirit and turned over my entire will to the monastery. And just as I had done during those moments hidden away in the crates when the ship fell into the hands of the Spaniards, I resigned myself entirely to fate.

And so began the Spiritual Exercises. All that we were permitted to do during this period was withdraw into ourselves, read, ponder, and attend the spiritual courses. We were supposed to draw close to the great soul of Jesus until we ourselves became part of his crucified body, attaining the absolute highest divinity that man can achieve. Yet, even when I finished the Exercises, I was still deeply and profoundly unsettled. During the confessional sessions that formed part of this spiritual program, I reformulated and reworded this feeling multiple ways, but nothing could shake the Morisco's secret from my mind.

I confessed to Father Savila that I did not yet understand the essence of the Ignatian teaching. How exactly was the soul of an embodied presence supposed to inhabit me? Could one consistently maintain such spiritual fitness all the time? And what was the solution to the many contradictions that surrounded man on all sides? He said, "The answer is inside of you. You just need to know how to find it, and that's the purpose of the Jesuit order's three great principles:

Communal life, absolute obedience, and openness to the world."

I struggled deeply with these Jesuit principles, especially because of Father Savila's cheerful, poetic manner in teaching them. I learned that he had reached the rank of abbot and had lived for twelve years in a cave, isolated and alone in the Sinai deserts. He had also been a candidate for bishop over one of the dioceses in the Basque region, but he preferred to remain involved in pedagogical work with Father Gaddis. The countless virtues of Father Savila were the talk of all the students at the monastery.

I mentioned to Siraj once that I wanted to ask the father myself if all these anecdotes were true, but he insisted that it was highly inappropriate for us as scholastics to ask the fathers such questions. Only someone of a higher rank would be allowed to do so.

I sketched out the three Jesuit principles in the shape of an open palm, placing each one on a finger. I put Father Gaddis' principle of argumentation on the index finger and, on the thumb, I included my own principle, which I called the principle of "the end". For me, this fifth principle was the most important. When Father Savila inquired about it, I said, "This pillar strengthens my resolve when the other principles are weak."

Naturally, he found fault with this and warned me against "innovation," because it splits hairs and distracts effort. I asked him what I should write on the thumb, and he advised me to cut it off!

I didn't cut it off. The word "innovation" confused me. Jesuits themselves hadn't been around more than a hundred years, and the principle of argumentation was entirely Father Gaddis's invention! However, I drew a sun next to the thumb, its rays covering it up, and I placed a cross at the centre. Next to each finger, I added symbols to help me remember what I had understood and its associated meanings. At the same time, it revealed the ideological malleability within the Jesuits. I wrote at the bottom:

"O God, who knows what is inside of me, when I know what is inside of thee, I shall love all mankind. This is my hand. Take it to do thy obedient will through absolute submission to thee and through the pure love of all thy creations and through joint work with all thy children. Guide me on the pathway unto the end, even salvation."

When Father Savila asked me to explain the Ignatian principles to him, I showed him my diagram and began to talk about my unease toward them. It was this same unease that made me realize I needed to experience the fruits of Jesuit spirituality first-hand—something I had not yet done.

I told him, "Once I personally witness the great spirit that pervades the Ignatian principles, then will they begin to be meaningful to me, and that will be thanks to the many people whose dreams and pains I will have shared and whose errors and trespasses against me I will have transcended. Yet can someone really enjoy his freedom without giving over a portion of it to others who also want to taste it? Can an individual truly transcend that Protestant spirit with its attendant scepticism, which originates within the values of personal freedom and independence? Yes, I serve the group, but not because the group has inherent value, but because I as an individual gain my personhood and my personality by being a fully integrated member in the group. If the group were the only thing to exist, then I would not exist."

Father Savila reminded me of things I had forgotten. Though why exactly, I was not sure. But I fully embraced the principle of absolute obedience during the first Spiritual Exercises and turned my heart over to the will of my teachers. It was not easy for me to do, but I was convinced by what Father Savila had taught. He continued:

"The principle of absolute obedience is essential to achieving the integration of the soul, which is prone to fracturing and splintering as it tries to prove itself to others in hopes of winning their approval. This principle alone is what allows the heart to open itself up to the whole world. How would you be able to observe the world if you were divided and torn between dozens of conflicting and contradictory facts? Absolute obedience stems from one central, accepted truth. And embracing it will be essential as you attempt to accumulate knowledge in a world full of contradictions."

He went on: "You will not be able to perceive any creative, holistic spirit, nor a guiding force within all existence until you surrender your soul to this grand principle that existed before you, surrounds you now, and needs your soul. Absolute obedience to a greater Will that knows what you don't, even about yourself, will steer you clear of the misery that awaits a soul full of itself or reliant on others."

For eight months, I zealously applied myself to the lessons and Spiritual Exercises. I didn't leave the monastery at all during this time, nor did I work in the printing shop until I had passed my foundational instruction, and then only for a few hours each night. My work there consisted simply of translating, installing the press and the typesetting letters, and editing pages after printing. I began to have a sneaking suspicion that it was all merely a ruse to conscript me into promoting the work of the Jesuits. If not, what was the rationale for spitefully expelling me from Spain upon discovering I had tried to contact the Morisco when I had left the monastery for good?

I refused to take any wages, and I didn't write my father a letter nor did I accept any compensation for the printing press. I was still attached to the idea that I would make something of a life in the monastery. Even after being freed, I adhered to the spiritual teachings of the Jesuits. Truth be told, I'll never deny the grace and kindness the Jesuits extended to me, despite the fact that my subsequent separation from them was one-sided. It was they who washed their hands of me and not the other way around. And yet their spiritual philosophy and theology were essential to my understanding of how God thinks about His children.

Chapter 9

I must admit that my time at the monastery—regimented though it was—and the absence of threats to my personal safety nurtured my budding Catholic faith, and I continued to fortify it through extended religious studies under the guidance of the monastery's teachers. However, as soon as I began to emerge from that cocoon, returning to experiment with freedom in a more natural environment, my former doubts came rushing back—the doubts that had nourished my rebellious spirit with an insatiable curiosity to explore the vague and unknown, untethered to all these complex theories and pre-packaged truths found in the books of ancient saints and philosophers.

I discussed this at length with Fathers Gaddis and Savila, saying to them, "The principles of openness to the world and absolute obedience are incompatible except under certain strict conditions. If any of these is violated, then the contradictions become plain as day. And these are the same conditions that feed people's doubts and hesitancy toward the Jesuits on account of their strict and methodical teachings."

I would brazenly question them, "How can we think to pass judgment on a boy for disobeying his father, who is beating his mother, after she caused the death of the donkey that provided the family's livelihood? Or let us imagine an even more complicated scenario than that!"

However, their response always hinged on the fact that the goal of the Ignatian teaching, at its core, was to rise above the messy details of life and create a holistic spirit inspired by the sacrifice of the Lord to overcome original sin. Subsequently, when we descend again to this world, we do not return as judges, but as divinely incarnated beings, overflowing with an abundance of tranquillity and serenity toward the boy, mother, and father thanks to our having surrendered to the wisdom of the Lord. "Everyone ought to apologize to everyone," they would remind me constantly.

However, this all presupposes that the family understands the Lord like the fathers and saints, or nearly as well. What I took away from the anecdote of the donkey and family is that, if it had been the donkey who kicked the mother in her side, breaking her ribs, the donkey would have had to apologize, too!

I hid my doubts and buried them deep within my soul, but they persisted, awakening all at once when the order for me to leave Spain arrived. After two and a half years in captivity, I wrote to my parents, hoping to put their minds at ease. When the Inquisition's decision came, I had only one day to gather up my things. Someone was assigned to escort and keep watch over me, accompanying me to the port where a ship would take me away to the Spanish Netherlands.

The decision came as a complete surprise. At first, I guessed the reason behind it was my refusal to set up a Jesuit order in southern England. By necessity, it would have had to be clandestine, and I confessed to Father Gaddis that a life of secrecy did not suit me at all—and was entirely at odds with Jesuit teachings. However, my guess was not exactly right.

When I met Father Gaddis on my last day, he asked what I intended to do after I left, and whether I would return to England. I told him that I wanted to stay in Spain for some time to be among my Catholic brothers and deepen my faith, which ought to be lived and not just based on theory, and to expand my network of religious relations. Only then would I think about returning to England.

Perhaps it was this comment that gave the Father a glimmer of hope that I would become a soldier in his service and a Jesuit missionary among the Protestants. I had the makings of an evangelist and a servant of the Lord. Father Gaddis said so himself on one of my last visits with him. The only thing I lacked was more zealotry and more time to study and deepen my Jesuit learning.

The Father also informed me that, as soon as he received permission to print the *Book of Hours,* he would send it to me so I could begin working on it. During my time at the monastery, I had translated the *Spiritual Exercises of Saint Ignatius* into Arabic, which they had received authorisation to print on the condition it not be distributed within Spain. I printed a small number of copies of the book, which turned out to be the only one the press produced during my time there.

Before this, I had never operated a printing press, and this book was the first I had produced in Arabic. Truth be told, had it not been for Yusuf the Morisco's Arabic lessons, I would not have been able to arrange the typeset, given its shoddy quality. The letters were worn down in some places, causing me a great deal of work in the end. Additionally, the font was based on ancient manuscripts, so the size of each letter was unwieldy, making it difficult to print a sensible number of words on each page. What followed the printing, though, was even more labour-intensive—filling in the missing parts and placing vowels over the letters as needed.

As for the decision to depart the monastery, it was more akin to a tacit agreement between two parties, each equally sheepish about the deal itself. The fathers (according to Siraj) looked toward my future serving as the leader of a Jesuit missionary group. As such, I needed to try my hand at living in the real world before embarking on more study. However, the desire to do so had to spring from within me first and foremost. Also, my anxiety and unsettled feelings, which were subtly reflected during my confessionals, caused them to not be entirely confident I would choose that path. In their view, the crux of the issue was that I wasn't useful to them if I simply remained at the monastery, and so they began to indirectly encourage me to leave, although still remaining in contact with Father Gaddis.

As for me, leaving the monastery was imperative, and not because I wanted to put Jesuit life to the test, but because I had my own projects and plans, the first of which was writing to my parents. I wrote them after my departure:

My dear father,

I pray to the Lord Almighty that this letter reaches you and that you and mother are in the best of health and spirits. I can't write much in this letter other than my deep yearning for you and our home in Truro. Please tell mother I am doing fine. During this long period, I was a prisoner and could not write. The Jesuit monks released me two days ago. I would like to inform you that I have converted to Catholicism, and I pray this does not cause you consternation. I will stay here in Spain for some time, though for how long I do not know. It depends on a weighty matter. The story is long, and I cannot go into detail here. However, I am undertaking a rich spiritual and intellectual experiment.

I was able to use the Arabic printing press myself—the one we purchased from the Dutch. The press saved me, Father. Imagine that. Had it not been for the press, I may have wound up as a slave on some

Spanish galley. It troubles me to tell you that I could not recover the press, however. Father Gaddis was ready to compensate us for its value, but I refused. I will work diligently, Father, to obtain a new set of Arabic type. I have learned so much about Arabic letters, and I promise you that I will repay your loss even if I am forced to carve the typeset with my own hand. I won't deny, however, that the letters we procured were unsuitably large.

While in prison, I thought back to Aunt Anna the Mohammedan. What made me think of her was a Christianized Moor named Yusuf bin Ma'mun bin Qassim Al-Hajari. He was the nephew of Afoukay Al-Hajari who taught Arabic in Holland thirty years ago. I don't know whether you have heard of him. I learned so much from this man, and we spoke at length during my time there. I can't say that I was entirely fond of him, but he has a secret that I will disclose to you at a later time. Now, however, I want to ask about the astronomical text that Aunt Anna copied for us. Was the author Al-Majriti? And if so, how did we come by it? And what are the other Arabic manuscripts in our possession?

As for what I know about Al-Hajari, the French captured him around the summer of 1618, and he remained imprisoned for about three years. Afterward, they released him so he could spy against the Spanish on their behalf. He eventually made his way back to Spain undetected, though he remained under the watchful eye of the French until he was caught red-handed by the Spaniards in possession of some reports and plans. They sent him first to one of the mines along the Mediterranean, then transferred him to a reformist prison where he has remained ever since. For a while, he was communicating secretly with a French publisher in Paris, sending him periodic news about Spain in exchange for his help in finding two Gothic women in the prime of their lives accompanied by an African servant. These two women were holding onto something extremely valuable, and he is quite certain that the two sisters did not depart France. Yet there are signs that indicate they may have arrived in Holland. What do I do father? How do we find these sisters?

Send my warmest regards to mother. I pray that we meet again soon.

Your dutiful son, Robert

Bilbao, 4 September 1639

After I left the monastery, I obtained employment working in the paper and wool market, thanks to a letter of introduction given to me by Father Gaddis. I thought it likely he wanted me to remain close by. Otherwise, how would he know that I had spent weeks trying to get access to indexes for a trove of Oriental manuscripts in Europe's largest libraries? How, too, would he have known that I was searching for someone to send me to the library of the El Escorial Monastery north of Madrid, that housed the Zaydani Library? And how would he know that I had written to the stationer who used to visit Yusuf? In a letter, which fell into the monks' hands, I apologized to Yusuf and told him that I had just recently been freed, and that I needed some important information from him as I awaited my father's reply.

The fathers didn't know Yusuf's secret. Consequently, they immediately suspected I was involved in forming Lutheran or Turkish underground cells, which made them grow vengeful toward me, especially Father Gaddis, who had hoped I would remain faithful to them. In their eyes, I had become like a dog that bit the hand of those who fed it.

Part 3

The Dutch Arabist

I wasn't convinced by what Professor Golius said. To disavow an idea doesn't necessarily mean you despise the person holding it. That's how I dealt with the Morisco. I learned what I wanted from him while neither liking nor hating him. To me, he was just another person.

Chapter 10

I doffed my shoes at the first-floor entry to the home of the "shy lady" (where I had been staying since my arrival in Leiden) and slipped on a pair of the felt-soled house slippers she required of all boarders. As we ascended the stairs to the attic, she recounted the house's long history. My weight must have caused the floorboards to creak and groan, which irritated the lady, because it kept interrupting her. As if to shame me into looking for accommodation elsewhere, she remarked, "The stairs are talking back to you!" I retorted that the stairs were fine by me!

As she showed me the room, she must have sensed that I was displeased, as she offered up that, "It's only temporary, until the room with a balcony on the first floor is readied within a week. Unless of course you married me and we lived together." She chuckled. I laughed too, surprised at this, given that she was called "the shy lady." I thought it was just a household nickname, but it became evident that this was what everyone called her.

The shy lady held onto a trace of her youthful beauty, which I imagined had once been the talk of Rotterdam, her former home. She looked to be in her mid-fifties, but still had all the pulsating energy and vitality of youth, perhaps owing to the many knickknacks in her home that she had to care for, as well as a small garden out back. With her keenness to wear clothes that made her appear young and stylish, even exposing her bosom and shoulders, she seemed to wrestle with a deep-seated, repressed lust. She admitted as much to me after several months, saying that she never had a husband who understood her needs and desires and, consequently, she preferred to stay far removed from Rotterdam.

A few days later, she moved me to the room on the lower floor with the balcony that overlooked the Prince William canal. She said it was the best room in the house. And it seemed so, being much more spacious than the first. I could tell that the trinkets in the room—and, more generally, throughout the house—weren't placed haphazardly. There was always a logic to it, whether it was to take advantage of the dance and play of light and shadow, or to facilitate movement about the house, or just to highlight some things over others. Yet perhaps above all else—as she once remarked—you found the *things* she cherished, if not necessarily the people.

I spent the first few days praising the shy lady's fine taste and the beauty and arrangement of her home, as well as the great attention to detail that Claudia, the housemaid, also displayed. I grew confident that the two women had also become more comfortable with me. Though from the start, my interest in old manuscripts had vexed them a bit, since they assumed I would be lugging piles of old books and dusty artefacts back to the house.

The shy lady did not care for antiques. In fact, she relished supervising the carpenters who often made new pieces of furniture for her. It was her greatest pleasure in life, and she was constantly replacing her furniture, selling the old and buying the new. She once confided in me that it was her way of living in a new and ever-changing world, and she certainly gave scrupulous attention to even the smallest details of this world.

I arrived in Leiden carrying a letter from my father to Jacob Golius, professor of Arabic and mathematics at the University of Leiden. I had gone from Antwerp to Amsterdam five weeks earlier and had no intention of staying in the city other than to look for a ship that would sail me back to England. Yet fear returned spontaneously the moment I saw Mr. Jos once again, as he was giving orders to the porters, hoisting gigantic baskets of piglets and geese onto one of the ships flying the Dutch flag.

I decided to linger in Amsterdam a bit longer among the libraries and booksellers, searching for any clue that might lead me to one of the manuscripts the Morisco had mentioned. I wrote to my father and informed him of where I had ended up and filled him in on what I hadn't been able to say in my first letter concerning the lost collection of manuscripts. I then asked him to send some money. By the time his reply arrived, I was begging and scrounging through garbage, destitute, as I searched for work that would save me from hunger and the cold. On more than one occasion, I threw myself at the mercy of Mr. Jos, pleading with him to hire me and waiting for his signal each time a job of a few hours became available. I was eternally grateful he did not recognize me, seeing how I was in such a state in which a person hoped no one but God knew who they were.

From my father's letter, it was apparent he was displeased that I had converted to Catholicism. He reminded me that, even though the Dutch were religious people, they didn't really care whether you were Catholic, Protestant, or even a Jew or Muslim. He rehashed the story of my grandfather, Owen, who refused the king of Spain's offer to become a naval captain if he would convert to Catholicism. I understood my father's reaction, but did he really think that the Dutch were tolerant simply for the sake of gold and not the Lord himself?

I told my father that Yusuf might know the precise location of the manuscripts and had been waiting for just the right time to inform me. However, I left prison just as events began to take a turn for the worse. If I could reach him, then perhaps he would guide me to their location. However, my father held the opinion that Yusuf's options were extremely limited and that I should forget him altogether and just concentrate on the two sisters.

My father wrote:

It seems that Erpenius obtained the Al-Majriti manuscript the very same year the Morisco was captured. Seeing that Yusuf had mentioned to you that the manuscript was with the sisters, then that would suggest they arrived in Holland, because Anna the Mohammedan copied it for us from Erpenius' text. It is a manuscript dealing with alchemy, not astronomy.

Perhaps it's best that you take advantage of being in Holland by visiting Jacob Golius in Leiden before coming home to us. We studied Arabic together under Erpenius and, when he passed away, Jacob succeeded him as chair of Arabic studies at the University of Leiden. Try to ask him about the original Arabic copy or if you might take a look at the Erpenius archives. However, be careful with Jacob. He is a man obsessed with manuscripts.

Jacob spent two or three years with the Dutch delegation in Marrakech and several more years in Syria, Iraq, and Constantinople, but hadn't amassed more than two hundred manuscripts. It's why you need to be cautious with him regarding the Morisco's library because he might attempt to seize it for himself. Don't broach the topic of the Al-Majriti manuscript with him directly, rather mention any other manuscript you might find in Holland and from there, drive the conversation toward the Erpenius collection and whether accessing the archives of this great intellectual would be possible for an amateur. Don't forget, you must be persistent and stubborn with Jacob.

I didn't call upon Professor Golius immediately after arriving in the city. In fact, it wasn't until three weeks later that I met him. During those first weeks, I visited the university library and came across the names of Jacob Golius and René Descartes in the lending records of the Latin translation of Al-Majriti's *Ghayat Al-Hakeem*, known among European scholars as the *Picatrix*. Although catalogued in the library, the Arabic original was nowhere to be found. No doubt this original was the first thread that would lead to Najma Al-Hajari and the Morisco's manuscripts.

I was now more knowledgeable about what I wanted and how I could approach Jacob without allowing his intellect to swallow me up and overpower me, as the warden had done to the Lombard and Father Gaddis with Siraj the monk. The shy lady had mentioned to me that the homes of Professors Golius and Descartes were opposite one another on the Prince William canal and just a few houses down from her home. In fact, this was not news to me. My choice of a place to live wasn't left to chance, and it had a story all its own as I made my way to Leiden whereupon I learned of René Descartes for the very first time.

Chapter 11

The day I went to meet Professor Jacob, I brought along some manuscripts I had procured in Amsterdam. Among them was a small, tattered pamphlet filled with drawings that explained how to perform ablutions and prayers for newcomers to Islam. There was also a Sufi *dhikr* manuscript written in an Andalusian dialect mixed randomly with Andalusian Arabic and Castilian Spanish, as well as a copy of the *Tale of Al-Miqdad and Al-Miyasa* alongside other works in Hebrew and Greek. I hadn't expected these manuscripts would make Jacob's mouth water, so I left them with him to peruse. Parting with them caused me no regret because a Jewish merchant had freely given them to me as a way to get rid of them himself. However, I did hold onto the important manuscripts for my father.

He opened the door to the vestibule where I and others were awaiting our turn to see him. He called out, "Robert George Febin?"

I thought he was going to invite me in, but instead he asked that I return that afternoon after he had finished interviewing all the new applicants. I felt slightly annoyed, but told him, "It's fine. I'll wait."

I could tell that my large satchel and the manuscript I was thumbing through had caught his eye, because the rest of the interviews proceeded quickly and, after less than an hour, he turned away the remaining appointments. He made short work of the last applicant when he opened the door and shouted, "Tell your father that the University of Leiden is not his family's personal fiefdom!" Then he invited me in.

Describing this man isn't terribly difficult, though on this occasion he wasn't attired in the usual garb worn by university professors. Anyone seeing him that day for the first time would presume without hesitation that he was one of the many art dealers that had begun to populate Holland. His moustache was light, offering little contrast to the tone of his skin, while his tightly cropped beard barely covered the tip of his chin. It was clear from his gait that he was trying to hide a small limp in his left leg. "It's been a long time since I last saw your father," he said as he made his way over to his liquor cabinet. "He never told me that he had *finally* been blessed with a son!"

With an effortless grace, he mixed a white wine with something he called genever while continuing to talk and gesturing over to a large mural above the cabinet: "Faced with the Spanish embargo, Prince William the Silent rewarded the people of Leiden for their steadfastness by establishing a Protestant university in the Netherlands. This painting, Robert, memorializes the salvation of the people who had been forced to eat rats and insects rather than turn over their city to the Spaniards."

He invited me to try out the concoction he had made, adding, "We have as many names for genever as the Eskimos have for snow! And you could spend a lifetime trying to find one worthy of being called a spirited drink."

I feigned surprise at the taste as he prattled on, "From among today's applicants, I accepted only one student. He was the only one whose answers I could not guess ahead of time. Everyone else simply wanted to be copies of Leiden professors!"

Retrieving some books on his desk, he placed them back on the shelf behind him and said, "For me, manuscripts are like a strong drink that immerses you completely. You have to set aside all the distractions around you and allow time to drift slowly by so you can truly savour and evaluate each text's importance. And, above all else, each manuscript's scent is unique, and each book must be dealt with according to its own unique rites and rituals lest you spoil that special moment."

He kept droning on about his former relationship with my father, back when they studied Arabic together under Erpenius. He began to ask questions, the answers to which I worried would anger him, so I began to show him the manuscripts I had brought. With great care and attention, he looked and turned them over one by one and said, "I suppose you did not come to show me what you have. Is there something I can do for you?"

I told him what I knew about the Al-Majriti manuscript and that I would be grateful if I could take a look at the original Arabic copy. "Why?" he asked.

"We want to compare it with ours so we can see what we could translate and print from the two manuscripts that would be of interest and use to a European audience, or even print the manuscript in Arabic to sell in the Orient."

"Your father's knowledge of Arabic is excellent. I couldn't believe it when he said that it was thanks to your grandfather who'd been held captive by the Arabs. Your father left his studies without much warning twenty years ago and went back to England. He offered his apologies to Erpenius but said that the course of study was not providing him much benefit. It was then that I discovered he had been receiving lessons from one of his workers. And now here he is, sending his son to me so I can give him an Arabic copy of the *Pictarix* because he wants to print it and sell it back in the East! Who would even think to buy a printed book dealing with talismanic magic!"

I was at a loss for words. I stammered out that we would select the most salient parts and went on to say it would unite the worlds of the academy and the market, something Oxford University did regularly by inviting my father to present lectures on the practical wisdom of the Arabs. However, it didn't seem that anything I said convinced Jacob one bit. He kept glancing furtively at me while I occupied myself looking at the contents of his office, with its antiques and works of art and other ornamental objects.

Jacob opened one of the boxes on his desk that had captured my attention. At first, I thought it was a book, but I smirked as I withdrew a piece of cake, pretending that it was an even more delicious discovery. He said, "Life has taught me to not trust two things: the Devil and the English. I can make you an even better offer, Robert. Tell me, what is the extent of your knowledge of printing and Arabic type?"

I asked him to test me, and I began to explain everything I knew about Arabic, manuscripts, and printing. We spoke in Arabic at length and, after he had confirmed my skills, he offered me an opening in his Arabic program and, at the same time, the opportunity to join the university print house as a technician. I accepted immediately. It would be a way for me to study mathematics and mechanics, an idea that had been planted in my mind back at the monastery, by the priest Juan Ándres.

He assured me that, with my skill in Arabic, it would not be difficult to pursue two courses of study at the same time. However, he asked why I wanted to study mathematics.

I explained what I could of Viscount Francis Bacon's method of critiquing Aristotelian logic and the necessity of inventing a new instrument to probe nature that relied on both the senses and experimentation. I also wanted to study René Descartes' method after learning that he taught at Leiden, in order to understand his theory of mechanical philosophy. Could Europe develop different views of nature from those already elaborated by Aristotle?

Later, Jacob explained the difference between Bacon and Descartes. Despite the fact that both of them critique Aristotelian physics, their methods were at odds with one another. He asked, "Are Descartes' ideas prevalent throughout England?"

"I don't know. However, on my way here, something occurred to me that I'd like to mention. By chance, I happened upon a Parisian woman returning to her city. My attention was piqued when I saw her working on a mathematical problem that the Amsterdam Institute of Sciences had distributed to applicants hoping to study there. It was an algebraic cubic equation. I began to chat with her a bit, and she explained that the geometric method for solving this kind of equation had already been invented by a French mathematician named Renatus Cartesius. She said that this method proved that arithmetic and geometry could be combined into a single science.

With a tinge of melancholy, she concluded, "I thought Holland would be more open-minded than France in accepting female students into their institutes of higher education, but I was unable to convince those idiots who believe only men can think. The professors at the Institute didn't even know who Descartes was, despite the fact that he has been in Holland for more than a decade. They even refused to accept the geometric method that I told them about and didn't dare accept a young woman to study in their institute.

I asked her about Cartesius. She said, "He's in Leiden. I tried to reach him at the university, thinking perhaps he could intercede on my behalf, but he didn't have an office. Later I found he lives on the bank of the Prince William canal, but I didn't go to see him."

After a brief silence, I stopped talking. I was delighted by this man's attention—this man who had transformed Leiden into the centre of mathematics for the whole of Europe. When it seemed that the wine had loosened him up a bit, I said, "For this very reason, when I arrived, I ensured my living quarters were near you two. Perhaps my good sir would kindly allow me to visit during one of his evenings with Monsieur Descartes?"

Jacob's face remained neutral, showing no reaction to the story. However, he repeated his offer of the job in the print house and explained the nature of the work. "You will be the link between me and the Elzevir family, which owns the university's press. We prepare the books here in the office and then the family takes on the printing for the university. We will discuss details later. However, to be forthright with you, I am trying to get out from under the printshop's control over my projects."

As he wrapped up our meeting, he added, "I will send a memorandum to the university administration regarding your matriculation as a student of the Arabic program as well as the program of mathematics and mechanics. Additionally, I will raise your name to the university deans so they will appoint you under me."

I thanked him immediately. I told him that I had been looking for a job to cover my expenses while in Leiden and had been hesitant to accept a job as a miner with the blacksmiths for five guilders a week.

He smiled while extending his hand to shake mine. "Please come back on Tuesday afternoon. We will talk about the contract, and I will try to arrange a meeting with René Descartes as soon as he returns."

With that, he handed me an entry ticket for the university auditorium saying, "I don't think I will use this, and it ends tomorrow."

I thanked him sincerely and, before leaving, said, "You will find me reliable and up to your standards, Sir."

I had not been happier since arriving in Holland. I needed to celebrate somehow and invited the housemaid, Claudia, to watch the presentation of a dissection in the university's anatomy theatre. With our single ticket, we entered the theatre after managing to convince the usher at the door that Claudia was the sister of Professor Jacob, and that he had asked me to accompany her to the show. The attraction that day was the skeleton of a gigantic fish. My luck was as good as Claudia's in guessing the name of this strange fish that anatomists themselves had shoe-horned into a number of scientific categories, owing to their puzzlement over its particular features and the functions of its organs.

On most occasions, anatomical shows were reserved only for students of medicine and surgery. However, on this day, the public could attend to watch. Sometimes they even displayed actual human cadavers, either pilfered by body snatchers from paupers' graves or purloined from among the executed and sold in turn to doctors. But at those times, the show was only for students of medicine and anatomy. I had heard that they even brought a pharaonic mummy a few months back. In any case, Claudia didn't find the whole affair very entertaining. A woman in her forties, it was as if she were escorting her son. However, she did enjoy the *kunstkammer* itself, which Dutch explorers and noblemen had filled to the brim with things they had collected from various places, making it a learning centre for natural history, peoples, and cultures.

Chapter 12

When Jacob told me that he would meet with Descartes that evening, and I could join them, I accepted on the spot. Earlier, I had sent Claudia to mail a bundle of tightly packaged manuscripts and a letter to my father because I had not written him since my arrival in Leiden. I wrote:

My dear father,

I write these words following a party I attended last night. Professor Golius invited me to the affair, an Easter celebration hosted by Mr. Abraham Elzevir and held for the workers in the print house and some important figures at the University of Leiden. I arrived two months ago and, as you suggested, paid a call upon Jacob. I went to see him as a collector of manuscripts and left him as a university student and technician in the print house. I had no other choice but to accept his offer. However, I failed to persuade him to show me the original Al-Majriti manuscript or even gain access to the Erpenius archives. As you said, he is extremely cautious.

I'm now uncertain that my decision was the right one. Things are progressing slowly here, and I have not achieved anything of note either in regards to the Morisco's manuscripts or Arabic typography. It was only yesterday that I met Mr. Elzevir, even though I will begin working for him next week. Jacob has assigned me nothing but the translation of some texts from the Dutch parliament and tracking down Arabic vocabulary in the Al-Sahah dictionary and other textual references found in various Arabic sources. He leans heavily on his students for help with the Arabic-Latin dictionary he's been working on for years.

I didn't know that Abraham was the owner of the university's press. I had thought he was just an employee. However, it has since become clear that the press is his family's personal property, which has made it more difficult for me to gain access to their Arabic type. I learned it was Erpenius himself who originally carved the typeset, but the letters later fell into the hands of Elzevir, when his widow sold them off after his death. I hope soon I will be able to become closer to Mr. Abraham—though I don't have high hopes. He is a gentleman nearing his fifties who sports a delicate black moustache turned up at the edges, and he has an ebony pipe that never leaves his mouth. Altogether, it lends him the air of a thespian keen to masterfully perform his role so as to not lose the aristocracy's confidence in his talent. I don't think he will pay much heed to me at all.

I had previously thought that I wouldn't need more than two or three weeks in Leiden, but it seems I won't be able to return to you soon. I've learned from a few people that Monsieur Descartes recently arrived in the city, coming from Amersfoort, where his only daughter lives. I'm still waiting for Jacob to introduce me after I made it known that I was interested in studying Descartes' method for critiquing the logic of Aristotelian essences.

I've attached herewith some manuscripts I managed to get a hold of in Holland. I gave a few to Jacob hoping to gain his trust, but I saved the choicest ones for you. I pray that you have not forgotten me. I continue to find myself in need of money. Although the university's stipend is sufficient, I sometimes chance upon valuable manuscripts that I cannot resist or bear the thought of leaving for others.

I pray that you give my warmest regards to mother. I am in the best of health and happiness and hope to return to you soon.

Your loving son, Robert

Leiden, 9 April 1640

That evening, I told the shy lady that I was going to Jacob's home to meet René Descartes. She reiterated what she had said previously, "Don't listen to a word Jacob's wife says. She's begun to loathe being the wife of a famous university professor. She says that the manuscripts see his face more than she does. Some people even say that, after she banned manuscripts from the bedroom, he began making candles infused with the scent of old books!"

I arrived at Jacob's home only to discover they were meeting at Descartes', which was directly across the way. As it turned out, I would not have to hear a word from Madame Golius that evening. I saw Jacob gesturing toward me from across the canal, so I retraced my steps back to the bridge and, when I arrived, I found them poring over several anatomical drawings of the human brain—the pineal gland specifically—that anatomy professors had made. I kept quiet after greeting them, and they motioned for me to take a seat. I listened to their heated discussion around the function of the pineal gland, which Descartes thought was the organ in which the human soul resided.

At best, my presence was tangential, and the gulf between them and me seemed unbridgeable. Several times, I had to catch the servant's attention to get them to bring me something to eat or drink. At that moment, I didn't understand why I was there with them. It would have been just the same without me. They were making history! And me? What was I doing?

As evening dissolved into night, I found myself asking to take my leave. However, Descartes stopped me, saying, "Robert, I was wanting to ask you about the woman you met on your way here. Did she say that the geometric solution to the cubic equation was the unification of algebra and geometry?"

"She said the unification of arithmetic and geometry, but maybe she meant algebra, because she was working on an algebraic equation."

Descartes turned to Jacob, "You know, my dear Jacob, we have discussed that very subject at length. This lady has inspired me with an idea that had never even crossed my mind. The matter of solving geometric problems algebraically is ancient and not entirely one of my own ideas. What she suggests is to execute algebraic operations geometrically, meaning that we add, subtract, and multiply the curves just as we do in algebraic equations. Any geometric problem involving the rate of change between two or more coefficients, we can render on a complex plane. Consequently, all the transformations that we perform in the abstract with algebra, we can also plot geometrically in reality. This lady has bridged the gap for which the Aristotelians at the Université de Paris had criticised me. God doesn't do any business behind our backs. God thinks mathematically."

Jacob slipped into discussion with Descartes once more, but I was annoyed and interrupted them. "But if you'll allow me, you didn't solve the lady's problem, Monsieur Descartes. She wants to undertake advanced studies. That is the issue at hand—not mathematics!"

"It's a delicate issue, Robert. Many ladies from royal and noble families study and attain a level of excellence equal to or even above that of men. However, they remain strictly within the confines of their palaces or homes in private study. As for universities, those are public institutions. I have heard, however, about a project that Christina, Queen of Sweden, is undertaking to establish a private college for girls. Jacob could propose that the university deans set up a private program for girls. I am sure that you would find a sufficient number of them if it was opened to all of Europe. In fact, I encourage you heartily to do so because the Jesuits have surpassed the Protestants in giving proper attention to women's education. However, I'm still thinking about the issue of uniting algebra and geometry. I need to look into this further," Descartes said as he turned back to Jacob who appeared engrossed in thought.

Finding myself on the margins once again, I asked for permission to head home for the night. I returned to my room with a question that was opening doors for me, "How do I get there?" I couldn't really say where *there* was. But I was sure that only the intelligent would raise such a question to avoid falling into what Galen called the "mill of the ignorant."

Chapter 13

It was a dreary morning and nothing could coax me out of bed. I was going to need a deep stirring within my soul to move it from where it had calcified years ago. Spring had come and gone, but my sense that Jacob had tricked me into staying did not. While I got nothing in return, he benefited from all my labour.

As I lay supine and inundated by feelings of despair, the milkman's voice echoed throughout the house as he harangued Claudia about my late payment. She replied that Mr. Febin had not yet received his monthly stipend from the university, and her remark spurred me to come downstairs where I found her smirking—a mix of mirth and censure. I asked, "Why do you insist on calling my wage a stipend! I work five to six hours a day for it." "So they take pity on you," she snapped back. Then, pointing to breakfast on the table, retorted, "You haven't even paid the lady of the house rent this month, nor have you given me anything in two!"

Truth be told, I disliked talking for long with Claudia. Her candour as she spilled out her woes always caught me off guard. Once, she told me that her husband had committed suicide after losing all of his savings during tulip mania three years ago, having fallen into debt to the tune of hundreds of guilders.

Anyone who managed to get to know Claudia would immediately sense her innate light-heartedness as she shocked you with odd bits of wisdom picked up here and there. I remembered one time in particular, when she described René Descartes as "the loftiest of philosophers but lowliest of mechanics." When he would come around to call on us, she would reach out to take his coat and say, "Pass me your theories!" Another time, I chuckled when Mr. Golius's cat came bounding through the kitchen window and she called to me, saying, "Come here. Professor Jacob wishes to see you!" While on another occasion, as we were gossiping about Jacob's wife, she took to her defence, calling her "the stone that Satan trips on as he makes his way to mislead Jacob!" Once, I foolishly quipped that her husband had probably committed suicide out of sheer embarrassment of her and not because of any financial hardship. She managed to eke out a smile, but I immediately regretted what I had said.

I fell asleep that night on top of a Latin manuscript by an unknown author. Jacob had tasked me with analysing it with the aim of discovering its origins, working out its date, and whether or not it was a translation of something else. And if so, from what language, where it was written, by whom, and how it might be relevant today.

I found some clues in the manuscript that pointed to the Toledo School of Translators, and it was dedicated to Alfonso X, King of Castile and León. Furthermore, I noticed the repetition of the Latin word *surdus* as an equivalent for the Arabic word *asamm*, which Latin translators used to define numbers the Arabs referred to as "deaf roots," or irrational roots of an integer. I also noticed the word "xay" was used over and over, although I did not know its meaning in Latin or even Castilian. However, next to it was the transliteration for its Arabic pronunciation as *shay*, indicating the word شـيء, meaning "thing." I hazarded a guess that it referred to the unknown quantity that Descartes called *x,* because Arab mathematicians had used something like that in algebra, which they invented.

I recorded my observations and planned to discuss them with Jacob during our appointment before his evening class on Arabic grammar.

However, that morning my soul kept dwelling on the depressing story of the Morisco's family. Outside of my conclusion that the two sisters might have made it to Holland, I had achieved nothing of substance—neither regarding the Morisco's manuscripts nor with Arabic typeset. And in spite of the trust I had built up with Professor Golius, he still would not allow me to access the Erpenius archives. Surely, he had jotted something down regarding the provenance of the Maslama Al-Majriti manuscript.

I asked Jacob about Al-Majriti once, but he paid no heed to my question nor to Al-Majriti himself. However, he alerted me to the fact that my father's manuscript was not the same as the one I had found in the university library. The *Picatrix* was not an alchemical text. But my father said it was the same copy! So either someone was deceiving my father or Najma had two different texts by Al-Majriti in her possession, although I didn't recall the Morisco ever mentioning that in prison. However, I kept wondering, "Even if there were two manuscripts with Najma, how did the second one fall into our family's hands? My father had said that Aunt Anna was the one who copied the manuscript for us. Was she lying to my father?

At this point, I asked Jacob to show me his Arabic copy, but he demurred. Then he went even further and declined to grant me permission to search the Erpenius archives, saying it would be a waste of my time to make no mention of the fact that the library administration had not yet indexed all of Erpenius' documents, and it was the policy of the library's special collections to not allow general access until everything had been catalogued.

In a later meeting, I tried to speak to René Descartes about Al-Majriti, but he too was indifferent, saying that his scientific method no longer accorded with the methods of Al-Majriti and the other astrologers. While their methods had a scientific veneer, it was not true science, because their analysis operated only on the level of mathematics. Fine...but did Al-Majriti write only about astrology? And hadn't Monsieur Descartes only until very recently believed it was an angel who revealed his scientific method during a dream he had while in the Black Forest, returning from one of the Habsburg battles? When I told Jacob this, he chuckled and made no comment other than to say, "René Descartes' dream explains the scientific method, but the scientific method cannot explain the dream of René Descartes!" And how can Descartes himself be so sure that the pineal gland is the nexus of the body and soul? What's the difference between that and astrology?

In reality, I didn't really care about the scientific method or the falsity of the astrologers' methods. Leiden's professors could champion sensory evidence as the foundation for experience for all I cared. What concerned me was how the Al-Majriti manuscript had made its way here.

Two weeks earlier at Jacob's home, I was puzzling through the spider web of marginalia in one of his Arabic dictionaries. Jacob pointed out the comments he had made, others in the style of an Aleppan copyist, and a third set Erpenius' own hand.

I asked Jacob, "What makes you combine work on both Arabic and mathematics? I don't see any connection between them."

"I don't. All I'm doing is searching for the roots of mathematics that have come down to us from the wisdom of the ancient Arabs. This accumulation of inherited knowledge from the Greeks down to the Persians, Indians, and Arabs is what created the scientific method. You go back to the origins of ideas to fashion the tools you will use in the future."

"Does that mean Arabic's sole importance is for mathematics?"

"You misunderstand me, Robert. The scientific method is what guarantees the continuity of advancement and prevents backsliding and vanishing as nations have in the past. How can we continue to progress without returning to the very foundations of human awareness? We must think like the Arabs so we can grasp all that has come down to us from them. That is why we learn their language."

I took the opportunity to ask him, "Can't we print the Al-Majriti manuscript?"

"While the author of the text you're asking about might have insisted upon the importance of visual examination and the mathematical analysis of manifestations, nevertheless he did not establish a clear dividing line between what he truly witnessed and what he could deduce. And his deductions were far greater than what he himself observed. Consequently, he padded his provable findings with the stuffing of his own best conjectures. Luckily, we have transcended all that, thanks to the method proffered by Descartes, whereby we now distinguish between what we can truly observe, measure, and probe and our own suppositions and educated guesses. What our students need today are texts free from any interference or distortion and that embody the very purpose of language itself: communication. What they don't need are books of magic or trickery."

"But it could be profitable. If the Al-Majriti manuscript does not have scientific worth, it may have commercial value. People want to know the future and the unknown. Nothing will stop them from buying up almanacs and astrological calendars to know what their astrological signs say."

Jacob skirted the issue, saying that they were an educational institution bent on building minds, and not wealth. "These facile generalisations by the ancients are no longer of use to us today, Robert." As he returned the dictionary to its place on the shelf, he concluded, "In science, the act of generalising is a dangerous undertaking and a skill that few who have not spent a considerable portion of their lives in laboratories among instruments and numbers can master."

As I was getting up to leave, he added, "Over the coming weeks, I want you to compile a collection of Arabic maxims and aphorisms that you will pull from three manuscripts that I have gathered myself and will hand over to you soon. Among them is an old print by Erpenius, but it is chock full of errors, and I don't think it accurately captures the spirit of Arab culture. Therefore, I would like you to prepare a new edition."

Chapter 14

It soon became clear that Jacob only wanted a lackey to execute his ideas. He didn't want a partner to share in the glory of possessing and controlling one of the largest collections of Oriental manuscripts in the whole of Europe. That morning, as the realisation distilled in my mind, my mood began to sour.

I had complained once to Descartes about Jacob's heavy-handedness. "Jacob controls everything, and it does not serve the interests of Arabic or the university in general. He is not investing at all in researchers who might carry on after him."

Descartes disagreed. "Jacob needs to see enthusiasm. You just have to understand the lens through which he views the world. A man who is comfortable with ambiguity and relishes long periods of doubt cannot be authoritarian by his very nature."

"Jacob only wants me to echo him."

"That means you are very close to him."

After some silence, he added, "Ten years ago, I found myself in your position. Jacob had just returned from the Levant, carrying a treasure trove of Arabic and Persian manuscripts. At the time, I was searching for a treatise by Apollonius on conic sections. The original was lost and all that remained was an Arabic translation that Jacob had obtained in Syria. At the start, Jacob kept putting me off, since I wasn't strong in Arabic. He only began to warm up to me after he saw the things I was trying to bring to life—things that do not easily fade away—like schematics, drawings, and ideas."

"You've perused the *Picatrix*. Is the book bad or of no use at all?"

"I can't say it has no use today. The matter depends on what you want to do. However, in general, the book is full of assertions that have required far more of mathematics than it can yield. The function of mathematics is to describe the world as it is and not to explain it, which is what Al-Majriti and other astrologers have endeavoured to do. They have explained the universe relying upon calculations of the planets and stars. I don't fault them for that. They were simply relying on their own personal abilities and a few primitive instruments."

When I went to see Descartes that day, I had brought along a few Latin quotations that had piqued my interest in Al-Majriti's *Picatrix*. Among them were his musings on the souls of planets and the transmutation of base elements into higher ones through alchemy (something he called "scientific magic"), the charting of astrological mansions to produce talismans derived from the rays of fixed stars falling on the wandering planets, and how soulmates are generated through the phases of the moon, Saturn, and Venus. Hence, the apportioning of afflictions and adversities of mankind that the talisman sought to combat.

As soon as he finished his critique of Al-Majriti, I showed him these quotes and said, "Why not let people entertain false hopes if for no other reason than to help them bear the trials and tribulations that assail them?"

Descartes smiled. My argument had reminded him of his first encounter with Isaac Beeckman, the Dutch philosopher who persuaded Descartes to abandon law and pursue mathematics and mechanics. The two of them ran numerous experiments on the effect of animal sounds on stringed instruments, and they would wake up early to observe the vibrations of fluids placed at varying distances away from the roosters of Leiden. After describing a number of experiments, he said, "And that's how mathematics was born."

Back in those days, people were all abuzz about the coming Day of Judgement following the appearance of the Great Comet of 1618. Unaffected, Beeckman and Descartes continued their discussions of mathematics and the attendant revolution it had spurred, which led to our understanding of the universe as one gigantic instrument as opposed to the antiquated notion that the universe was divided between a fallen, corrupt world and a higher, incorruptible one.

Their discussion stirred up a French woman who was returning to France from Leiden where she had defended ancient astrology—just as I was doing now. This lady carried a satchel filled with astronomical instruments, manuals, and charts. With these, she was going to prove the primacy of mathematics in understanding the upper worlds and the role of these instruments in transmitting that knowledge to the world below, in order to diminish the effects of corruption and change.

I began to question Descartes more about her, but he could only remember that she refused to identify herself. However, the instrument that she was carrying was none other than the Al-Zarqali tablet, the *Saphaea* that the Morisco had described to me in prison. I was taken aback. Was it possible that Descartes was talking about Najma Al-Hajari? He even indicated that she might have been a Huguenot escaping religious persecution in France, but had been forced to return to France despite Beeckman advising her not to, because her life would be in peril.

Beeckman had given her an address in Leiden for one of his friends interested in Arab astrology, which made me think this woman was perhaps Najma. And, after she met Erpenius, she had for some reason decided to return to France.

I recalled what Descartes had said as I thought about my meeting with Jacob that afternoon. It seemed then that Najma had made it to Holland. But where was her sister Hind and the servant Hasan? And what about the library of manuscripts? I didn't know!

When I went to see Jacob, I found one of his assistants reshelving books that had piled up on the office tables. It was Jacob's way of ensuring his staff became acquainted with the titles and authors. As soon as I entered, I arrayed the manuscript in front of him and began to explain my observations, concluding, "It seems that this is Gerard of Cremona's translation of a work by Ibn Mu'adh Al-Jayyani for calculating circular triangles from the 12th century."

Jacob praised my perspicacity: "This work is related to the mathematics of twilight and the duration of sunset. Many attribute it to Ibn Al-Haytham, but you have done well to realize the work is from Andalusia and not Egypt. We have many Arabic works here that are only in their Latin translation. I've been hoping we chance upon the Arabic original."

At this point, I asked Jacob again about the Al-Majriti manuscript. I told him what Descartes had said and asked him, "Could this lady be the one who gave Erpenius the Al-Majriti manuscript?"

Jacob ignored both my question and the commercial justification for printing it. He said, "That still does not explain your obsession with this manuscript, Robert. But I will think about it."

He placed in my hand manuscripts of maxims as well as an old edition of Erpenius' book of proverbs. He said, "Before you begin to typeset it, I want you to show me the pages you've organised and edited for clarity. We will print the book on royal quarto paper. And since there are no more than two hundred pages, we can sell more copies of the book. Draft an announcement so we can inform our Arabist colleagues and Europe's intellectuals about the book."

I asked for his permission to go to Amsterdam to spend the money my father had sent me. He agreed and asked me to stop by some booksellers, especially Jewish ones, to look for any Hebrew translations of works by Ibn Yunis, Al-Tusi, or Ibn Beja.

As I left, I tried to root out any gratitude I may have felt toward him. He had said, "I'll think about it." But I had a sense he was just taking advantage of me for his own projects, and I was nothing more than a tool in his hands. Such a feeling only underscored my need for an all-encompassing Jesuit perspective and outlook to save me from both his demands and my own ego. Fine. Let Jacob add his name as he liked to the book of maxims, which would be the fruit of my hard labour. In any event, no one would care about the book if my name appeared on it in place of Professor Jacob Golius.

Chapter 15

Jacob finally granted me permission to sift through the Erpenius archives while he looked over the printing plates I had arranged for his book of maxims. The work had progressed much more quickly than Jacob had expected, and he wanted to reward me. I told him that Erpenius would be my reward. This time, without any hesitation, he agreed, especially since he was delighted by the Hebrew manuscripts I had brought him from Mokum (as the denizens of Amsterdam called their city). He was particularly happy about the treatise by Joseph ibn Nahmias of Toledo, which was on the astrological works of Al-Tusi. He told me that Ibn Nahmias was the bridge between the Tusi couple and the Copernican solar model. "Now I can think like Copernicus," he said as he handed me a small chit to give to the university's bookkeeper so I could be reimbursed for my expenses.

I had visited him on several occasions in his office as I worked on the book. In the beginning, it was to seek his guidance on some of the religious sayings attributed to the false prophet. He asked me to be selective and only choose ones that were secular in nature and related to the life and customs of the Arabs, including their food and peregrinations. I needed to be careful to set aside any that seemed dubious and show them to him.

I raised his hackles by referring to Mohammed as a false prophet, and a long discussion ensued in which he defended Mohammed. He didn't regard him as a prophet *per se*, but as a man who successfully cultivated a civilized nation out of a desert people and imbued them with morals that transcended even our own. "They do not allow anyone to profane Jesus or his mother the Virgin," he said, gesturing toward a book printed in Leiden from a Byzantine copy that rehashed the Byzantines' deep-seated hatred of Mohammed.

I told him that I had looked through that book once in the university library, and there were many things that defied logic, especially the anonymous author's allegations that Mohammed used chicanery to win over his followers, like training a pigeon to stand on his hand or make his coffin hang suspended mid-air.

Lifting his left leg with his hand and placing it over the right, Jacob commented, "But here in Holland, the gullible relish that sort of thing. I didn't agree to print the book when it was presented to me, but the council of deans wanted to ingratiate themselves with the population by showing that the university, though Protestant, had not become pro-Turk on account of the Catholics.

"But that doesn't stop Mohammed from being a false prophet. If he's not, then we should believe in him."

"That's a naive deduction, Robert. When one is endowed with a scientific spirit, it is best to not take sides in any battle. It doesn't matter whether Mohammed was a true or false prophet. In the end, we need the sciences of the Muslims—not their faith."

I wasn't convinced. To disavow an idea doesn't necessarily mean you despise the person holding it. That's how I dealt with the Morisco. I learned what I wanted from him while neither liking nor hating him. To me, he was just another person. Though perhaps my inability to determine whether he was Christian or Muslim made it easier to discount him, especially in light of what befell me because of him. I no longer needed him. Unless of course he could offer a shortcut to the lost library.

During one of my sessions with Jacob, I showed him the Arabic letters used in the Elzevir printing press and compared them to the elegant and clear calligraphy in a hand-copied manuscript. I said, "Elzevir's letters are atrocious. Oversized. Difficult to typeset. And just ugly. On top of that, there are so few of them that they barely fill four panels." I was trying to convince him that we needed to cast a new and better set of type, but he said it wasn't as simple as I thought, though he would try to make it his next project.

Jacob's word was final, and he often turned away the unserious from the archives on the pretext they had not yet been catalogued. So, as soon as everyone discovered he had allowed one of his students to access them, I became the centre of attention. Some turned green with envy. Others had more sincere intentions, such as Lukas, the young Dane, who had been studying Arabic under Jacob, and for years had been trying to gain access to a collection of Levantine texts that had secretly arrived long ago from Heidelberg, shortly after that city fell to the Catholic armies.

The young man kept crowing on about the importance of propagating knowledge, but after I probed him deeper in conversation, he acknowledged that he was a member of a secret society called the Rosicrucians and was searching for the Hermetic sources of magical Oriental manuscripts, telling me all about the founder of the order, who travelled in ancient times to the lands of the Arabs in Syria, Egypt, and Morocco, and who had brought back many works on magic, alchemy, Sufism, and the occult sciences. Most of them ended up in the Bibliotheca Palatina in Heidelberg. After that city fell, its holdings were transferred to the Vatican, save for a few that a group of Protestants had managed to smuggle to Leiden.

Lukas asked for my help in accessing the archives. I told him that

I had barely received permission myself after months of waiting and haranguing Jacob. And then, I was only granted access to the documents related to Erpenius. I told him I would try, though I ended up dropping the issue entirely, later apologizing to the young man. The truth was that this collection was complicated enough, and I did not want to occupy myself with other things at that moment. Or, at least, I thought I would postpone the matter of helping him for a while.

The Erpenius archives were located inside a storage room that was set off in a corner of the special collections room on the library's ground floor, connected by a corridor that led on one side to a locked room primarily used for storing maps and paintings, and a small warren of rooms set aside for researchers. I reserved one of these rooms and used it after picking up the Erpenius boxes. Apart from some papers, documents, and notebooks, there were no books or manuscripts in the collection. I was dispirited. When I mentioned it to Jacob, he glumly said that "Holland lost the Erpenius collection to the duke of Buckingham after his widow sold it off. And that's why to this day I don't care much for the English!"

At first, I had a hunch that the Al-Majriti manuscript was in that sold-off collection, but Jacob assured me that it was still with him. Though I found some important things in the archives, I did not find much. Or, at least, what I did find only served to complicate matters further.

I met up with Jacob and Descartes the evening I returned the Erpenius boxes. That morning had been a stormy one for Descartes. He had given a lecture in front of a vast, elite audience of Leiden's professoriate and the philosophers of Holland. I even noticed some women in the mezzanine, which was quite a rare occurrence. Descartes was expounding on what had led him to refute the Aristotelian notions of prime matter and subjective essences—a topic that set off a heated debate between Aristotle's supporters and his new opponents. Things quickly devolved to the point that some threatened Descartes with eternal damnation and being forever denied the sight of God. And as sparks started to fly, the university administration was forced to intervene and end all discussion, demanding the whole affair be taken up by what they called the "Republic of Letters" that circulated among the elite of Europe at the time.

During our meeting, I found the two men rehashing the dispute that had inflamed the morning. Jacob asked me about the archives, and I told him I hadn't found anything of interest. Most of what I had found was Erpenius' notes on his lectures and research and some scraps related to unfinished projects. Jacob reconfirmed what he had told me earlier: that he was surprised I had been so insistent on accessing this archive.

Truth be told, I did not reveal that Erpenius had mentioned a French lady by name and had listed her address in the city of Meaux. She had been the guest of a cloth merchant in Leiden and had asked Erpenius to work with him as a translator, assisting him in various projects related to Arabic. However, she suddenly vanished without ever receiving payment for the Al-Majriti manuscript.

Shockingly, the name that Erpenius mentioned was the very same name that Yusuf the Morisco had given his wife Najma before they had separated: Madalena Despucci. And it was the very same one that Descartes had mentioned in connection with his friend Isaac Beeckman. Erpenius also referred to the Al-Zarqali astrolabe and charts. The other notable thing was a letter from my father to Erpenius, confirming what Jacob had told me before. My father terminated his courses early and informed Erpenius that he was returning to England. It was at this time that Madalena disappeared, following her encounter with Descartes and Beeckman.

Her disappearance coincided with my father's own return to England, after finding an instructor to teach him Arabic, which meant he no longer needed Erpenius or to leave his work behind in England. Why had my father never told me this? It also accounted for the differences between my father's manuscript and that of Erpenius. The source of both was the same—Najma Al-Hajari—but it appeared that she had been in possession of two works by Al-Majriti, not just one.

I wrote to my father at once and asked if a French lady had taken refuge with him while he was studying Arabic with Erpenius and if that was the reason why he stopped his studies and returned to England. I told him of my suspicion that she was Najma and that she may have lied to him when she said the Al-Majriti manuscript was the same as the one Erpenius held, but for a reason I could not yet determine. I also asked him if she had said a word to him about their manuscripts or about her sister Hind and servant Hasan.

I wrote that she had probably been hiding the secret of the library and looking for the right opportunity to leave England, to search for her husband and sister. Yet where did she go? I closed my letter with another hunch. Could it be that Aunt Anna was this very same Najma Al-Hajari? There were more than enough shared traits between Aunt Anna, who had passed away, and Najma Al-Hajari. Both were Muslims who kept their Islamic faith hidden. Both shared an interest in Arab astrology. And they shared a physical similarity, according to what the Morisco had told me about his wife Najma.

After a very full day, Jacob asked me to focus on making up what I'd missed in class while working on the book of maxims and to begin thinking about producing new Arabic type, a project that would be difficult and take months. Yet there were still a few lingering questions from his archives, like Erpenius' letter to Jacob when the latter was in Morocco, as well as the news clipping that Erpenius held onto concerning the printing of Abu Bakr Al-Razi's *Comprehensive Book of Medicine*, known in Arabic as *Al-Hawi*. It had been printed by a Florentine mentioned in a Dutch periodical that covered events in Italy. I still had my suspicions about Najma Al-Hajari and needed to confirm some more information, which obsessed me and kept me up all night to the point that I ended up gripped by a terrible feverish sickness.

Claudia attended to me in my febrile state. When fever struck, she had a custom of placing a bundle of opium over a pitcher of highly concentrated beer in the invalid's room, saying that the odour wafting from it would dehumidify the room and freshen the air enough to relax the sufferer. That was why, when Professor Golius and Descartes came to see me, Descartes' first comment upon entering was, "I smell the scent of Avicenna," prompting me to ask why.

He eyed the pitchers and said, "Avicenna, or Ibn Sina, was the one who introduced opium into European medical treatments. He dedicated a whole chapter to its benefits in his book *The Canon of Medicine*." Then he added, pointing to one of the pitchers, "This is one of his remedies."

During my sickness, I sent off two letters. The first was to the address that Erpenius had noted down for Baron Despucci in France. I wasn't sure whether the baron himself was still alive or whether the address would still be the same after all these years, but I told myself that perhaps this would all lead to something. I wrote to him, asking about Najma and Hind. Did he know where they were? Because I had important information to relay about Yusuf. I also asked about the name of the merchant who had brought them to Holland.

The other letter was to the Florentine printer in Tuscany, inquiring about *The Comprehensive Book of Medicine*. Did they really print it? And would it be possible to locate the nun from Aragon who oversaw its printing, or else Daoud Al-Afriqi, David the African, both of whom were mentioned in the clipping dated February 29, 1624?

Once, during my sickness, Jacob visited me, accompanied by Balthazar Moretus, a scion of the family that owned the most famous press in Antwerp. It was an unexpected visit and perhaps the most momentous thing that happened, at least until my father's letter arrived. Or perhaps it was discovering my standing in Jacob's and Descartes' eyes, given their multiple visits to me during my sickness.

My father's letter replenished some of the vitality that my fever had drained from me. He wrote:

Our dear Robert,

Perhaps you have noticed that your departure from us has entered its fourth year. We know that you are doing all you can to get back the Arabic printing press and Oriental manuscripts. A few weeks' visit to us won't prevent you from continuing your search, however. There are so many things that you have missed over these years.

We had been just about to leave Leiden when a lady came up to us, introducing herself as Madalena and saying she had been sent by Isaac Beeckman. She told us that she had lost everything and pleaded for our help. After staying with us for a few days in Leiden, we brought her to Truro. This person was your caretaker, Anna the Mohammedan. We didn't learn her story until shortly before she passed away. But it was indeed Najma herself, a fact confirmed even more now by your letter. We have no reason to think she was lying to us. We loved her. All of us did. As you know, she became part of the family. Had you come back to us directly, we would have told you her story.

She had mentioned something about manuscripts, but we didn't take her seriously. We had no idea there were so many of them. She herself hesitated in telling us about her family, at least until death approached. As for the similarity between the Al-Majriti manuscript that she gave us and the one Erpenius told me about, it had been merely a guess on my part. We apologize if we didn't tell you everything we ought to have. Had you come back to us, then this conversation would have taken a different course. However, from afar, we didn't want to weigh you down with details that could affect your state of mind while abroad. There was no way for us to imagine that her husband was still alive, and we surely could not have imagined that you would meet him.

She asked us to change her name so she could begin a new life. She hid her faith out of fear of Catholic zealots. We agreed that she would be able to practice her religion as she pleased, but out of concern for her safety and to avoid looks, she would do so within the home. Meanwhile, in front of everyone else, she would appear Christian.

That's everything there is to the matter. We sincerely hope that all is well with you and your studies. Please do not fail to send our regards to Mr. Golius.

Deepest love and affection,

Your father,

Truro - August 18, 1640

Despite my joy at receiving my father's letter, it filled me with doubts. A strange sadness pulsed through me when I learned that Najma, Yusuf's wife, had passed on years ago, while Yusuf remained in prison unaware. And the most painful thing of all was that Najma had been my nanny when I was a child!

Part 4

Storms in Leiden

He was fond of saying that talent honed in secret made you an asset for the whole world, whereas talent that selfishly sought attention and fanfare only made you think of yourself and would create enemies and provoke jealousy.

Chapter 16

I was in bed sipping on wild chicory broth Claudia had prepared when Jacob entered, presenting a bony young man by the name of Balthazar. I didn't find either him or the topic that brought the two of them to me in the first place terribly interesting, and I was in no mood to discuss Arabic typography. The fever had sapped my energy and had a stranglehold on all my senses. I felt like someone listening to a song in an unfamiliar language, trying to be moved by it, but the lyrics would not oblige.

Jacob entered the house in his usual manner, leaning on his right foot for a moment, birdlike, before giving the left one a push forward. The shy lady was not home that day. She often felt anxious when someone crossed the threshold with their left foot, interpreting such an act as a bad omen. Making his way toward my room, Jacob commented wryly that, "It is easier to persuade a cat to smile than to convince the shy lady that horoscopes are nothing but ancient superstitions.

He introduced me to the young man who, judging from his physical weakness, was sicker than I. However, they stopped by out of necessity since Balthazar would return to his city, Antwerp, that very day.

I had not expected Jacob to have already begun preparations for casting the Arabic typeset. Yet, from the sound of it, it seemed that he and the young man had already discussed the topic at length, agreeing that a metal engraver working at the Plantin-Moretus press would execute the carvings based on drawings I would provide. My damnable fever had put me in such a sour mood during their visit that mustering as much inhospitality as I could, I barked, "But I can't travel to Antwerp."

The day was sunny, and the shadows cast by the canal danced into the room allowing me to maintain just enough poise to graciously excuse myself. They realized their presence had been ill-received and saw themselves out. A few days later, after receiving my father's letter, my spirits began to lift, and so I set about sketching the typeface.

Carrying my sketches with me, I went to see Jacob at home and told him that I was now ready to head to Antwerp. He was in the company of Descartes, who was himself preparing to depart Leiden for Amersfoort to attend to his sick daughter. The two men were going over some objections an English philosopher had made to Descartes, though I had never heard of the man before that moment. The objection concerned a thought experiment whereby a demon of superhuman power is able to deceive man's senses and delude his understanding of the external world. This awful idea seized me with horror as I imagined myself lost in an interminable labyrinth manipulated by a supernatural being. "But we are able to learn and understand reality," I told them. "Can we not confront this all-powerful demon together and expose his trickery?"

"Of course. And that's what the principles of the scientific method should yield." Descartes spoke before thinking, and then added, "At least on a theoretical level."

Jacob turned to me while casting an eye over the drawings I had made. "Don't tarry too long in Antwerp and end up missing your coursework," he said before pointing out a few minor flaws in my drawings. Afterward, he pressed me about my previous inquiry concerning the lady who gave Erpenius the Al-Majriti manuscript.

"How did you discover it? And why were you asking about her? And who is she in the first place? Don't tell me that it has something to do with your father's business."

"I actually don't know her. Descartes mentioned he had met her before, and I found reference to her in Erpenius' archives." Jacob wanted more from me. But, trying to change the direction of the conversation, I added, "I think Isaac Beeckman sent this lady to my father. Didn't my father mention something about her to you or Erpenius?"

Jacob shook his head, but acknowledged that it explained why he had left university so abruptly that year without completing his Arabic studies. Jacob still suspected I was keeping something from him, but I tried to explain that my question stemmed from curiosity and nothing more.

At that moment, Descartes suggested, "You should ask your father, but I don't think he would have done what he did unless this lady had stolen his heart. She certainly was beautiful." I tried to ignore Descartes' comment, even though it provoked within me the same misgivings I had with my father's correspondence.

I left for Antwerp the same day Descartes left for Amersfoort. At the way stations along my route, I made the modifications Jacob had asked for in my drawings. At one of the final stops, an elderly lady began hurling insults at me, though I couldn't fathom why. She relented when I shouted back, "I'm not a Spaniard, Ma." To make amends, she opened one of the egg baskets she was carrying to her children in the city, and I was only able to rid myself of her by taking one egg for each of the curses she had spat at me. I gifted those eggs to the senior Balthazar after I told him the whole story.

The story made Anna laugh. Anna was the young woman who sat in on my meeting with Balthazar, the director of the press. He introduced her as the wife of the son who had paid a call on me earlier in Leiden. Her devastating Flemish beauty produced the same effect as the fever that had overtaken my body and sapped all my strength, leaving me completely extinguished, save for a desire to become one with her immaculate dress. My heart pounded erratically and each beat pulled me closer toward her. I barely managed to restrain my hand from reaching out. With all this beauty, she was as delicate as if the Lord had created no one else but her.

Her outsized personality filled his office as she explained to me all it would entail: the cost of engraving, how long it would take, and how often I would have to visit Antwerp. The sweetness of her voice flowed with the tranquillity and purity of the river Maas in springtime. For days, my heart remained consumed by her. That is, until I discovered she was the cause behind my firing from the University of Leiden and the reason why Jacob and Abraham Elzevir began to treat me so coldly. She had even informed on me to the Spanish authorities who ruled the city, which prevented me from being able to return to Antwerp because of the ban against me.

I only found this out after returning to Leiden, where I discovered things had taken a turn for the worse. In Antwerp, I had asked the younger Balthazar to give me one of the German casting moulds that the press used so I could draw a technical schematic of all its parts—something I do whenever something catches my eye. However, my behaviour raised alarm bells with Anna, and she told her father-in-law.

I could never have imagined that behind such immense beauty hid the soul of a viper. She smiled at me during the entire meeting, especially as the elder Balthazar regaled us with the story of the Typographia Savariana—an Arabic printing press established by the French ambassador to Constantinople, François Savary de Brèves, at the turn of the century in Rome, after his return from the East. He had eventually taken the printing press and its technicians with him back to Paris. When he passed away, the press stopped functioning for a time, before the Imprimerie Royale purchased it from the inheritors, and it was subsequently sent to Antwerp for repair of its defects. However, as it made its way to Antwerp, a gang of Dutch Protestants in disguise stole the press.

The astonishing part of this story was that the press remained with the Dutch for years. When they gave up trying to use it, they sold it off. And I was the buyer! The printing press that wound up with Father Gaddis was none other than the very one that Balthazar was talking about—exactly as Father Gaddis had said during our first encounter. So the man was telling the truth, but how did he know all that?

I asked the director, "Do you know the name of the merchant who bought the press, Sir?"

"What merchant? You mean the Englishman? Yes, I know him. His name is George Febin. He owns a successful printing press and paper mill in the south of England. He had corresponded with me in the past, hoping to find the technical drawings of Robert Grangnon, the French sculptor who engraved the typeset for Typographia Savariana in Rome.

The director stopped talking suddenly and turned to me, "Wait a moment. Did you say that your name was Robert Febin?"

"I am Robert George Febin, Sir. I'm the one who procured the printing press from the Dutch merchant in mid-February three years ago. I will never forget the date I fell into the hands of the Spanish and became their prisoner. On behalf of my father, I offer my apologies, Sir. We had no idea who the true owners of the press were."

"I'm truly astounded—not only by the coincidence that brought you to us, but also to learn that Mr. Febin finally produced a son! I think you're a little older than 20, right? In reality, the Savary de Brèves press wasn't ours. But it was a fine opportunity to produce copies of the typeset for ourselves. You would be doing a service to the French if you negotiated with them for the press. They are still hoping that they will get it back one day. In the whole of France, there is not a single Arabic press!"

I was surprised to learn that France did not have any presses capable of printing in Arabic, despite producing the most famous typeset engravers for Levantine printing. I said, "It would be an honour if Monsieur Moretus delivered my name to the French so I could serve them in this matter," and then began to think of a way to reach the Morisco in exchange for information I would present to the French about their press.

They set to work engraving the hand punches and, by the time I left Antwerp, they had finished four of them. I checked the quality and promised them I would return in one month's time. When I got back to Leiden, I learned that Descartes' daughter had passed away, and that he might not return before winter set in. In my absence, a letter from the family of Baron Despucci had also arrived, referencing Najma's death, about which my father had already told me. It also mentioned the name and address of the cloth-seller who had taken Najma to Leiden. The merchant himself had died, but his widow had been living in France since the summer. The letter concluded with the signature of the baroness, who wrote that she would like to see me.

I tried to meet Jacob the day I returned. However, his wife deflected me. The following day, I went to see him in his office at the university and found him upset. He told me that the university refused to print the book of maxims unless he removed any saying tainted by even a whiff of religion or praise for the Arabian prophet. He then told me that someone at the Plantin-Moretus press in Antwerp had told Abraham Elzevir about my trip and my assistance engraving Arabic type. Abraham dutifully passed the information to the university administration, and they interrogated Jacob about my reasons for being in Antwerp.

"I was in an awkward position to say the least," Jacob said, "So I told them, 'Let's await his return and ask him.'" Then he noticed the schematics of the moulding casts in my hands.

"I can drop this job and work with you personally. We can set up a press that would surpass Abraham's in both precision and typographic elegance. The only thing I'm lacking is German casting moulds. The university has nothing to do with that. And the Plantin press can go to hell."

"We must think long and hard. We can't upend the entire printing industry in a workshop that's set up overnight. Let's meet in the evening. Not today, but tomorrow night."

After he excused himself to get back to all his work, I left Jacob and headed to the ironmonger. I showed him my sketches of the casting mould and all the various pieces involved, and I went into detail for over an hour before asking him if he could reproduce it. When I finished, he said, "My boy, you're nattering on about something that could be done perhaps 100 years from now. Even if you brought me the pieces themselves, and I made a herculean effort, I still wouldn't be able to create them for you or promise that it would work properly in the end. How do you expect me to transform something sketched on paper into cold, hard steel? Metal does not understand paper!"

I went back and forth with him as I tried to determine what exactly he would need to undertake this project. "Steel," he said. "I don't have any. When I do need it, I usually send a mock-up of the piece I want—carved in wood—to a factory in Nuremberg specialized in hardening iron with coal to create cast iron. However, because of the wars there, placing and receiving orders has become nearly impossible, not to mention how the cost of producing steel has soared. Its market price is now eye-watering. Your contraption here involves more than twelve steel pieces assembled ever-so-carefully, not to mention the brass track inside the spring connecting the upper and lower pieces. That track's purpose, I reckon, is to draw in air to push the moulding piece and ultimately press on the metal letter. These tracks are delicately hollowed out from inside. I don't think anyone here in Holland could create that. I'll have to ask. It's not an easy task, Sir."

Chapter 17

Dispirited, I left the metal worker. I thought it might be worth visiting Monsieur Elzevir to allay any apprehensions he was having. I had worked for him for many months on the book of maxims, but thought I ought to first coordinate my response with Jacob. Yet it took several days before I could actually cross paths with him, and it seemed as if he were trying to avoid me on purpose. When I finally found him at home, he immediately asked me, "What is it with you and Spain?"

Caught off guard, I stuttered and stammered. "The apple doesn't fall far from the tree," he said, just before cutting our meeting short. "You're just like your father. Always hiding something. I won't stand here while you keep hiding your story from me."

So, I told him everything, starting with how I had fallen into the hands of the Spanish after the naval battle off Lizard Point. "The Jesuits," I said, "are the reason for my expulsion from Spain. I didn't want to cooperate with them on their secret plans."

Jacob kept the interrogation going for an hour. He wasn't convinced by anything I said. Toward the end, he told me that someone in Antwerp had denounced me to the Spanish authorities there, making subsequent travel perilous. Then he added, "For the foreseeable future, it is best that you stop working at the university and dedicate yourself wholly to your studies. You're enrolled in two programs and have already missed so much. For now, we will set aside the idea of an Arabic press, at least until things settle down."

As I was about to leave, he added, "Do you know what got us in this predicament? You raised the elder Balthazar's alarm by sketching the casting mould. His son's wife told him, and it set him off. He was the one who relayed it to Abraham. Perhaps you were ignorant of the fact that the university's press actually began as a branch of the Christopher Plantin press, and the connections between the two remain strong to this day."

"But we can buy these moulds from Mainz."

"Perhaps. We will discuss it after the New Year."

I left thinking about how he had urged me to be discreet about the whole matter before I departed for Antwerp. At the time, I didn't understand why he said, "I don't want to lose you." He was fond of saying that talent honed in secret makes you an asset for the whole world, whereas talent that selfishly seeks attention and fanfare makes you think only of yourself and will create enemies and provoke jealousy.

At the time, Jacob was the only professor occupying two chairs and had recently been nominated for membership into the university's council of deans. For that reason alone, I could be sure that he was not going to sacrifice his new-found prestige for the sake of some reckless English lad. From then on, I heeded his advice and dedicated myself strictly to study and nothing else.

As for the French printing press, it was a full two months after my return before I received any news. Finally, a representative of the French embassy in The Hague paid a call on me. I explained that there was a prisoner I wanted released in exchange for information I could offer. When I told him that the Spanish held the press, he scoffed, saying, "You want us to negotiate with the Spanish to give up both a prisoner and the printing press? In exchange for what? That's a fleecing, not a negotiation."

"France is a kingdom, Sir, and I am simply one man. My only concern is setting free a prisoner whose imprisonment and banishment from his family was caused by France. I can tell you exactly where the press is located. I worked on it for a year and know it like my own self. If France is serious about recovering it, then you will do the impossible for it."

Looking me squarely in the eyes, he said, "And how? What do we say to the Spanish? We want your printing press and a prisoner you're holding? In exchange for what?"

"I don't know! That's the job of the king if he really wants it back!"

I asked him for assurances that the Morisco would be included in any deal to recover the printing press before I gave any additional information. Later, I realized how short-sighted and naive I had been. It was more than enough for them to learn that the printing press was in Spain. After that, they could determine exactly where it was through their own devices. And indeed, they did, and they negotiated with Spain to recover the press, which I learned several months later through Father Mersenne, the monk Descartes had suggested I visit in Paris.

I heard nothing more from the Moretus family in Antwerp. However, when I visited Abraham Elzevir to apologize—hoping that he would employ me after the university had let me go—he told me that the Plantin-Moretus press had stopped producing the punches I had designed due to how tricky and intricate they were.

"If I had been on site," I said, "they would not have stopped. We can make them here. We will buy the moulds from Mainz and set to work."

"You never learn your lesson, Robert. I was going to hire you to work with me had you not destroyed the trust between me and Professor Jacob."

I left, having lost face, and I had to wait for something positive to happen that would restore my dignity. Finally, at the end of January, something did happen, as I finished my two courses of study, receiving a diploma in Arabic language and mathematics.

That very day, I went to see Jacob to apologize and thank him for all his support and encouragement. At the same time, I asked for permission to take my leave and head back to England. Instead, he proposed that I join the Arabic faculty as a lecturer for beginning students in Oriental languages, on account of my excellent knowledge of the language. I told him, "But I only have a diploma in Arabic." "On the contrary, your knowledge of Persian is nothing to sneeze at. And you can speak Turkish and Hebrew. Over the coming while, you can work hard to obtain diplomas in these languages as well." "I'll think about it, Sir. But for now, I must go back to England, then I'll see what I can do."

At the onset of winter, I received another letter from Baroness Despucci. By then, Leiden had been blanketed in clouds for weeks, nearly extinguishing the sun, which dampened my reaction to her letter. She said that she was still impatiently awaiting my visit and informed me that the cloth merchant's widow had returned to Leiden.

After Christmas, I visited the merchant's widow and learned something quite interesting. Madalena had been in the first months of pregnancy when they met her. In light of that, I thought back to my first visit with Jacob, as he expressed his astonishment that my father had *finally* produced a child. The elder Balthazar in Antwerp himself had the same reaction. The word *finally* snagged at my heart though, at the time, I gave it no more thought. Yet there was something odd about the overlap between Najma's pregnancy and my own birth month! A clutch of dark thoughts rattled around inside me, disturbing what little tranquillity I'd had during these otherwise lethargic times.

As I departed Jacob's home for the last time, I said, "There is still a matter that preoccupies me and troubles my mind." I told him about my visit to the cloth merchant's widow and her remark about Madalena's possible pregnancy. Given Descartes previous insinuation that my father had become embroiled in an illicit relationship with Madalena, I added, "For some time now, suspicions have swirled inside me that I could be the illegitimate son of my father and Madalena. My birthday corresponds with the ninth month of Madalena's pregnancy, if we assume she was two months along, according to the widow's best guess."

"It is a strange coincidence to be sure, but you can't be the child of George and Madalena because she would have already been pregnant by the time he met her—assuming that Madalena was indeed pregnant in the first place, and the widow wasn't just imagining things. It's more likely that your mother was pregnant at the same time. But what surprises me most is why your father never told me about you, despite our long correspondence. News like that ought to inspire immense joy after waiting for a son for so long. Maybe you should write to him and ask. Or ask when you get back home."

As I left Jacob's place, I was mulling over another piece of information that the widow had disclosed. Madalena had written several letters from England to Baron Despucci and his wife. It was the widow's deceased husband who delivered them to the baron. Perhaps if I got ahold of those letters, then I would learn important things about Najma. And so, for several days, I remained befuddled about whether to return to England or go to France to meet the baroness who insisted I visit.

I went immediately to Descartes, seeking his advice. But since his daughter's passing, he had slipped into a depression and gone into seclusion. Even after returning to the city, he neither received nor visited anyone. And while we tried many times to raise his spirits by inviting him to join us, he declined each time. Only for the New Year's festivities did he finally open up, inviting Jacob and me to his house to show us his automaton Francine—a doll-like figure he had made to resemble his daughter and dressed in her clothes. He constructed her to make mechanical movements through a system of springs, gears, and pulleys, letting her walk forward and backward and turn around without falling down. She even moved her head and eyes to the left and right. She could smile, too—the way young girls coquettishly smile to get what they want. He even asked if we perceived any difference at all between his deceased daughter Francine and this marionette!

At his home, I found him dissecting the corpse of a rabbit and a fish and comparing the skeletal systems of the two. Laughing, he said, "My servant is awaiting the fish to grill for supper this evening, but I don't know if there will be anything left of it."

I told him about my diplomas, my meeting with Jacob, and my intention to return to England. I asked his opinion about studying theoretical philosophy, and he said, "If you are going to study

Aristotelian philosophy, I would advise against it. After allying itself with Christianity through the work of Saint Thomas Aquinas, it has saved us from the darkness of the Platonists and run its course. Now, it has become sterile, and is no longer suitable for Europe. Here in Leiden, there are excellent professors who are teaching the new philosophy that takes into account the heliocentric system of Copernicus, the laws of Kepler, the discoveries of Galileo, the developments in mathematical and mechanical thinking, and the latest results in the anatomical sciences."

When I asked for his thoughts about Jacob's offer for me to teach Arabic, he said, "Grand ideas do not germinate by staying in one place."

I then asked about the topic that brought me to him in the first place, "Was Madalena pregnant when you met her?"

As he washed his hands and called for his servant, he said, "Does that have anything to do with studying philosophy or teaching Arabic?" He asked this with a glint in his eye that irked me a little. However, he went on, "I don't remember all that well. However, her fear and anxiety were very clear. Given that she didn't return to Erpenius, perhaps it was because of the pregnancy. She must have had a reason and feared telling someone."

"But do you believe my father had an illicit relationship with her?"

"I didn't say that. All I said was that she was beautiful. If she *were* pregnant that day, it would have been impossible for him to be the father. He had not even met her yet."

I wrote to my father and asked him about Najma's child, and who I was exactly. I told him about the congruence of my birthday and Najma's pregnancy and confessed that this matter consumed my thoughts, more than the Morisco's library or even Arabic type. Then I told him that I might not return immediately to England, but would make my way to France to meet Baroness Despucci. Until I had committed it to paper, the idea of not returning to England hadn't been finalised in my mind, but, as I discovered more reasons to go to France, it soon became clearer and clearer.

Chapter 18

France came to me in my dreams four or five times

Each time as a young girl, different from the one before

Speaking to me 'til morning.

As the sun rose, she transformed into a window overlooking one of the four directions.

From her tales, French was written and

In the last dream, the ancient Latin man died.

With this poem in mind, I entered France. I don't know who had composed it, but I kept singing it, perhaps to remind myself that it was the French (not the Italians) who reaped the fruits of Latin humanity.

With me in tow, the coachman passed a lofty hill, on top of which stood a small, roofless hut. The driver came to a halt along the ridge, informing me that one of the ladies in Meaux had asked him to fetch a stone from Sons of Thunder hill for her."

"Who are the Sons of Thunder?"

"Don't quite know, Sir, but the woman said that she had the bone of Saint Son of Thunder's big toe, and it was smuggled out of Spain by a monk."

I asked him to take me back so I could pick up a stone myself. When I arrived at the baroness' home, I introduced myself and gifted her the small rock. She tossed it to the side and said, "How can an Englishman like yourself believe in such superstitions, Robert?"

Then she asked, "So, is Yusuf still alive?"

"Yes, but he's in a Spanish prison. That's where I met him."

She asked me to describe him, perhaps to confirm my story, which made me somewhat uncomfortable. What right did we have to reduce an entire person—his hopes and dreams and hard-won life experiences—down to a few inadequate descriptors? However, I sidestepped the request and said, "Perhaps the years of torture have effaced his former features."

She gave my description very little thought. However, as I began to talk about Najma, and how she had been my nursemaid as a child, she cried out, "Are you her son? I don't believe it!"

"What makes you think I'm Najma's son?"

"I don't! I was only asking."

Here, she excused herself a moment, saying, "Wait here, I'll show you something."

She came back a short time later, carrying a portrait of Najma with me cradled in her arms. "We have that painting too," I said. "But she is not my mother. She was just my caretaker."

She excused her faulty memory and added, "I remember she had sent us a letter telling us that she was pregnant. After a few years, she sent us this picture, and I thought the child was her son."

I asked about Najma's letters. "Can I see them?"

"She never sent us letters directly, except for one which my husband quickly destroyed. But then her letters began to arrive via the cloth merchant. The baron would visit him sporadically, and he would shred the letters before returning home. He only ever brought back this one painting."

"Couldn't these letters still be with the merchant's widow? Or perhaps her deceased husband kept them somewhere, or the baron held onto them himself?"

"The baron no longer has the wits to tell the difference between the living and the dead. He doesn't even recognise himself anymore. However, he assured me that he had destroyed the letters immediately upon reading them. If he had handed them back to his friend, I don't think he would have hidden that from me. And I don't think the widow would keep the letters hidden if she knew where they were. I know her very well. She stayed with us until midsummer and left just a short month ago. She's my friend, and we would spend time together every day. I truly miss her now. However, her children and grandchildren are first and foremost in her life."

Then, pushing back tears, she added, "I loved Najma and her sister and Yusuf more than my own children. My children don't visit me any longer. All because their father is a Calvinist. How can anyone's religion permit them to cut off their parents?"

I tried to comfort her. When I asked if she knew anything about Hind and Hasan the servant. She shook her head and asked, "Can't you help get Yusuf out of prison?"

"I am trying to reach him," I said, "but it's nearly impossible." I let her know that I had come to France for that very purpose.

I told her that I might visit the cloth merchant's widow another time to inquire after the letters, and she asked me to send her greetings. She repeated how much she missed her and implored me to ask her when she would come back to visit.

I asked the baroness to describe Hind and Hasan, which she did as best she could. Then she said, "If Hind were still alive, by now she would be in her late thirties. She certainly would be a beautiful woman, taking after her sister."

"Is it possible that Hasan rid himself of the sister and absconded with the library?"

"Impossible. Hasan was devoted to that family and would sacrifice his life for them. Also, the library was huge, and they had to bring it down from the mountains in several instalments. The baron lent them a large cart and horses for that very purpose."

I asked the baroness if I could hold onto this picture that connected me as a child to Aunt Anna, or Najma Al-Hajari. After some hesitation, she agreed. "I loved this young girl and her sister Hind. Yusuf was a strong young man too. I told him that they could stay with us, but he refused to be a burden on us. Some weeks later, Najma returned to us, terrified. She said, "I have no one left." She was crying and broken-hearted. I beg of you, Robert. Do all you can to help Yusuf. The Spanish lost their good sense when they expelled the Moors."

As I left the baroness, I thought back on all she had said. The tragic event Yusuf mentioned in prison not only broke apart Yusuf and the two sisters, but the two sisters from one another, leaving Najma alone and the manuscripts still with Hind and Hasan. And it began to appear that this library was much larger than I had ever imagined.

Hasan and Hind didn't return to the baron's home, as Najma had. Consequently, it was highly likely that the two of them remained hiding in France or adrift on the high seas, carried off to a Mediterranean shore more accepting of those who were different. But could they transport such a large number of manuscripts with them?

As I entered Paris, I bemoaned the labyrinth I found myself lost within. The more I progressed toward uncovering the secret of the Morisco, the more I discovered just how complicated it truly was. The only thing in Paris that managed to lighten my burden was knowing its maze was even more complex.

Chapter 19

Armed with a letter of introduction from René Descartes, I went to see Father Mersenne. At first, when I told Descartes my plan was to visit the Imprimerie Royale to inquire about an engraver who could teach me the craft of cutting Arabic type, he had hesitated to write it. I also wanted to find out anything else I could about the French printing press. I still hadn't heard anything since meeting that representative back in November.

It was Descartes who suggested I meet Father Mersenne, in light of the strong relationship he enjoyed with Cardinal Richelieu, the king's chief minister, and to whom he had gifted one of his most important books on theology. Descartes was also of the opinion that something deeper lay at the root of the father's scientific and theological interests. I suggested that perhaps I would ask him about the secret society of the Rosicrucians. I knew that, in the past, he had many heated ideological debates with this society and found fault with their mixing of science and magic in what they described as "salvation."

When I went to see Father Mersenne, he was robed in his cassock, even at home. As he read the letter of introduction, he asked, "So tell me, what would you like to know about the Imprimerie Royale?"

I told him I knew where the Savary printing press was located, and that I had previously discussed the matter with a representative of the French embassy in The Hague, but that I had received no further information about it.

The Father looked me in the eye until I began to fear even a blink would rouse his suspicions. He asked, "How did you learn about the press?"

There was no way to avoid telling him my tale and, when I finished, he said, "So you know Father Gaddis. He's one of my acquaintances as well. I'll be upfront with you, my boy. I was the one who corresponded with Father Gaddis to recover the press. I found out about the matter several weeks prior, through Cardinal Richelieu himself, after some of the printers raised the issue and asked him to intervene. Thanks to my acquaintance with Father Gaddis, the Cardinal assigned the task to me, and so I wrote to him. Shortly, we will send a Jesuit professor from the college in La Flèche to negotiate its release."

"My father, it was I who told them where the press was."

"It sufficed that they knew it was in Spain, even if it took some time to determine precisely where, though frankly all it took was for one copy of the Ignatian Book of Prayers to fall into the hands of the trustees of the Imprimerie Royale."

"Father, do you know that I was the one who printed that book, even though they refused to put my name on it. They had the press for more than a year, but never learned how to use it."

The father asked the secret behind my deep interest in the printing press. I admitted to wanting to reach the Christianized Moor languishing in jail in San Sebastián, with whom I had been imprisoned for months on end, and who had entrusted me with something important that I could not reveal. The father asked me to return a few days later, saying he would see what he could arrange. I told him where I was staying and left, my head still churning with thoughts. What could I do?

I stayed a week in my accommodations, never venturing further than the foyer where I scrutinized faces in all their tones and various features. Suddenly, everything began to remind me of Yusuf Al-Hajari and his cousin, Najma. My feelings and emotions were all a jumble. At one moment, I wanted them to stay as far away from me as possible. At the next, I wanted to be as close as I could to Yusuf so he could guide me to the lost library, which seemed to have become more and more difficult to access.

I spent many subsequent days in Paris wondering why I was there at all as I continued to wait for Father Mersenne's increasingly tardy response. After a week, it dawned on me to visit the Bibliothèque Nationale to look over the catalogues of Oriental manuscripts—if there were any. But I found nothing. Not even at the Université de Paris. France was nearly devoid of any Eastern manuscripts. How strange. It was as if there was no interest at all. And so, I thought, if I can't locate Arabic manuscripts, it is also highly unlikely that I would come across a talented engraver to teach me his craft. When Father Mersenne finally summoned me, I went to see him and shared my impressions.

In short, he told me that the matter involving the Morisco was impossible. France could not intervene in an internal Spanish matter, nor could Father Mersenne ask Father Gaddis to do so, even in a personal capacity, despite their long-standing relationship. The wars and enmity between Spain and France were too great. However, Father Mersenne introduced me to the priest who was heading to Spain to meet Father Gaddis and who was planning to first pass by San Sebastián. The priest suggested that I write what I would like, and he would attempt to deliver my letter to the prison. I told them about the stationer who used to visit the Morisco and said it would be better if the letter were delivered to him instead.

I began to leave and promised I would write the letter. Just then, I remembered to bring up my search for a type engraver. I told the father, "I fear I won't be able to find an engraver to teach me Arabic type casting since I was unable to find a single Arabic manuscript in Paris."

The father gave me the address of a craftsman along with a letter of introduction. Then, as I was about to leave, he commented, "We French are the European nation most sincerely convinced of our right to inherit the wisdom of the East, Robert. France is full of Arabic manuscripts. However, most are held privately by Arabists in their personal collections. They don't donate or make them available to public libraries. I personally benefited enormously from an Arabic manuscript composed by the Brethren of Purity, concerning acoustics and music, during my work on the *Encyclopaedia of the Physics of Sound*. I used to take advantage of all the Maronites and Copts who would pass through Paris and ask them to translate some sources for me."

I left the father, pondering his lofty calling. He was a man who combined his religious core with the experimental sciences in a manner that I imagined was expressive of God's will for creation, through which man could discover and understand His marvellous workings while glorifying and revering the Almighty. It was an impression I distinctly did not have in Leiden. In Holland, the pursuit of knowledge was to make a living, nothing more.

The next day, I went to visit the engraver's workshop. To be honest, what I took away from our meeting was enormous. I learned how to painstakingly engrave steel and how to repair letters worn away by time and use. I asked about cast iron, and he said that he procured it from Germany. Both Germany and England had developed ways to produce cast iron commercially, but the process was laborious and exorbitantly expensive. And, on average, an ingot of 100 ounces was barely enough to produce 20 letter punches.

By the time I was ready to return to Leiden, I had engraved 12 hand punches and cast seven letters, imitating the font styles from the Al-Maydani *Book of Proverbs,* as I found their clarity and ease of drawing most suitable. Unsurprisingly, these punches and letters exhausted my resources, and I tried to get Father Mersenne to lend me some money, at least until I got back to Leiden and could repay him. However, I discovered the hard way that he followed a Catholic ascetic tradition whereby he eschewed ownership or possession of anything beyond his most basic of necessities. Truth be told, that only elevated him in my eyes. A man of his erudition and social standing— yet he maintained such a simple life.

I inquired about the casting moulds at the Imprimerie Royale, and the engraver said that they currently used modern ones produced in France. They could be taken apart and put back together again easily, and they surpassed traditional moulds that took much longer to produce. I asked him how one could procure these moulds, but he said you had to first have a licensed printing press—they weren't sold to individuals. However, he did give me the address of a factory in Paris, and I said goodbye, though not before successfully persuading him to give me one of his worn-down moulds.

During my time in Paris, I stopped by Father Mersenne's regularly and began to assist him in some of his experiments on acoustics. Some years back, he had published an eight-volume work on the science of sound, and he remained consumed by this science even now. On a later visit, I found him talking with a priest about the Jesuit college's plans to prepare missionaries for service. They also delved into the lively debate surrounding a drink that some explorers had begun to bring back from the East called coffee. While Father Mersenne leaned toward repudiating it, drink undrunk, the priest had no qualms about embracing it, particularly after the Vatican proclaimed the brew permissible for Christians.

I returned to Leiden shortly after receiving a letter from Professor Jacob warning me against dallying for too long. Studies had begun two weeks before, and I might not be able to join the new philosophy program if I were delayed much longer. Saying goodbye to Father Mersenne, I packed my bags and promised to stay in touch.

Chapter 20

I was quite pleased with the type I had cut in Paris and by the fact that my letter destined for Yusuf the Morisco was now wending its way to him. Yet, upon my return to Leiden, I read a letter from my father that filled me with confusion and left me simmering with doubt about Najma's child.

I showed my hand punches to Abraham Elzevir, saying, "All it took was a bit of patience." At the same time, I replayed in my mind the tale my father had recounted in his letter, confirming that Najma's child had passed away as a weeks-old infant after falling ill with intestinal worms and being prescribed a dosage of medicine normally reserved for adults. My mother was pregnant with me at the time, and, as she deeply felt for Najma, she entrusted my care and raising to her. The coincidence of the births, my father explained, was nothing more than a happy accident.

Cheered by the fact that Abraham said he would reconsider the matter of the Arabic type, I left his place though still turning over my father's words.

I vacillated between visiting the cloth merchant's widow or paying a call on Professor Golius. Jacob must have sensed my hesitation, because he came to visit me straight away in the shy lady's home, bringing with him an old manuscript which he displayed before me, saying, "This is the Al-Majriti manuscript you've been pestering me about for a year now. Now tell me what does this writing mean? And how about this sentence? And these comments here?"

As he thumbed through the pages, he pointed out sentences and words scrawled in the margins in an unknown language. From the handwriting, it was clear that the marginalia had been added later and written in Aljamiado—the very language that the Morisco had taught me in prison. From the looks of it, the comments were likely Najma's, jotted down before she handed the manuscript over to Erpenius. How often I had pleaded with Jacob to show me this manuscript, and now here he was, bringing it to me of his own accord, standing over me and wanting to know everything.

"It's Spanish," I said, "but written in Arabic script, Sir." I perused the side notes, page after page. Written on the right-hand edge of the third page after the leather cover was: "I am Najma bint Ahmad bin Qassem Al-Hajari. I arrived in Holland bereft of kith or kin with all paths blocked before me, having lost my husband and my sister in the Pyrenees mountains. O Lord, may you protect and aid me." At the bottom of the following page, she wrote, "Mr. Erpenius does not want to help me." Two pages later, she wrote something that truly shocked me, "I'm pregnant with my cousin Yusuf's child. The child will be born without a father! Like our Lord, Isaa, peace be upon him." She wrote the name of the Lord as Arabs do. Then, a few pages later, scrawled at the top, she noted, "The cart remains with my sister Hind and with Uncle Hasan. I don't know where they have gone. I went back to where we had become separated, but they were nowhere to be found." At the bottom, she wrote, "If they didn't make it to Holland, then maybe they went to Tuscany." Turning the page, she continued, "Devastated and broken, I returned to the home of the baron who had given me his surname and taken me with him to the north of France. From there, I made my way to Holland with the family of a cloth merchant, but I'm pregnant and I can't tell them about that." Then she wrote on the last page of the book, "O Lord, save me for the sake of your beloved Mohammed." On the final two pages, she repeated what she had written on the first two.

Jacob's astonishment vied with my own. Madalena was not her real name. Although I had to affect astonishment at that, since I already knew her real name. Fortunately, she hadn't written anything concerning the manuscripts.

"So, she was pregnant after all, by a legitimate husband whom she lost in the south of France."

"Yes, my father confirmed the pregnancy, but said the child died mere weeks after birth."

"Judging from what she wrote and her name, it stands to reason that she's a Muslim. Could she be one of the Moors whom Philip III expelled from Spain decades ago?"

"It's quite likely. Perhaps they had planned to seek refuge in Holland because of the freedom and religious tolerance here."

Then, trying to recall, Jacob asked, "What did she write about her father's name? Ahmad ibn Qasim Al-Hajari? That name rings a bell. Is it not Afoukay? The Morisco whom Erpenius met, who taught him Arabic?"

I took this opportunity to bring up a letter I had found in the Erpenius archives, dating from the time of his final illness. "I found a letter Erpenius wrote to you when you were in Marrakech. He told you about his suspicions that Afoukay had daughters whom he left behind in Spain. It seems that Erpenius had come to the conclusion that Madalena was none other than the daughter of Afoukay Al-Hajari, something she must have denied and which explains her trepidation and unwillingness to return to Erpenius."

"Erpenius is the one who introduced me to Afoukay. And he wrote a letter of introduction to him when I journeyed to Marrakech, and I even stayed in his home for some time. Thanks to his role as an advisor to Sultan Zidan Abu Maali, he helped me gain access to Andalusian works and rare Levantine ones as well. I still remember asking him whether he had daughters back in Spain, but he always denied it. And so I thought that it was just the imaginings of my professor Erpenius. Afoukay never talked at all about Madalena."

After a short pause, Jacob added, "We had still been in contact until a short time ago, but lost touch after the assassination of the Sultan Al-Walid bin Zidan. Perhaps he fled Marrakech. The religious scholars had faulted him for Al-Walid's overweening reliance on Dutch and French soldiers, and he had even been plotting to recover the Zaydani Treasury from the monastery of El Escorial in Madrid, going so far as to ask my advice. But I told him that Holland and Spain were not lacking in wars."

Jacob turned to me, observing my flushed face and quickening heart. "But where did you learn Aljamiado, Robert? You said previously that you fell into the hands of the Spanish, but you didn't say anything about your story there. You remained a prisoner there for more than two years. What else are you hiding?"

I moved a bit to avoid Jacob's piercing gaze, and I poured a drink for each of us. As I walked toward him, drink in hand, I said, "I previously told you how I had fallen captive to the Spaniards and imprisoned for nearly a year in San Sebastián before the Jesuits freed me to work on their Arabic printing press in the Monastery of the Divine Incarnation in Bilbao. I picked up Aljamiado from some of the Moors in prison."

"That explains the secret of your interest in this Morisco lady.

You've been searching for her all along."

"Not searching *per se*, more motivated by curiosity. I came to Holland to be far away from my father."

"So how did you free yourself from captivity?"

"I told you: The Jesuits expelled me because I refused to form a cell for them in England, and because they feared I would do the opposite and create a Protestant underground network or work on behalf of the Ottomans in Spain."

"For the Turks? Why would they think that? What's your relationship with the Ottomans?"

"Perhaps because, while in prison, I showed a modicum of sympathy toward the Moors."

"Did you meet Yusuf, Najma's husband?"

I nodded as I whispered "Yes," trying to conceal the answer in my throat.

As each one of us nursed our drink, a prolonged silence filled the room, extending longer than was comfortable. Breaking it, Jacob said, "I don't understand why you didn't tell me that from the beginning. It's been more than a year since you arrived, and only now do I come to find out part of your real story. What else are you keeping back, Robert?"

"Nothing, Sir. I just didn't find a reason to tell my story. I don't know. It's unimportant."

"There's more to the story. That's certain. Perhaps the rest of it lies with your father. Or with you? Who knows. You must write to your father at once. I would be pleased if you told me anything you find out. I, too, have become interested in this Najma Al-Hajari. My path has crossed hers through three friends: Erpenius, Afoukay, and your father George. And you're now the fourth."

Jacob got up to leave while I was left tossed about, as if by a tempestuous sea of thoughts—each one a monstrous wave nearly sweeping me off my feet. I didn't wait for Jacob's odour to clear the room before rushing over to the home of the widow.

Darkness shrouded the home as her eldest daughter opened the door. Fortunately, the widow hadn't been asleep and welcomed me with a faint smile and good humour. I passed along Madame Despucci's greetings and told her that she missed her terribly. She asked, "So, you were in France?"

"Until just yesterday. She's impatiently awaiting your return. She asked me to find out when you would return to Meaux."

She turned to her daughter, as if reminding her of some long discussion. Then she said, "She is an extremely fine woman. She's the reason I stayed in France until winter. She feels lonely and depressed now that her husband has gone senile and her children no longer visit. I don't know when I will return, but it won't be before summer."

"To be honest, that is not the reason for my visit at this late hour. Rather, I wanted to ask you again about Madalena Despucci. You once told me that she was pregnant and was corresponding with the baron's family through you. Did your deceased husband store these letters anywhere? I'm guessing he would not have destroyed them, but instead returned them to you after reading the contents."

"I don't believe so. If he had, he would have told me. In any case, we found nothing of her letters among his papers."

"Is it true that her child died in infancy?"

"No. That's impossible. The child grew up with her until her passing. She even let the family she lived with name him, despite wanting to call him Joseph."

"Did you know that she wasn't the daughter of Baron Despucci?"

"Yes. The baron's family saved her and brought her with them from the south of France. She was a Spaniard who had fled the barbarity of the Catholics. Her real name was Najma."

Choking back my voice, I asked, "Do you know the name of the child?"

"I think his name was Robert. She sent us a portrait of him in her arms."

As I desperately searched for some deep hole to crawl into, so I could escape this bitter truth, I asked, "Couldn't the child have belonged to the family, and she was just the caregiver?"

"Yes, I suppose so, but why then would she deceive us and say he was her child, later adopted by that English family?"

I left the widow's house. And though my feet propelled me forward, I felt as if I were in retrograde. Tossed out to sea and frozen. Unable to make my way back to the ship, like on that dreadful day years ago. It was as if my cellmates were pummelling me again and again, blow after blow. Wending my way to the home of Professor Golius, I kept thinking about how I wished I were some neglected tree in the garden of the Monastery of the Divine Incarnation, or a sheet of paper in Jacob's library tossed aside and forgotten, or that Father Gaddis' spirit somehow would possess my body, making me a copy of him to perform the will of the Lord.

I finally reached the professor's house. In my mind, it seemed to have taken an eternity and somehow, along the way, I had transformed into something nameless and unrecognisable. His wife nearly cursed me up and down when I knocked on the door at that late hour of the night. And maybe she did, but I was oblivious to it all.

When I saw him, I immediately blurted out, "One of Yusuf's hunches about me turned out to be true. I'm not English." I slumped into a chair in the back garden of his house. "I am the son of Najma and Yusuf. I was in prison with my real father and neither of us knew it. How is that for twisted fate!"

A short silence reigned until I cleared my throat, dislodging more words, exactly like the Morisco when he spoke. "This explains why I have no siblings. And why my hair is jet black unlike everyone else in my English family. And why I am shorter than both my parents. To say nothing of the many other habits I have that can only be understood by my having Arab roots. Perhaps I am the Morisco's secret and not..."

I trailed off and shoved my hands between my knees.

Jacob expressed his inability to fathom George's reasons for keeping this hidden. Perhaps, as he entered his seventh decade of life, he began to fear the dwindling years or the very real possibility he would be unable to find someone to inherit the family's printing house or take on its responsibilities, especially if Robert became estranged. Jacob thought this all aloud while urging me to accept my fate and not be too hard on my adoptive parents.

"But, Sir, do you know what it means to be a Moor? It is the last thing in the world I would want to be. They are a people without a homeland, stripped of an identity and belonging to nowhere. They don't know whether they are African or European. Are they Berber or Goth or Galician? Arabs or Spaniards? Christian or Muslim? They are a people crushed and torn asunder. Their present has been stolen from them and consequently their future. How can a people survive, unable as they are to pass on a homeland to future generations? I don't want to be one of them!" I said as I searched desperately for a new body for my head.

Jacob tried to soothe me by speaking about the multiplicity of homelands. "No one inhabits one nation, and not everyone has the same idea of what that even entails. The Moors are certainly not the only people scattered about. Many have lost their lands, but they haven't lost their soul. Their music, art, poetry, and myths infuse their spirit and are passed onto future generations, like the Jews who for 2000 years have been scattered across the earth but have never lost their identity. Even their habits of food and dress are passed down to their children. You bear the name of the family into which you were born. You're English by virtue of the land. What is a homeland, other than one's childhood, the faces one has known, and familiar sight and sounds? You're not the first Morisco, nor will you be the last Englishman!"

Chapter 21

By the time I got back to my room, I had begun to find my equilibrium. I wrote to my parents at once, berating them for having kept the truth from me, but also reassuring them that this knowledge would not affect our relationship. Despite all that had transpired, I was still looking for a way to produce an Arabic typeset for my father's printing press, alongside my efforts to discover just where the manuscripts were.

I told him that the younger sister, Hind, might have taken refuge in Tuscany, according to Najma's notes in the Al-Majriti manuscript. And she very well may be the Aragonese nun mentioned in the Erpenius archives, in connection with the printing of the Al-Razi text by a Florentine press.

I told him I would remain a little while longer in Leiden. I was still trying to get Abraham to cast new Arabic letters as I awaited the delivery of my letter to Yusuf Al-Hajari in jail, although my hopes in the Jesuits was starting to flag. And, in any case, I was going to start teaching Arabic at the university while studying the new scientific philosophy.

Over the days that followed, I began to make peace with the revelation that my real parents were Moors who had escaped the ruthlessness of the Spanish. It was natural that I held on to a measure of love and longing for them that I could not shake. I had spent the first part of my childhood with Najma and over nine months in a prison with Yusuf, where I had been born again.

During this period, I visited Abraham, and, after several attempts to convince him, he finally relented, agreeing to produce a new set of Arabic type for his press and a set for me as well. Jacob assured Mr. Elzevir once more that his attempts to set up a printing press were for his own personal projects and not to compete with him for commissions from the university. He intended to install the printing press in his house just as Professor Erpenius had done. And so, Abraham agreed to dedicate a portion of his shop to casting Arabic type and all it entailed.

And this meant everything: including the procuring of a furnace and tanks in which to store lead, tin, antimony, along with copper ingots used to manufacture matrices, in addition to equipment for the extraction and forging of iron. Lastly and most importantly, he said that he would not begin gathering the necessary equipment until he could guarantee his ability to procure the French casting moulds about which I had told him.

Abraham wanted to order the moulds from the French factory by post, but I advised against it and suggested instead that he travel there himself. Otherwise, they might dawdle if he wasn't on site to harangue them to get to work. Though, to be honest, I suggested this course simply because I was looking for someone to return the debt I owed the engraver and to order new steel ingots.

A month later, the Jesuit priest who was supposed to deliver my message to Yusuf sent me a letter, regretting to inform me that the Spanish stationer had for years now been banned from visiting the Morisco. It was clear that the priest had written the missive from the monastery after meeting with Father Gaddis and after conveying my regards. The father mentioned to the priest that his soul was still heavy toward me, and he was unwilling to violate an order of the

Inquisition by allowing the letter to be delivered, especially after the warden determined that he was trying to escape from prison.

I was disappointed because I had hoped this message would reassure Yusuf and buoy his spirits. Further increasing my despair was Abraham's fruitless trip to Paris after failing to persuade the factory to sell him casting moulds on the pretext that his printing press was Protestant and the law did not permit selling anything that could fight against the words of Christ or Holy Roman Church—especially in light of the fact that the Elzevir press had printed one of Galileo's treatises and a book by Descartes on the mechanical system of the world—both of which were banned by the Catholic Church.

Mr. Elzevir relayed all this back to me as he handed over the ingots I had requested. Though a setback, he said he wasn't giving up and had written to Balthazar, informing him about the punches I had made and telling him the two printing presses could now work together. To be frank, I can't deny that I was losing hope with these Arabic letters. Anyone else who had faced failure after failure would have washed their hands of the idea and been done with it, but despair is never final until the soul reaches its absolute limit.

I reached that limit as summer drew to a close. We gave up hope of ever receiving approval from the senior Balthazar—despite the fact that his son had visited me in Leiden and promised to respond soonest regarding the matter. However, in the end, it seemed that he had been unable to win over his father. Or perhaps he could not convince that viper of a wife, whose personality and control over him was obvious. Her devotion was to the Catholic Church and her allegiance to the Spanish throne.

In Paris, Abraham picked up three ingots (equal to about 500 ounces), which was enough to carve around 100 letter punches. I continued with my work, but in the end, despair got the best of me, and I eventually gave up, although not before carving more than 70 letter punches.

After returning to Paris, the Jesuit priest sent me an apology along with my letter to Yusuf, expressing his regret that he had been unsuccessful. I responded at once, after realizing I no longer wanted to remain in Holland or return to England. I declared my desire to join a missionary delegation to the Levant, telling him that I was prepared to face any and all conditions—whatever might be asked of me by the Jesuits.

Autumn had barely begun when the priest's response arrived, turning down my request, because I would have to first study in La Flèche for two years at the very least. My father's letter also killed off any desire I might have had to stay in Holland, especially since Descartes had already departed for Endegeest castle. He had recently published a new book, *Meditations on First Philosophy*, and wanted to devote himself to responding to scholars and scientists throughout Europe who had begun to rebut his theses.

I visited Descartes in his lodgings not far outside of Leiden. I wanted to say farewell before making my way to Florence, and to request a letter of introduction from him, as I hoped to meet Galileo. I found Descartes engrossed in a matter that he claimed would change science itself—a unification of mathematics and logic. I didn't understand most of what he said to me except when he jokingly asked, "Have you crossed paths with another lady who brought up such a dangerous idea as this?"

Descartes told me that Father Mersenne knew Galileo better than he did, and there had been some communication between them in the past. In reality, though, it was one-sided, because Galileo never responded to the father's letters, while also noting that he himself only knew Galileo through his books. He then asked me about the Rosicrucians and what Father Mersenne had said about them. I told him I had forgotten about the matter altogether, but would ask the father when I saw him again.

Leiden had become a desolate wasteland for me—all of Holland really—because I had achieved so little of what I'd set out to do. My father's latest letter completely destroyed any desire I had to stay at the University of Leiden. In it, he apologized for hiding the truth that I was the son of Najma and Yusuf Al-Hajari. She had wanted to call me Yusuf, but she let him choose the name, recognizing that it would be easier on both him and me in the long run. He also urged me to continue looking for the younger sister, Hind.

As I said my goodbyes, Jacob suggested—as Descartes had as well—that I visit Father Mersenne to ask for a letter of introduction to Galileo. It was no secret that I was hoping to meet this man whose ideas had shaken the very foundations of Europe, so much so that his thoughts and experiments established a bright dividing line between traditionalists and the new scientific movement being expressed and debated in letters exchanged among proponents of the new philosophy and the new experimentalists.

As winter descended, I departed Leiden, heading first toward France as I made my way to northern Italy. Throughout the journey, the image of my aunt Al-Hajari, filled in with details from Madame Despucci, remained at the forefront of my mind. Would I find her there in Italy? Would the manuscripts still be in her possession?

Part 5

The Heart of Florence

A small aperture opened between our hearts—an opening through which the ancient gods of the Babylonians, Egyptians, and Greeks could see the world of mankind once again. It was an overwhelming sensation. This kiss was the ultimate telos of my life.

Chapter 22

Antonio the Portuguese was Genoa's only bookseller. I began to frequent his shop regularly while waiting for my ship to depart once again, as it conveyed me from Nice to Pisa. The shop was just a few steps from the park of Signora Prigionera, nestled at the bottom of Vico Way. At the opposite end of the path sat Saint Syrus' Basilica. Yet wending your way to Antonio's bookshop left you with the distinct impression that you had departed Genoa proper altogether, as the cobblestone footpath quickly began to turn to dirt.

Periodically, I had to pass by a building attached to the rear of the Basilica of Saint Syrus. According to town legend, this chamber held the saint's mummified relics, interred at the very spot where he had performed his miracle at the well, banishing a basilisk. Located in ancient times outside the city walls, the basilica was eventually moved behind the ramparts after relentless attacks by Arab Saracens.

Antonio dismissed the old tale as I tried to verify its details. He was an elderly Jew, and his hearing had started to go, forcing me to raise my voice when I spoke. I perused his shop and shelves, looking for any titles I might recognize, but in the end I came up empty-handed. I did, however, relieve him of a few ancient Hebrew texts that his father had lugged with him from Portugal decades ago.

According to him, Marseille and Rome were the prime destinations for anyone on the hunt for Arabic manuscripts, or even Hebrew ones for that matter. "Genoa is done for!" he would repeat over and over. Once, nearly screaming so he could hear, I asked, "So why are you still here?" As if chipping away at a boulder, he said, "You will never find a people more patient than the Jews."

I can't say for sure how long I had been in his shop that morning when a man caught my eye hounding a woman who was obviously trying to get away. I quickly collapsed the distance between us, wondering if it could possibly be Álvaro Elzin, the soldier who had worked under Captain Simon. After a moment, I began to worry others would think I, too, was chasing down that poor harried lady. When he reached Cross Street near the park, and just before reaching Rifalo Road, which led to the eastern docks, I shouted "Hey, Señor Álvaro!"

Almost as if I had disturbed some sort of spiritual isolation, he whipped around toward me, clearly annoyed. "I don't know many people here in Genoa," he said, shielding his face from the dust kicked up by a passing carriage on the road that separated us. "Who are you?" Álvaro ignored the litany of curses the coach driver let loose upon him. He tried to recall my face, to decide whether or not the matter was worth sacrificing his amorous pursuit.

"Robert the Englishman? The lad with the printer? Right? Europe really is tiny sometimes," he said as he withdrew the pipe from his mouth and opened his arms to hug me. He placed the pipe back in its place, trying to hide the small mole on his upper lip. "What are you doing here?"

"I'm on my way to Florence," I said, apologizing that his "bride" had made her escape. "The ship stopped here for provisions."

He laughed, then adjusted his cap, with its curved brim and clutch of feathers tucked just above the left ear, noting that he had become a captain. He scratched his head and asked, "How in the world did you free yourself from captivity? Had I killed you that day on the ship, I would never have run into you here now!"

"It's a long story, my good man. From the looks of it, it appears that you're either an admiral or vice admiral."

With a touch of pride, he said, "Me and Cap'n Simon fell into the hands of some Ottoman pirates and the only thing that saved us was that I'm circumcised like the Mohammedans! Out of respect, they let us go and returned us to our vessel. From then on, I've been a vice admiral."

"Are you a Moor?"

"Who knows. But I still remember what my mother used to say whenever I harangued her for circumcising me. She would say, 'Every one of your grandfathers was purified by the angels.'"

Again, he asked, "But how did you get out of prison?"

"The Jesuits let me go. I have no clue how they got wind of me or the printing press. I worked for them for a while before they let me go."

"Cap'n Simon is the one who told them. We used to drop anchor in Bilbao, and he was trying to ingratiate himself with the Jesuits. But what's awaiting you in Florence?"

"I'm carrying letters from France to Galileo."

"Were you just in old man Antonio's shop?"

"How'd you know?"

"I seem to recall hearing Galileo's name come up when the town shut down his bookshop a year ago. They discovered Antonio was selling books that the Church had banned."

Trying to redirect the conversation, I asked, "And what about you? What are you doing here?"

"I parted ways with Cap'n Simon awhile back, though he's still working the Bay of Biscay. I left in the hope of having my own private ship, but it never panned out. Nowadays, I'm a quartermaster for a captain from Venice. We work transport between Genoa, Venice, and Smyrna. And sometimes Iskenderun."

By now, we had reached the bustling port. He asked, "When do you head out?"

"Maybe in two or three days. As soon as the ship finishes getting loaded. What about you?"

"Not for two weeks at least. We have to find more deckhands. There's always a slew of them just before winter, but our arrival into port was delayed, and so we've been hard pressed to find unemployed sailors," he said, readjusting his pipe. "Demand in Genoa for cotton, silk, and eastern spices spikes in winter. That's why we were so late."

As if waiting for me to volunteer for the job, he repeated, "I don't know if we're going to find any sailors now!"

"Maybe you'll find some in Nice. There were so many there when I departed."

Casting off, he said, "It's alright. You'll find me in the sailor's inn if you need any help." As he headed back, he looked all around, chatting up three or four men on his way: "Looking for any work on the high seas, mate?" I sensed his desperation. An eye like his could spot a sailor from a mile away—those jocular friends of the fair winds with their bohemian vagrancy and faces like ravenous eagles.

I sat and thought for a while about the strange coincidence that brought me back in touch with Álvaro. He was dreaming of his own ship. Would he make captain one day? His appearance certainly wouldn't help, I muttered to myself as the voice of a young boy performing acrobatics to attract passers-by into his father's nearby shop drifted to my ears.

I had arrived in Genoa a week ago, having come from Nice. In the beginning, my plan was to follow the Alpine trails toward Florence, but in the end I decided to head southward. Mediterranean ports share the soul of the Moors. Alpine slopes, on the other hand, remain unrelentingly European. It is in these very ports that the European soul begins to dissolve and fade away, alchemically transmuting the Mediterranean into something truly cosmopolitan.

Before departing Paris, I made one last call at the Bare Pinetree tavern. Rumour throughout the city was that an Armenian had begun to import an Oriental drink called coffee and, ever since witnessing the debate between Father Mersenne and the priest, my curiosity had been piqued. I wanted to try it.

As I entered the bar, a worker was showing the door to a drunkard who was raving loudly: "Let that bastard Richelieu kill me if he wants. I'm a Calvinist, and I'll die a Calvinist." Someone from inside the bar was shouting to the waiter, "Give him some coffee and maybe he'll come to his senses and realize he's sending his family all to hell." The response came: "Arton isn't here. And he's the only one who knows how to make the stuff!"

I asked the waiter about this Armenian, Arton. He rebuffed me. "Who told you Arton was Armenian? He's Austrian. We import coffee from Vienna."

"I heard that you brought it from the East. I was keen to give it a try," I said, as if somehow apologizing.

"Vienna would never have been able to withstand the Ottoman siege had the population not managed to smuggle coffee inside the city from the Turkish encampments," he said. "Now that it's become part of the fight, the drink is no longer considered Oriental!" Swatting away a fly buzzing around him, he added, "Come by tomorrow. Arton will be here."

Fine. I would have to satisfy myself with some beer instead of coffee. Perhaps, I thought, it was one of Father Mersenne's small mercies.

After leaving Father Mersenne's place earlier, I had been at the engraver's before making tracks to the tavern that afternoon. When I met the engraver, I brought along some of the punches I had made and laid them all out in front of him. He praised my work and offered a few observations, such as how the edges of the letters could extend slightly beyond their base to mimic handwritten script, such as the upper stroke of the letter *kaaf* (ﺱ) sliding seamlessly into the space above the letter before it.

"That's the clear advantage of steel. You needn't worry that the strokes will bend or snap off, and it makes it easier to add ornamentation and embellishment to the letters. If you're planning to sell books to the Orientals, it will be a losing proposition if they can produce something more resplendent and decorous by hand themselves," he said, while advising me on the merits of magnifying glasses, such as the ones used by goldsmiths to carve smaller, more intricate, and more precise letters.

I left the engraver's thinking about something my father, the Morisco, had said. It was something Jacob had mentioned as well, about Easterners' antipathy toward printed material. It was beginning to look like we would need more than 200 individual punches just to appeal to the tastes and aesthetic sensibilities of the Orientals!

My mind turned all of this over and over as I made my way to the bar in the Saint Germain neighbourhood. The sadness that had hung over me ever since I'd cinched up my satchel, saying goodbye to Claudia and the shy lady and departed Leiden, finally began to lighten and lift.

It hadn't been the satchel or tears that made me sad, but rather the feeling of being distracted, unable to concentrate, which had weakened me to the point where I couldn't decide what I wanted for myself. As my journey to Tuscany progressed, I began to collect and distil particular questions within myself, right before skirting the township of Tilburg in Brabant, which we bypassed (on the advice of fellow travellers) given the sharp divisions among the inhabitants— between those who saw their roots firmly in the Netherlands, and thus in union with Holland, versus those rooted deeply in Catholicism as championed by Spain.

"The question of roots," said the man who warned us, "tears them apart, and war could break out at any moment." He added, "In such a state as theirs, they ought to allow their roots to branch off how they like and not how their forefathers would have dictated. Otherwise, they will be the cause of their own destruction, and they'll be finished off."

I thought back to the question of roots as I laid bare my sorrow at the Jesuit college's rejection of my petition to join in the service of the Lord to Father Mersenne. I told him that it was just one more deprivation after a string of so many. Jokingly, he said, "The Order of the Jesuits is not the word of the Lord. They are just a system operating below the Word."

The father had been busily commenting on his friend Descartes' recent publication, *Meditations on First Philosophy,* when I told him of my intention to go to Florence and to meet Galileo if possible.

"Seeking an audience with him has lately become difficult. His house arrest in Arcetri aside, old age has also begun to take its toll. However, Clemente Settimi, the secretary appointed by the Church to assist him, will help you get in touch."

Just then, the rumours about Father Mersenne that spread in Leiden came rushing back to me, but I felt that asking about them might pain him, so I broached the subject gently. "Something has been weighing on me, father, but I fear raising it will make you think poorly of me."

"What makes you think that, my son?"

"There are rumours swirling around Leiden about your strained relationship with Galileo. It's been said that Galileo did not deign to respond to your letters because of his belief that you chose to ingratiate yourself with the Church at the expense of scientific knowledge."

"That statement is not without merit, but it does not bother me. My heart is pure before Galileo. In a letter to some of his Parisian friends—and before he lost his eyesight—he said that he had been unable to read my handwriting. What I see is that he didn't respond to me because he felt I had not sufficiently defended him among the followers of Latin Averroism here in Paris. Especially in light of how I maintained the right of the Church to defend the word of the Lord. On the other hand, I am not a follower of Averroes, as they imagine. After all, we are all sons of the Church."

"But they also say, father, that you don't believe in Copernicanism, which makes you a hypocrite within mechanical philosophy, for which you are among the most ardent supporters here in France!"

"But even if I don't believe in Copernican ideas, that doesn't mean I am against the budding scientific movement in Europe. I am part of this movement. The truth, my son, is that among Lutherans there are some who try strenuously to put the Church of Rome in opposition to science, and they raise the trial of Galileo as a banner. The matter, however, is not as they would like. Science operates best outside all of these polarizations. I disagree with Galileo and also with Descartes in the matter of attaining certainty. Both of them believe—or want to believe—that science is what creates certain knowledge. My response to them is that all that science does is make us more precise—but it cannot ever bring us to complete certainty."

"Is the issue somehow connected to your own imposed self-effacement and asceticism, Father?"

"You're a bright and astute young man, Robert. I know what is rolling around your mind when you ask that question. The knowledge I possess is pursued simply for itself. It is a pure good when we seek it to understand who we are and where we are. Going beyond that, however, the pursuit of knowledge can lead one astray. And that is why I take the followers of Galileo to task. They seek knowledge to gain riches, either through proximity to the wealthy or to those with power, or by selling what they can produce. Knowledge that generates money only increases the darkness and shadows of the soul. I defended the Church because I knew Galileo was intent on amassing wealth and gaining the prestige of the world. He was seeking treasure and fame. This stands against the very spirit of Christianity, which calls for people to rise above materiality and what is between their hands, because what God offers is far greater and purer for the heart. To be honest, my son, European Christianity has become avaricious and covetous, thinking of nothing more than wealth and riches."

The father didn't need to justify himself to me. He was among the prominent scientists in all of France, and my heart sank to see him defend himself like this. I apologized. "Forgive my audacity. It's just that the mention of Galileo made me recall all I had heard about you two."

Then, beseechingly, I asked, "Will you provide me with a letter of introduction to meet Galileo?"

He asked me to return the next day, and so I left. When I came back, he handed me two letters, both for Father Settimi. One was for Galileo, and the other was my letter of introduction. I nearly lost these letters, as well all my notebooks and documents, when my bag almost fell into a deep ravine near the Fort of Saint Andrew on the outskirts of Nice, close to the Mediterranean.

Chapter 23

Off in the distance, the hills of Arcetri loomed before me, hinting at the bitter cold that would test my ability to bear whatever crossed my path as I made my way to Father Clemente Settimi. Only the cypress and birch trees were capable of withstanding such iciness, set as they were around the frozen pools and ponds that flashed into view from time to time. I descended to the left as I approached the Church of San Matteo and then climbed up into the hills once more, where the perfume of herbs and winter lilies filled my nose with a bit of hope as it implored my hands to warm it up.

My breathing grew more laboured as I neared the turn leading to dei Giullari Street. As morning dovetailed into midday, I grew further and further away from the river Arno, before nearing it once again as I made my way toward the mountain heights, where the scent of acacia overpowered all other odours. And although the path was rugged, it actually proved to be something of a shortcut and avoided the Church of San Leonardo, infamous for its pamphlets and fiery sermons that railed against Galileo's ideas and books.

I kept walking for several minutes before I arrived at the oak tree flanking the gate that led to Galileo's house and Clemente Settimi's office, which was set off to one side. From a distance, I glimpsed two men standing beside the oak near a post-box. Draped in sorrow, they appeared to be seeking solace from the tree and, for a moment, I felt that winter had stripped this oak bare of any power to offer comfort at all.

I slowed my pace as I neared them, but remembered that among Florentines such behaviour was improper, so I marched up to them directly, wondering if I had not seen them somewhere before. Greeting them, I introduced myself by saying, "I'm Robert Febin. I met with Father Settimi two days ago and have a letter for Galileo from Father Mersenne in France. He asked me to come today. Perhaps the scholar's health has returned?"

"Galileo is dead!" lamented the younger one.

"We're awaiting the coffin now. It's quite tardy," added the older of the pair.

"Though I did not have the honour to meet Galileo alive," I said, "I would be honoured to escort him to his final resting place."

"That's fine. As long as Father Settimi knows you. The funeral will be a small gathering. His family is sensitive about provoking the ire of Rome," one said as he looked off into the distance. The younger one added, "I'm Vincenzo Viviani, and this is Evangelista Torricelli. We were students of Galileo."

For several moments, nothing but silence reigned as I awkwardly fumbled with Father Mersenne's letter for Galileo. Father Clemente had asked me to hold onto it until Galileo regained his health. It was to be the final letter from Mersenne to Galileo. Who would read it now?

"Are you Spanish?" Vincenzo asked.

"No, I'm an Englishman making his way through Europe."

"I saw you in the Medici Library. You were asking for an author, a certain Maria of Aragon. Books by women are nearly impossible to find. And you can assume what you want about those who go hunting for them," he said, almost apologetically.

"Perhaps your information is lacking, Mr. Viviani. In fact, the person I asked about was a Spanish copyist of books and may have worked in the library in the past."

"So," Evangelista shot back. "You're not just taking a tour of Europe, then."

"Pardon me, good sirs, for not divulging what brought me to Florence. I was in the library searching for primers on the Tuscan dialect along with some dictionaries. My inquiry about the lady arose within the context of some research I have been working on since first setting foot in the Netherlands."

"Forgive our nosiness, Robert. Your acquaintance with Father Mersenne, coupled with your desire to meet Galileo, raise suspicions that we just might be standing before a unique and enlightened mind who is trying to debase himself or hide behind something," Vincenzo said, trying to press me.

"I was looking for a manuscript of *Al-Hawi* by Al-Razi. I have reason to believe that the Spanish lady made a copy of it years ago for the Florentine library," I said, trying to find an escape from these meddlesome questions that were pushing me to prevaricate. I added, "Is it true that the library's real architects were engineers and not Michelangelo himself?"

From that point on, discussion between us took off naturally, ranging from books and authors to the new scientific movement and the history of the city, until true bonds of friendship began to take root. A week later, at the memorial service organized by Father Settimi for the family and students of Galileo, it wasn't necessary for him to introduce me to the two of them.

Galileo's family had been unable to fulfil his last wish—to be buried next to his father. Instead, he was honoured with nothing more than a paltry two and a half metres in some side gallery, off in a remote corner of the Basilica of Santa Croce, which only increased everyone's sorrow during the memorial service at his home.

"If knowledge is not valued and honoured here," Vincenzo said, "then it will depart Italy for other parts of Europe!"

I helped myself to several drinks from the wide-bottomed fiasco bottles, which looked like rain-filled clouds. I went back three or four times, both before and after the eulogies given by Father Settimi, Vincenzo, and others. Each time I did, I discovered a new taste.

Father Settimi presented me to a nobleman of the Ricardio family, one of the august families of Florence. The man was no less sophisticated than the rest of the city's nobles, though his excessively florid name put me off a bit. However, when Father Settimi informed me that the man was looking to hire someone to oversee the large library at his palazzo and mentioned that I might be the right man for the job, I began to call him Sir Ricardiana. We agreed I would pay a call on him at his palazzo to look at the library and get a sense of the nature of the work, and that I would decide afterward.

Later, Clemente inquired about the manuscript by Al-Razi in the Library of Florence, known among Florentines as the *Biblioteca Medicea* and sometimes simply as the Laurentian. I told him, "I haven't yet had any success. The book isn't available, and the librarians don't know anything about it!"

"You should ask Alessandro de' Medici himself, the eminent head of the library. I'll ask Vincenzo to introduce you."

I thanked him on the spot and asked, "Will I find anything pertaining to the Orient?"

"You won't find anything directly. Arabic manuscripts aren't accessible to the general public, nor are the catalogues available yet," he said, urging me to temper my expectations.

During the memorial service, I met Margherita Viviani, Vincenzo's younger sister. I must admit, she had caught my eye earlier, at Galileo's funeral. Later, I discovered that she lived with her brother in Galileo's residence even though Fernando II, the grand duke of Tuscany, had granted them a home near Galileo's villa. Though I couldn't be sure if she had noticed me at the funeral, my intense interest in her had nonetheless imbued the solemn occasion with an air of romance.

From the moment her brother introduced us, I could not conceal my fascination. Her delicate and refined nature had entranced me when I bumped into her while pouring myself a drink. She suggested I try a bit of the Chianti. She had no need for such a sweet and kind disposition in order to make the world revolve around her—her beauty alone was sufficient to make her the centre of attention. And the rarefied scientific milieu in which she moved further bestowed a graciousness upon her commensurate to her beauty, which could only be fully appreciated by those of noble spirit.

I gave myself over to poetic excess and broke through the mordant atmosphere of the memorial by proclaiming to Vincenzo, "The very ice of Arcetri will melt before her beauty." I imagined her smile at me as a bridge narrowing the distance between us, but I soon noticed she extended that same smile to everyone, which made me cease feeding her grapes and stroking her hair in my virginal imagination.

Chapter 24

I took up residence in a small pension in the middle of Florence, separated from the Ponte Vecchio by a narrow path, the same path that led to the Society of Sisters. The house itself was an endowment, set aside for young girls entering a monastic life after their entire families had passed away, either from plague or war. Since the proceeds from the house subsidised the operations of the Society, every time I paid rent, I had to knock on the door of the Society's ancient building, which had undergone more than one renovation. I also came to find out that the building itself had previously been a clinic before being annexed to the convent in the neighbourhood directly behind the Medici Villa.

The sisters would regularly gather at the Society. It was their way of connecting the interior life of the convent to the wider outside community. They often organised activities for mothers and young girls, sold their products, and introduced them to the life of nuns. Many who desired to join the ranks of the sisters began their journey in this Society and, truth be told, those considering leaving the convent began planning their exit from there as well, for not just a few chaste love stories (bandied about by young Florentine men) had their beginnings within that building.

I once asked Margherita about the Society of Sisters. She described it as a "cloud of the Lord raining down life-giving water upon Florence." Fine. I suppose I should remark here that Margherita composed poetry. I once said that her poetry put her beauty to shame, which made her laugh and ask, "Is that a compliment or a critique?" I said, "Am I winking?"

Night grew deeper, and so I departed the memorial to return to my accommodations. And though I was accustomed to walking in the dark and the path was not entirely devoid of light, Vincenzo and Evangelista refused to let me go alone. As we made our way along the trail, Vincenzo told me that he could not stand in the way of his sister's wish, filling me with euphoria—more so even than the happiness I felt the time Father Settimi handed me a manuscript and told me it was a copy of Surah Yusuf from the holy book of the Turks, and I realized that a part of the Qur'an had finally fallen into my hands at long last.

Father Settimi had told me that the copy arrived in Italy by way of some Maronites from Aleppo or Lebanon who were guests of the Maronite college in Rome. I knew that Master Erpenius had printed Surah Yusuf and even made a Latin translation of it, which Jacob described as "decent" though in need of a few corrections. His intention was to reprint it as part of the many projects he planned for his printing house, though Jacob had never shown me the Erpenius copy, nor had I been able to find a copy of it anywhere else.

Young girls, some accompanied by nuns, were beginning to leave the Society just as we reached the street leading to my place. Evangelista stopped to speak to one of the sisters, who it seemed was an acquaintance. We waited for him at the entrance to the house where Vincenzo cracked a joke that Evangelista had come along with us for her sake alone. When he caught up with us once again, he apologized, saying he had known the nun since childhood and she'd entered the convent when she turned 15.

Viviani asked him, "Does she still only want to marry a soldier returning from war?" Evangelista said she had begun to set conditions that the soldier also be a Spaniard. Vincenzo laughed. "She won't find any of those except in the streets of Milan." I didn't quite understand what they were talking about, but, inviting them to come inside, I asked, "Isn't she rejecting both love and war by living in a convent?"

The two young men stayed up with me until midnight. The few things I had brought with me to Florence steered the conversation toward my tales and adventure: from typesetting to Erpenius' Arabic grammar and Jacob's not-yet-published Arabic-Latin dictionary, to make no mention of all the other manuscripts and books I had lying about, including a collection of works I intended to post to my father but had not yet, given my malaise whilst among the canals of Leiden.

I visited Lord Ricardiana several days later at his palazzo near Giovanni Nere piazza. To its north, Bande Nere park separated the palazzo from the piazza that always hustled and bustled with all manner of carriages, itinerant merchants, and porters. From a window in his palazzo, you could actually see the park and Piazza Giovanni, and Ricardiana would use a special telescope to watch events taking place there and sometimes in the park. He was always on the hunt for someone who could fashion successively more powerful telescopes so he could see all the way to the Medici Library, which was just a few buildings and a horse stable beyond the piazza to the south. He ceaselessly crowed about the strength of his telescope, saying, "You can even see a pigeon standing on the head of the statue of Giovanni the Terrible."

I didn't hesitate for a moment before accepting his offer to enrich the library with manuscripts and rare Oriental works. However, I did baulk at taking up residence in the palazzo. I preferred keeping some distance from the coddled world of the wealthy. Doing so would allow me more freedom, although there was more to it than that. I wanted to get closer to the Viviani family. Also, with time, I discovered Lord Ricardiana's rationale for me staying in the palazzo for as long as possible was to entertain him and keep him company. But I hadn't come to Florence for that!

So, it wasn't long before I suggested to the nobleman that we cooperate with the Medici Library so they would allow us to copy some of the works in their collection. After some initial hesitation, the gentleman agreed. For a long time, he had thought he was a competitor to the Medici Library and therefore they would not cooperate with him. I have no clue where that idea came from, because there was no comparison at all between his holdings and the Medici Library's. Not only that, but in the letter of introduction he provided me to present to Alessandro de' Medici, head of the library, he had written that we at the Ricardio library had no objection at all to teaching them the tricks of the trade, how to catalogue a collection and otherwise maintain manuscripts. That's what prompted Alessandro to refuse the request outright, disavowing that they had any Oriental works, and subsequently forcing us to go together as he muttered to himself, "Either me or Alessandro!"

That day, the piazza was overflowing with inventors showing off their latest creations alongside amateur craftsmen and engineers, as well as noblemen and those simply looking to pick up some bauble or trinket for their loved ones. I suggested to Lord Ricardiana that we stop and take a look at some of the new ideas but he refused, saying that time was short despite the fact that he never felt any rush while spending hours observing the piazza through his incredible telescope!

When we arrived at the Medici Library, Alessandro welcomed us into the book depository, which was situated in the basement. It held a wooden box filled to the brim with a collection of jumbled manuscripts, all of which appeared to be in Arabic.

On numerous occasions, I had seen Alessandro on my visits to the library, but had never met him face to face until now. Each time I came across him, he was engrossed in some aspect of his work, which was natural given how many visitors came to the library each day. It had become a principal destination in Florence for visitors from Europe and elsewhere. Alessandro relished the exertion and exhaustion caused by all the work, but it was not hard to notice a slight hunch developing on his back, the result of his advancing years. He was examining this storage room when we entered.

Introducing me, Lord Ricardiano offered our assistance in sorting through and organizing the collection in exchange for permission to copy some of the works. Alessandro had no qualms and said, "There is no problem at all. I am just trying to find out how this box made its way to us."

As we went upstairs, Alessandro said, "We had been dealing with a nun at the Monastero delle Murate who was studying medicine and apothecary and would copy manuscripts for us in the past, but she was consumed by her medical studies, and soon after, when the plague struck, all contact ceased. After it receded, the convent returned this box to us. It seems no one has rifled through it much, likely because it's all in Arabic."

The wheels of my mind kept turning over this nun mentioned by Alessandro. Could it have been my aunt Al-Hajari? We reached an agreement with Alessandro that I would begin working for him in addition to my work with Ricardiana. However, as days went by, I discovered that my true place was in the Medici Library—something Alessandro also remarked on once he learned I had letter punches in my possession. He began to seek more details, and I told him of my attempts to carve them and set up an Arabic printing house in Leiden. "You should transfer here to us," he said. "I will inform Duke Lorenzo about this at once."

I could identify three manuscripts in the Medici collection thanks to things Yusuf had told me in prison. Among them was a section of the Al-Razi text, which meant that Hind and Hasan had indeed arrived in Florence and were the likely source of all three—and perhaps the other manuscripts in that box, too. But where were they now? And where was their trove of manuscripts itself?

I asked Alessandro about the nun of Aragon, who had copied manuscripts for them in the past, and about the previous project reported in that Dutch periodical about the printing of the *Al-Hawi* text by Al-Razi. He told me, "The project withered on the vine due to problems we encountered with the typeset we had. As for the nun, her name was Maria of Aragon. She had taken refuge in the Monastero delle Murate after arriving in Florence from France. I have no idea why she was called Maria of Aragon. I thought she was French."

Alessandro insisted, however, that the library had not circulated any announcement of that kind and suggested that we ask Duke Lorenzo de' Medici about these manuscripts, whom Alessandro had been trying to meet for a while now. The duke was the superintendent of the library and the innumerable possessions of the Medici family, as well as the nephew of the Grand Duke Ferdinand II, ruler of Tuscany.

After the Easter holiday, Father Settimi invited me to the Galileo family home for a gathering of his former students. He encouraged me to transfer to the Medici Library after learning of my own failure to set up an Arabic printing house, which, for reasons I can't fathom, he was pleased to hear. There seemed to be a strange competition among the Italian duchies for the soul of the Orient.

He asked me about the Surah Yusuf manuscript, and I told him I had difficulty understanding some of the strange terminology given that I was reading it for the very first time. However, you could easily note the glaring contrast between the Quranic version of the story and the account in the Holy Bible. I cited some of my discoveries in the story of Yusuf, specifically how the Qur'an referred to the ruler of Egypt as *king* rather than *pharaoh*. I didn't try to hide my infatuation with the astonishing narrative or my surprise at the ability of the prophet of the Muslims to write a story with such beautiful detail, such as whether Potiphar's lusty wife yanked at Joseph's shirt from behind or in front as a means to establish his innocence—a detail missing from the Bible's story.

Vincenzo and Margherita came over just as I was telling Father Settimi how the two narratives complemented one another. The father warned me against giving too much credence to the account in the book of the Turks. When I told the father that I might suggest Alessandro print this surah in a multilingual edition, he was not encouraging and said, "Printing excerpts from the book of the Turks is not as easy as you might think. The Mohammedan narrative of the story of Joseph appears to be quite at odds with the Old Testament. You would need to insert refutations in the book eviscerating the Quranic story and avowing the Holy Bible's version. If not, then you certainly won't receive permission to print it. You're in Italy after all, not Holland!"

I told him that even in Holland it wasn't an easy matter, and I abandoned the idea. Perhaps my interest in Surah Yusuf was due to its intersection with the story of my father Yusuf the Morisco, who was also cast into prison unfairly. At this point, Vincenzo interjected: "I have a better idea for you, Robert. Something related to Galileo's scientific legacy. How about you visit us at home so I can show you exactly what I have in mind."

I could not have hoped for anything more, originally thinking that the invitation came from Margherita and not her brother. So I agreed and jokingly said, "An unfinished thought is an unconfessed sin." Margarita laughed and confirmed her brother's invitation.

Chapter 25

The hour approached midnight at the Viviani residence. A certain tranquillity had quietly descended on the house, lending it the peacefulness of a temple just before worshippers begin trickling in. When Margherita walked in, I was poring over some papers and reshuffling them while I remained hunched over, copying the final manuscript in the collection of David the African.

She had told her brother that this Englishman could copy Arabic manuscripts with such agility that it was nothing short of an art. Or art itself. She noted how much she relished the opportunity to watch the quill glide and pirouette in my hand, like Canary dancers in a nobleman's palace. It was indeed a rare skill in Europe, even more so in Italy, and Vincenzo and his sister opened the doors to their home and offered me their total support.

She observed that I wrote as if oblivious to time itself. I admitted that I didn't write so much as I drew a picture—a method developed by the Moors over generations to preserve a heritage that was beginning to disappear. They drew the language as if it were a picture without understanding the content of what they were reproducing. One needed only to grasp the basic orthographic conventions to appropriately render each letter with all its swoops and curves brought into being through skilful handling of the quill. And with some training and practice, you quickly got to know the quirks and style of the original author. Once you understood how the amanuensis worked, then the process of reproduction became nearly mechanical.

I would say, "The single most important factor in copying quickly comes down to the kind of feather and parchment used for the task. Personally, I found the best are plucked from a live goose's left wing at the height of springtime. The quill's strength lies in the angle of the feather's inclination, the flatness of its writing surface, and its slight curve at the top. Combined, these factors determine the quality of the stylus. As for paper, I was most accustomed to and comfortable with the improvements Venetian stationers had begun to introduce to traditional Baghdadi paper. Adding used cloth—linen in particular—to the pulp from stone pine trees, and then heating the mixture while applying pressure produced paper renowned for its strength, durability, and even a certain suppleness."

My ears learned to identify the cadence of her footsteps perfectly. I memorised them like a dance with precise choreography. As a result, I was always prepared to greet that radiant face of hers that exuded such warmth and vitality.

She understood quite well the effect her footsteps had on my heart, and she tried to protect it by treading lightly. That day, she came down the stairs and went directly to make some hot soup. Bringing over a bowl to me, she stole furtive glances in my direction as she pretended to tuck into her meal. Finally, she gave up and asked, "Have you begun writing the letter to your father?"

"It's still early. My father does not have a need to know that I'm talking with you."

She smiled at my reply. I tossed my quill to the side and sipped the last drop of the soup that whispered her care for me. "Not yet," I continued. "I will write to him as soon as I finish the manuscripts at the Medici Library."

She said that she had begun sifting through Galileo's papers and notebooks and was able to narrow down to four experiments we could easily test. "The experiments themselves should not be our main objective," I said. "Rather, the questions that lead to the experiments themselves. The *why* behind them and the facts that preceded them. That's how we will help the reader to think like Galileo himself."

She was caught off guard a little and I quickly followed up with, "That's how Jacob and Descartes taught me to think back in Leiden."

She asked me about René Descartes. "How deep of an impact have his ideas and philosophy had in Holland? Are his enemies as cruel and relentless as Galileo's?"

"He has certainly made a lot of enemies. Some who would even like to see him dead, but he also has his supporters. And he certainly does not enjoy clashing with the Church. In fact, quite the opposite, he is open about his devotion to Catholicism—even going so far as to write his books primarily in Latin, unlike Galileo, who used Italian. However, the educational environment in Holland is different than it is here. Universities and colleges in Holland rely on their own financial assets, funding both from the government and private companies, in addition to tuition fees. They don't rely on gifts or endowments from wealthy patrons, whose funding ends where their interests stop."

Margherita was now giving me her full attention, so I continued: "I attended more than one course with Descartes. His opponents outnumber his supporters, but he can stand up to them without fearing for his life. Some discussions are stormy, as was the case when he rejected the possibility of attaining certain knowledge, thus implying we must doubt everything since our senses are deceptive. Descartes asked, "What prevents a demon from tricking us and our senses and in fact deluding our vision altogether?" It was his way of proving that the authenticity of existence took precedence over matter and the body. However, this kind of doubt, which he hammered on during his lessons, frightened the religiously inclined, and so he ended his discourse on what he called systematic doubt. To be honest, I don't even know what this kind of doubt is!"

That evening, I plunged deeper into conversation with Margherita, talking about my adventures in Leiden and the university there, and the differences I had noticed between Holland and Italy. As dawn drew near, she bid me farewell, saying, "Your place in my heart, Robert, continues to grow larger and larger."

A few weeks prior to all this, Alessandro had asked me to take a closer look at some of the boxes that had been discarded in the library basement. He assigned two workers to help me out and, after several days, I handed him back a list of what I had found. Alessandro couldn't quite recall the source of these boxes, placing the blame on his fading memory. Among the collection were five Arabic manuscripts, while the rest were in Greek, Syriac, and Coptic. Among the Arabic texts was the lost treatise on Apollonian cones that Descartes had mentioned in Leiden.

I mentioned it to Vincenzo during one of my initial visits to the house, and he asked, "Are they part of the treatises by the sons of Musa bin Shaker?"

"Yes, and translated by Thabit bin Qurra."

"This is a momentous discovery, Robert. For more than ten years now, Jacob has promised the scientific community in Europe that he would publish these treatises translated into Latin, but has not gotten around to it yet."

"Jacob translated them orally for Descartes, who had begun to take a deeper look at Euclidean geometry," I said.

"And that is what I hope you will do for me as well. We will publish these texts so they'll be available to all engineering students, and we won't have to wait around for Professor Golius to grace us with them."

I agreed immediately. Here was yet another basis for getting closer to Margherita.

I told them how I intended to copy some of the Medici manuscripts for my father, but would wait first for my anticipated meeting with Duke Lorenzo de' Medici. I asked them about the duke.

"He is a connoisseur of both art and science. And, thanks to his proximity to the elder duke, he is able to render us great services. In fact, he was the one who supported my nomination to work with Galileo. And when I suggested that Margherita come with me, he didn't hesitate for a moment. Thanks to him, we receive a yearly stipend from the duchy in addition to this home we're in now."

It was later that Margherita explained in detail the project they both wanted to work on. It involved compiling a scientific guide to Galileo's experiments alongside the latest questions raised by these experiments in the field of natural philosophy. The guide would be available to students, scholars, and dilettantes alike, and it would serve as a neutral introduction into the new natural sciences.

I loved the idea and pledged my services to it. Our shared interests became the key that opened the door to my subsequent discussions with Margherita. From that point on, true love began to find a path into my heart. It was a love that had quietly smouldered within me for a number of months before maturing and evolving into a language all its own.

Time passed quickly, and Vincenzo offered that I spend the night with them. I declined the invitation, because the next day I had to work at both libraries. After my meeting with the duke (which proceeded far better than either I or Alessandro had hoped), I went back to Vincenzo and Margherita's house. Their congratulations and excitement were far sweeter than anything a stranger in a strange land such as myself could hope for. With Alessandro agreeing to let me copy Arabic manuscripts for myself outside work hours, Vincenzo agreed to borrow them from the Medici Library in his name, something I could not do myself because I was not Tuscan. And that was how it came to be that I asked Vincenzo to let me stay with them in their home for a period of time.

Chapter 26

Like the concentric rings of an onion, what appeared at first to be a single residence with a unified facade was in actuality three homes nestled at the bottom of dei Giullari Street. No one could say for sure where this road actually began, with its many serpentine twists and turns, which started as small meandering paths radiating out from the city centre before ultimately flowing toward the ring road. The city's administrators themselves were hard pressed to determine whether the road was part of dei Giullari Street or had once been part of an old fort now collapsed and in decay in the middle of the road. If the beginning of dei Giullari Street was unknowable, its far-flung and perhaps forgotten terminus ended at these three houses, the first of which was where the Viviani family called home.

Though the distance between the house and the oak tree was less than 200 yards, if two people were standing at both ends, the curvature of the path and density of the thick trees would block their view of one another. And it was precisely at that bend in the trail that Margherita confessed her love to me.

We were leaving Father Settimi's office one day as spring was just beginning to turn to summer. The birch trees—with their renewed verdant leafiness and silvery wide trunks—basked luxuriantly in the sun's rays, which shot through the branches and slaked the blossoms' thirst for sunlight. With us were some instruments and equipment, so we could run new experiments we were thinking of including in the scientific manual we were still working on. She said that she had told her brother Vincenzo first, and he had urged her to reveal how she felt about me. I dropped what was in my hands so I could kiss her near the cypress tree that was covered in creeping moss. It was my first kiss.

That kiss clung to my soul as if it had no end. As if time had ceased. In that instant, my heart released all its worries. Suddenly, that minute became one long moment of anticipation. Like a baby on the cusp of birth, hesitating to leave the warmth of its mother's womb. A moment so long that the moss creeping up the trees inched toward us searching for the sun. Or a moment lasting long enough that dei Giullari Street finally ironed itself out so that one standing at the top could see a person all the way at the other end.

Everything resolved and clarified in that instant. When my tongue touched hers, the surrounding foothills came to understand that language itself had become obsolete. A small aperture opened between our hearts—an opening through which the ancient gods of the Babylonians, Egyptians, and Greeks could see the world of mankind once again. It was an overwhelming sensation. This kiss was the ultimate telos of my life—the very objective of all Jesuit teaching, all the principles of mathematics and mechanics, and all the experiments of Galileo and Father Mersenne combined into one perfect whole. All the knowledge and learning of the world had prepared me for that one ultimate goal: to kiss the girl I loved.

As we approached the house, Margherita said she had restrained herself before finally surrendering to her feelings. Part of the hesitation was her sense that my presence in Florence was not a mere coincidence. Rather, I was searching for something greater than just an old manuscript or nun I had once known. And something whispered to her that I was only there temporarily and would soon return from whence I had come.

I didn't reveal my tale at that point, but waited till after returning from the Monastero delle Murate. That evening, she was attending an event at the Society of Sisters. I waited for her at the Arno River, across from the cathedral of Florence. When she met me, we talked about everything—except for love—the sole thing that brought us together at that moment. Perhaps it was because pure love transcends all need for language.

Sitting side by side on the riverbank under trees the Florentines called Cosimo cypresses, Margarita began to wax poetic, describing the Arno as "a cemetery serpent snaking stealthily into the cities to harvest the dreams of mankind." She recited poetry to guard her femininity, or to place a boulder capable of resisting the roaring waves and thus allow me to protect her from my truth. Yet everything we did and possessed and enjoyed together quickly stripped the soul bare of the defences we had built around ourselves.

"Up until his final breath," she once said, "the poet fights to protect his exposed soul." Perhaps that was why she immersed herself so deeply within the natural sciences and experiments.

We stayed up all night beside that river, until dawn was just about to break. All that was lacking was the moon, which was illuminating other lovers' dreams on the other side of the world.

Our conversation led us once again to the natural sciences. "Not a single intellectual in Italy believes the earth is flat," she said, affirming that nature was unyielding to all our man-made convictions. She spoke of a priest in Venice who taught philosophy, one of the main agitators against Galileo. The same year Galileo was put on trial, he published a book, refuting Galileo's methodology and championing instead Aristotelian principles. The Church published hundreds of copies and distributed them all for free. When Galileo got hold of a copy, he said, "Antonio Rocco will perish, long live Galileo!" As she spoke, a drunkard tossed his hat into the river, catching her attention. He shouted, "Tell my girlfriend that I love you. No. I mean I love her!"

Pedestrians began to slowly dwindle away until there was no one left save for a few inebriated souls stumbling out of the bars looking for their wives. At that moment, she asked me, "Why does man think he is the centre of creation?"

"I don't believe that. Maybe it's just men in taverns who do."

We spent the whole night singing the praises of the river and, as we drew closer to speaking of love, I found myself candidly telling her why I had come to Florence in the first place. I told her my whole story from my imprisonment with Yusuf the Morisco up to what Sister Luisa had revealed to me in the Monastero delle Murate. As soon as I finished, I found her asking me the same old question as Professor Jacob: "Is that everything?!"

I was not entirely sure it *was* everything. I seemed to have lost the ability to know whether there was more to say, so I just nodded. Naturally, those closest to me know my nod means I've run into a dead end and by now Margherita had known me for months— perhaps since my first meeting with the duke.

Alessandro had spent days preparing for that meeting to ensure it went off without a hitch. He asked me to bring along the letter punches, the casting mould from France, and a manuscript of Razi's *Al-Hawi* while the head of the printing press brought the well-eroded Arabic typeset that could no longer be used, as library workers carted in the boxes Alessandro had requested.

Alessandro poured some warm milk into the coffee, the taste of which brought a smile to Duke Lorenzo de' Medici's face, expressing his satisfaction. After several sips, he remarked, "My dear Alessandro, you really ought to try hot chocolate. Some missionaries returning from Mexico said it was delicious, and I cannot wait to give it a taste. And if it's as good as they say, we will offer it to our cousin the grand duke.

Before the duke arrived, Alessandro noted that the Medici were the ones to thank for Pope Clement VIII's sanctioning of coffee. After all, there had been a fierce debate in Europe over it, some even going so far as to consider it the drink of the devil. In fact, coffee had begun to take the place of wine and beer at the tables of wealthy Italian families. Perhaps if Father Mersenne had known that, he would have changed his opinion. I myself had tried it when I first arrived in Florence, though I had not anticipated how its taste, when mixed with hot milk, would be akin to a lover gently rapping at the door of his beloved, who coquettishly refrained from opening the door but whispered that the window was open!

Making his entrance with a servant in tow, the duke directed his first words to me. "Ah, so here is the Robert that everyone is talking about." Then he added, "Is it true that you have mastered five Oriental languages without ever traveling to the eastern lands?"

I was at a loss for words. I figured he was testing my humility, but then I remembered Vincenzo's remark about the duke, and I thought that perhaps this was just his way of speaking to artists and craftsmen.

"In reality, seven languages, my Lord. But, I'm only fluent, or nearly so, in three of them."

He smiled. "Did these languages teach you such modesty as well, Robert?"

I wasn't quite sure what he meant, but he went on, making his way toward the director's office. He noticed the cases holding the old Arabic type. "Where did you learn to print Arabic?"

I hesitated a little as I presented the punches, which he began to inspect. Where to even begin? Before saying anything, the duke removed a small gold chain from beneath the white collar under the silk caftan draped over his shoulders. Dangling from it was a magnifying glass, which he used to scrutinise them. Before I could say anything about the events that had brought me in contact with the Arabic printing press, the duke reformulated his question. "Alright then. What do you lack, Robert, in order to set up an Arabic printing press here in Florence?"

"Basically, casting moulds, Sir," I said, eyeing the head of the printing house who, continuing along in the same vein, placed the worn-down French mould in the duke's hands. "The old moulds we have are made of wood and entirely unsuitable for large Arabic type," he said, while showing an example to the duke.

"I don't think it's casting moulds we lack!" the duke said as he turned to Alessandro and finished his thought by giving the order to transfer me to the Medici Library full time. "The Ricardio family will have to find someone else." Then he added, "It's better that we make the moulds ourselves. There is a factory in Venice that produces equipment for printing. I know the owner quite well and he owes us a visit. I will tell him to send to us one of his iron casters, and you two can discuss what can be done."

Next, Alessandro showed him the boxes of manuscripts, including those of David the African. I asked him about this David as I laid before him the text of *Al-Hawi*. He said, "I'm not sure I knew him. At least, I never met him personally."

"I need to ascertain and verify some facts about him, because he may have been hiding a much larger trove of Oriental manuscripts!" I said, as if revealing an important secret in exchange for something even more valuable.

Alessandro was stunned to hear me say this, and he focused intently on the duke's response as he was mulling it over. "Personally, I don't know anything about him, but there's a chance that the head of the paper mill in Siena still remembers him. David worked for him nearly ten years before passing away during the plague. If you bring us these manuscripts, Robert, I'll reward you handsomely. I want to make Florence the capital of Oriental manuscripts in all of Italy. I'll send you at once to the head of the factory if you'd like." "Of course, Sir," I said and thanked him. In my heart, however, there was a twinge of sorrow, knowing now that Hasan, or David the African, had passed away. Who was left for Yusuf now other than me?

Alessandro wrapped everything up by saying, "We have discovered we have a collection of no less than 40 Oriental manuscripts in multiple languages, and this is the index. We will now be able to examine them in depth and publish them." "That is all well and good," said the duke, "but we do not want to clash with the Jesuits or the bishops of Rome. They cooperate best when you are forthright and don't hide any secret intentions."

Chapter 27

I returned from the Medici Library that day after doing my best to avoid Alessandro's prying questions as he tried to find out more about the collection I had mentioned to the duke. "Why had you never told me about it before?" he asked, to which I replied, "I'm not entirely sure about the manuscripts to begin with, or even how many of them there are!"

"But you've been searching for them since the beginning?"

"Yes, but like someone looking for a needle in a haystack."

Alessandro didn't hold back his smile and kept nagging me about the trove, not relenting until I said, "The lady of Aragon and the African came to Florence more than 20 years ago and were a mere two steps away from the Medici Library, and yet you all knew nothing about them! It deserved being kept a secret!"

I walked back to the Viviani house to find Vincenzo waiting for me, so he could tell me about the nunnery. I had mentioned that my relationship with the Medici Library might grant me access to the convent as well, having learned earlier from the duke and Alessandro that the convent and library often cooperated in the maintaining, binding, and illuminating of manuscripts. There were even workshops and a laboratory at the convent to produce the gold threading used to embellish the opulent books.

I didn't conceal from Vincenzo my hesitation in visiting the convent. Perhaps it would be easier if I asked one of the sisters at the Society, because they might be more forthcoming than those in charge at the convent. In reality, my hesitancy went beyond that, but I didn't quite know how to articulate it to Vincenzo or perhaps even to myself. Something Father Savila had told me, when I once dared to ask about his miracles, still lingered in my mind. I remember him cheerfully replying, "Monasteries are abodes of silence."

At that point, I couldn't yet fathom the coincidence that would transpire to bring me into contact with Sister Luisa just days later, as I knocked on the door of the Society of Sisters to pay my rent. The young lady who opened the door asked me to wait before a nun in her forties appeared and asked, "Are you the Englishman asking about Maria of Aragon?"

I told her yes, and that I thought Florence knew more about me than my hometown back in Truro!

Without much fanfare, she said, "I'm Luisa, Maria's guide at the convent—or I was—from the time she joined us until she left our company. I want to know why you're asking about her."

"So that means she's no longer at the convent?"

"Maria left the convent a long time ago, after the plague began to subside in Tuscany. Enough with your questions. I want to first know who you are."

"I can't tell you everything now, but there is a chance that her older sister worked for my family as a caretaker and took care of me as a child."

"Her sister Madalena?"

"Yes, Madalena Despucci."

"Alright," she said briskly. "I can't stand here long. I leave tomorrow for Milan on a religious assignment for the convent and won't return for a month. However, I want you to return to the convent as soon as I send for you. Do you plan to stay in Florence for long?"

"If I was intending to leave, I'm now forced to remain," I said, hoping she would stop dithering and just tell me what she knew. She demurred, however, and said she had to get permission from the mother superior, who was currently away for several days.

That encounter weighed heavily on my soul and might be the reason I hesitated in visiting the convent. With neither Hind nor Hasan in Florence, I spent the ensuing weeks wondering what I could do besides just wait for Luisa's return.

More than a month later, I received Luisa's summons along with an apology for being delayed in the north. At the appointed hour, I dashed over to the convent. It so happened to be the saint day of Rita, the patroness of impossible causes, which meant I had to remain silent and solemn, though I had no idea whether I convinced anyone of being either!

The convent was just outside the city centre. In a previous life, it had served as a military fort to rally the troops for the later Crusades. As the crusaders slunk back from the East, the new humanists began to oppose armies and warfare entirely, and so the fortress was converted into a convent for nuns. A product of the new age.

What struck me about this convent was its giant wooden gate, in which was set a smaller door that resembled a chink in a small straw hut. The strange thing about this inset opening was how it consisted of two identical doors opening in opposite directions. The thickness of both equalled that of the giant gate. As I entered the convent, the deeper meaning of that stayed with me. It reminded me of Janus, the god of gates in Roman mythology, who looked out in two directions, inside and out and front to back all at the same time.

An elderly nun welcomed me at the gate with a sparrow-like smile and brought me into a large circular auditorium, the ceiling of which arched three to four storeys above us, giving the sense that you were entering a gigantic cylinder, unable to see anything other than the cascade of sunlight pouring through the clerestory windows high above. I had no idea how those openings were engineered to produce such fanciful shadows on the walls during the day, when the sun was at its most incandescent.

The play of light and shadow was truly Christian, allowing you to easily imagine the great battles of the saints and the tribulations of the ancient followers of Christ. I was pondering it all when Sister Luisa entered, coming from the same narrow corridor that the elderly nun had just led me down.

She apologised again for having to leave on urgent business and said, "You know, those who enter monasteries and convents do so searching for new beginnings. To regain the serenity and peacefulness of childhood. Is it not then our duty to help them bury their secrets and forget them?"

It was evident that Sister Luisa had forgotten how worked up I had become that day at the Society of Sisters when she told me the lady of Aragon had left the convent. This reassured me, to a degree, because it meant she wasn't going to pin me down with awkward questions of the sort that forced one to lower their defences. However, one question caught me off guard. "Can you describe Maria to me?"

"But I have never met her."

"I can't believe you're searching for someone that you have not at least imagined in your mind. Describe that image to me."

I wrestled to come up with an image of Al-Hajari. Just then, the elderly nun entered and brought over two cups of water infused with wild mint. I began to describe Maria of Aragon, from what I had gleaned about her from Madame Despucci. I described a woman nearing her forties with a thin body and sunken chest and a mole on her right shoulder. Her hair leaned toward chestnut and had a slight wavy curl to it.

Then, quoting the baroness, I said, "She prances like a timid doe, eating sparingly, as if there were an enmity between her and her food!" When I stopped talking, she said, "You knew about the mole. Do you not know her real name?"

I found myself here unconsciously saying, "Hind Al-Hajari. That's her real name."

"And now I can tell you her whole story."

As I left the convent, I thought more about that room with its shadows and small double door than I did about the many details Sister Luisa had provided about my aunt Al-Hajari. Something was telling me, "Nothing she said rivalled the importance of knowing where my aunt is now. That's what brought me to Florence in the first place." Luisa regretted that she had been absent from the monastery when the lady of Aragon made her final departure, because she had to go to Milan to take care of her parents who had fallen ill because of the plague.

Luisa's description of Hind closely matched what Madame Despucci herself had said. Hind was peaceful, pious, and full of humility before God, and not prone to speaking. Before taking her final vows to become a nun, she spent three years as a novice at the convent. In fact, her first request to join the convent was rejected because nobody knew her or could speak on her behalf. However, on the second attempt, she was accepted into the fold, helped by the fact she had revealed details of her past, confirming that she was not in fact French. She also opened up about her fears and distrust of people given all the catastrophes she had experienced following the loss of her family.

"It was her tearful sobbing that led to her acceptance into the convent. At first, she worked in the workshop restoring manuscripts and spinning gold thread. Only later did she begin studying medicine and the apothecary arts, at the hand of some medical practitioners who visited the convent. And from then on, she began to make the rounds at hospitals in Florence. However, near the end of her stay at the convent, she was nearly dragged before a tribunal on the charge of practicing medicine without a license. But as you know, it is almost unheard of for women to receive such credentials."

As for David the African, Luisa said, "An African man used to come by and see her. She called him Uncle David, but that wasn't his real name. She introduced him as a peasant who had worked for her family in Aragon and was all that remained of her family. But she wasn't telling us the whole story. Her family was Christian and left Aragon when she was just a little girl, seeking refuge in the mountains where they lived as vagabonds, moving from one place to another until finally arriving in France. In the end, though, most of them were captured while she somehow managed to escape with David's help, and she remained in hiding until eventually reaching safety in the duchy of Tuscany."

After my meeting with Luisa, I began to think about David, now deceased. The duke told me where he had worked, but I had made no effort to look into it further after learning that Maria of Aragon had departed Florence for some unknown destination.

Furthermore, the visit by the Venetian caster of moulds, which came at the duke's behest, resulted in nothing substantive—he admitted that imitating German moulds was simply impossible. So, the duke ordered the purchase of five moulds from France.

Margherita noticed how deflated I was when we met up by the river, and I told her about Maria of Aragon. The next day, I intended to remind the duke of my desire to visit the paper mill in Siena with Alessandro, but instead I found him telling me about the arrival of the French moulds and an invitation addressed to me from the Maronite college in Rome. So I had to temporarily delay my work casting the type and prepare to head to Rome.

It wasn't until midsummer that I could continue looking into the story of David the African. Upon returning from Rome, I found a letter from Professor Golius in response to one I had sent him before I had departed Florence.

I had nearly completed carving the punches following the visit of the Venetian, who had provided me with ingots of English steel. For some time, I searched for embellishments and decorative flourishes that could be added to beautify Arabic printed material, but it was not easy. And though I had discussed this very topic with the Morisco in prison, executing it without a master craftsman to help was practically impossible. Eventually, I gave up on the idea.

Before leaving Florence for Rome, I had written to my father and Jacob informing them of how I was doing. My desire to keep searching for my aunt had begun to flag, but upon my return from Rome, I read Jacob's response and found myself reinvigorated once more, and in a race against time to find the secret of the Morisco!

Part 6

The Lady of Aragon's Trail

I met her cousin Yusuf in a Spanish prison. I saw the guards whip him for five days straight. I never heard him scream once. He kept his head raised to the sky, lamenting this injustice to the Lord in whom he so firmly believed. Yet the Spaniards chose to view him only as an infidel.

Chapter 28

The invitation from the Maronite college reached me by way of Duke Lorenzo. Not wanting to disappoint him, I accepted immediately. It was Rome, after all. That most poetic of cities. Why not add it to the beloved harbours of my heart?

I sailed out of Florence and floated up the Arno on a riverboat, which first directed one away from Rome, before bending toward it once again. Where the river begins to roil, boats would stop at the last ferry station, not too far from the Tuscan hills where the Arno and its sister river the Tiber begin their slow descent. From there, some travellers on their way to Rome take carriages to the first port on the Tiber while others continue their journey by land.

The invitation (according to the letter) was to instruct Maronite students on the Arabic printing press and to reach an agreement with the Sacred Congregation for the Propagation of the Faith, which wanted to modernise its old Arabic typeset. At least that was what I'd thought. However, no sooner had I arrived than it became clear to me that the matter was altogether different.

My arrival coincided with the Pentecost festivities, according to the calendar of the Eastern churches. Though I was exhausted from my travels, I wanted to attend the evening carnival in the Orthodox amphitheatre, where I watched groups of students pour into the main arena carrying banners and flags representing the various parishes to which they belonged. What truly caught my attention was the slogan raised by the delegation from the Chalcedon Church of southern Iraq. In clear, distinct Arabic letters was written, "The Word came down to the river and the river was cleansed. The Word ascended to the clouds and became obscured."

I kept that phrase in mind during the morning meeting two days after my arrival, in the presence of the dean of the college and three Maronite professors. One of them—the most senior—asked me, "What did you read into that phrase?" I said, "I'm not sure, Father, though the baptism of Jesus by John the Baptist in the river Jordan did cross my mind. Was it because this young man was without sin that he became the one to baptise that river, which has not 'ceased to harvest the dreams of mankind'? As for the ascension of the Word, it could signify that the Lord ascended upon a cloud, obscuring his glory that had begun to spread out while on earth."

The father praised my answer. However, later I wondered if the Word was only beneficial to people whilst it dwelt among men, but after ascending to heaven, it became clouded over and obscured, allowing everyone to understand the Word in his own way and from his own perspective.

Adjusting his red skullcap, one of them began to speak, echoing the words in the letter. After many long years, the Monastery of Qozhaya in the Qadisha valley of northern Lebanon had acquired a printing press capable of printing in the Garshuni language, Syriac letters used to write Arabic to camouflage it from the Ottomans. It was rarely used except now and again to print books of psalms, and so they wanted to replace it with Arabic letters instead.

I expressed my readiness to help them out, but the matter of casting type remained contingent on agreements that needed to be taken at a level much higher than mine. I was nothing more than a print technician for the Medici family, and there were already lots of orders for Arabic type flowing into the Medici printing house in Florence. In addition to the printing press itself and my father's press, there were orders from the Imprimerie Royale in Paris and the press in Leiden, to say nothing of a fifth order from one of the wealthy noblemen from Kazan in Russia, the press of the Sacred Congregation. And now, the Maronites.

"Perhaps," I said like one trying to ward off a ghost, "even two years won't be even enough to meet all that demand." However, one of them chimed in, saying, "What's two years for a printing press that hasn't worked for 20?"

My discussions with the Maronites lasted until the afternoon and were riddled with interjections as I tried to understand the relationship between Arabic and Syriac. A dispute rose among them when I asked which was older, Arabic or Syriac? The argument could have quickly devolved into a brawl had it not been for one of them who pulled me out of the room to hand me a letter sealed with wax. He whispered, "Father Gaddis sends you his warmest greetings and says to read this letter when you are alone."

I didn't absorb everything this man had said. I thought he was one of the instructors at the college, but lo and behold it turns out he was a Jesuit sent by Father Gaddis. The man returned to the debate, and I followed, although a gigantic question mark hung over my head. My thoughts remained consumed by this letter until I could no longer pay attention to most of what was being said except when they delved into the Mohammedans' extreme sensitivity toward anything new coming from the Europeans. I stayed with everyone until the bell began to clang, announcing midday prayers.

I began to wonder, as I made my way toward my room, *Was Father Gaddis a guardian angel watching over me?* I stumbled, as if I had only begun to learn to walk. I made it to my room after crossing what seemed to be a vast distance. I opened the letter and began to read:

My son Robert,

I know that you, as you are reading this letter, find yourself at the Maronite college. Perhaps you are surprised that I knew you were in Rome. The truth is that I am the one who orchestrated it all. The Jesuits administer this college, which targets Eastern Christians, in order to instruct them in the true teachings of the Catholic Church and out of concern for their susceptibility to Protestantism. Your meeting with the Maronite fathers and the issue concerning their ancient printing press are nothing more than side matters to why I want you. Your help will be appreciated and acknowledged for its sincerity and clarity of conscience.

I know that, in the past, I was very sharp with you, but you have never been far from my thoughts. And your cooperation with me in what I intend to ask will have the happy effect of rescinding the ban on you from entering Spain and will greatly facilitate your communication with Yusuf Al-Hajari. And perhaps I will exert great effort to free him, if first he joins in the service of the monastery, as happened with you. We will, however, look into all of that later.

Firstly, I pray that this letter remain between you and your soul alone. Nobody knows about this matter save for you and some of my assistants in the monastery.

I dispatched Siraj to the Maronite college about a month ago as I contemplated sending him as a missionary to the Arabs in the Arabian Peninsula, owing to his striking resemblance to them and his understanding of their moods and natures therefore, making him the most capable of influencing them. However, it seems that he was not at peace with the idea. Unfortunately, and contrary to his nature, he was not candid with me. I had chosen him on purpose, hoping it would help him rectify his feelings toward his former people. However, I don't think my choice was a success, even though he excelled at the Maronite college in learning Arabic, the beliefs of the Muslims, and the inconsistencies of the Qur'an, while being surrounded by other Maronite students and learning from them how the Muslims, especially those from the peninsula, think.

After Siraj departed the monastery, I could not find my personal seal anywhere, and doubts and suspicions swirled within me. So I began to investigate, coming to the conclusion that it was Siraj who had absconded with the seal. However, I didn't have decisive proof. And since whoever possesses this seal will acquire expansive power and authority, I fear he could harm himself if he were to use it. So I am asking for your help, first because you're the only one who knows Siraj, and second, because you two lived together for more than a year and a half and you have his confidence. I arranged for you to stay in Rome to assist in the service of the Arab Christians and consequently he will not worry that you're pursuing him. I'm relying on you to recover the seal using your clever intellect. Yet I beg of you: Do not underestimate Siraj's cunning. His current internal crisis will make him weaker and perhaps lead him to commit some stupid mistakes.

In conclusion, I'm hanging this great hope on you to recover the seal. If you do so with minimal losses, then your place in my eyes will be lofty, because I still see Siraj as the right young man to evangelize the word of the Lord in the Hijaz, Yemen, Oman, or Bahrain.

I pray that our Lord blesses you.

Father J. I. Gaddis

Bilbao, May 18, 1642

I folded the letter after having read through it multiple times. It was definitely a surprise. So, Siraj was here in the Maronite college studying with the Eastern Christians. How had I not bumped into him over the last two days?

Suddenly, all the impressions I had formed of Siraj fell to pieces. It seemed that the seed of Arab rebellion was still alive inside of him, though he had tried to bury it with his hatred for Arabs and by showing total allegiance to Father Gaddis. I was not going to be able to find a way to win over Siraj except by being completely frank with him about the seal. However, the priest who handed me the letter suggested I introduce him to Siraj from afar and, one morning, the two of them would pass by the auditorium where I was giving instruction on the printing press, and thus he would come across me by coincidence. But I was surprised that Siraj had vanished completely, even from the student dormitories, and was nowhere to be found.

Perhaps he had caught sight of me and run off before I could meet him. Or perhaps he was experiencing extreme anxiety. I felt a tinge of disappointment because I truly wanted to help Father Gaddis. This would have been an opportunity to regain his trust. However, my chagrin lasted only a week before I found someone passing me a letter saying that a thin young man of average height had handed it to him. Far from anyone's prying eyes, I opened the letter and read it.

My dear Robert,

This is Siraj—the one you came looking for. I know that I made a stupid error in stealing Father Gaddis' seal. I disappointed him as you yourself had done before. Perhaps your spirit seeped into mine. You managed to escape to where you were free, far from any system that imposed its will on you. While here, I am still thinking that I am serving the Lord, but my soul keeps telling me that I am only serving the will of Father Gaddis. He never did me wrong. Rather, I was the one who erred, but I do not love the Mohammedans. I hate their religion and their character, their infighting, and their dissimulation. It does me no honour that I am one of them. Why did the Father refuse to change my name? And why does he want to send me to these people now?

I've placed the seal in a small opening at the base of the eastern wall of the college's ramparts, near what's left of the withered oak tree. From the stump, count 24 paces, then dig a little in the clay brick, and there you'll find the seal. I never used it once and never even thought of using it. Even now, I don't know why I stole it. Don't look for me. I am nothing more than a lost soul wandering aimlessly on this earth, and I have only grown more anxious ever since my ordination as a theologian. I want to forget what I am and who I am and what I desire. After all that has happened, I have nothing to give to excuse myself.

Farewell, Robert.

Nearly two hours later, I was in the presence of the Jesuit priest, handing him both Siraj's letter and Father Gaddis' seal. "He is a defeated man," I said.

"He doesn't yet know himself, but his place is not on the path of monasticism. The good monk does not leave the monastery, but leaves behind the taverns and markets and numerous troubles of life. Without experiencing the sufferings of Christ, he will not be able to serve His word," the priest said as he thanked me and confirmed that he would send the seal to Spain. I asked him to send my regards to Father Gaddis.

Chapter 29

Siraj didn't make an appearance the whole time I was at the Maronite college, though, just as I was about to leave Rome, our paths crossed. My carriage was turning alongside the canal when I asked the driver to halt so I could take a better look at the emaciated young man who had been surveilling me for some time before running off. I had never seen Siraj without his black cassock, which only made his weakened state all the more shocking. He looked like one of those homeless gamins working away as porters in the markets, barely able to earn a shilling. I don't know why, but at that moment I realised that religion didn't suit him. Without his cassock, he was much closer to his personal truth.

He kept scurrying away, though I quickened my pace behind him, calling out to him to stop. He finally halted in his tracks and gave me an enormous embrace filled with a silent pain. I said, "Welcome, my brother, Siraj." In return he said, "I'm not polite enough to apologise."

I reminded him of what Father Savila had recited to us one day at the monastery. From the word of the Lord, "In all truth I tell you, you will be weeping and wailing while the world will rejoice; you will be sorrowful, but your sorrow will turn to joy."

He said he wanted to go along with me, and we climbed into the carriage together. There was no place for him anymore among the Jesuits. "It's a complicated organisation! Absolute obedience is a principle that requires you to learn how to forget. Forget who you are."

"You must imagine yourself continuously as a novice," I said. "Openness to the world means that you are always learning, in other words, always ascending and arising. And absolute obedience here doesn't mean to people, but to principles. Your task is to find the principles worthy of strict obedience, then you yourself will become the principle."

With a hint of deep-seated anger, he said, "Yes, it's as if the Jesuits feign to let you discover principles you believe to be true, but in the end the principles are nothing more than what they say is the truth."

"When you reach a certain level of divine understanding," I said, "it means you have become capable of creating your own personal truth. All that is then required is that you find a place for it among other truths."

"How though?"

"I'm not sure I know, but what I do know is that every person can change. You can have influence over another person no matter how great his knowledge or power or even his obstinacy. The Jesuits are open to others. You ought to write to Father Gaddis and tell him your feelings and what you would like to do or what you're lacking in knowledge. Even when you confess your sins and guilt, you are changing something. You're looking for a place to lay your truth."

"The truth is, Robert, that I find their openness to be nothing more than so much talk."

Rain came down in sheets the whole journey home, and we were forced to stop in hostels along the way, because the horses were not able to continue with the journey. I imagined that Father Gaddis had sent this torrent as a warning for what I had done, something I did not want to reveal to Siraj, nor could I even be honest with myself about my motivation for doing so. I had sketched Father Gaddis' seal before giving it back to his messenger.

I liked to draw anything that might prove of value in the future. I was once forced to rip up some sketches I had made of the ceiling decorations at the Bibliothèque du Roi in Paris after someone caught sight of me drawing and became upset. I didn't understand why, but the official explained that it had to do with the fact that the houndstooth pattern—no longer used in building since the coming of the Gothic style—contained secrets of the Sassanids. I told him, "But it's right there at the main entrance! I can draw it from the outside." But he just expelled me while shouting, "Get lost!"

We were quite delayed on our way back, but it was a chance to engage in a long, meandering conversation. When we neared Florence, I asked Siraj, "What are you planning to do?"

"What can a monk do?" he asked, almost as if pleading.

"If I were you, I would forget about being a monk. I would remember one thing, and that's that you must do whatever it takes to live. Later, you can exert yourself to draw closer to your truth which, on the final day of judgment, you can lay before the Lord when you see Him and say, 'This is what I can offer to you, Lord. Forgive me for what I was not able to do.' Is that not divine salvation?"

"Does the Lord listen to us, Robert?

"Do you doubt it?"

"Yes. Perhaps He does listen, but not directly, and only once the voice has reached Him through an intermediary closer to Him than we are ourselves. Why then do we need the Son? In all of our festivals and prayers, we speak with the Son. The Son is who speaks with the Father. This ascending chain simply means that we are merely nameless, faceless beings in the eye of the Father."

I told him that I could hardly believe that Siraj had been consecrated as a priest. "Didn't the Lord say: No man cometh unto the Father, but by me. The Father and the Son are one. They are just different levels of grace. When we pray to the Son, we are also praying to the Father. The Father hears us as if we are speaking to him."

"Yes, but didn't you once ask Father Savila, 'Do all understand the Lord to the same degree?' I see this intermediary as nothing more than ancient paganism that has filtered its way down to us. Have you heard of the anti-Trinitarians, Robert?

"Not much."

"I read about one who was put to the stake in Geneva at the turn of the century. Imagine his suffering, differing little from the pains and anguish of our Lord Jesus. What caused him to insist on his opinion? Was it not the spirit of Christ? Why then did we put him to the flame? Why did we disown him and his followers and do so even today? It is something else, I believe, that has no relation to faith in the spirit of Christianity, but that is connected to the system generated by it. It is as if we believe in the creed of the system and not in the spirit of Christ himself. And if that is not true, then why do we burn at the stake the anti-Trinitarians? Christ himself was neither burned alive nor did he kill anyone!"

"Perhaps what you are saying carries some validity. Would Christianity have been able to survive had it not branched off into denominations and systems? It becomes soft and malleable, susceptible to dissolving into any environment possessed by the order. Pragmatic nations are the ones who never cease to produce religious divisions and create factions. Unbending monotheism will drive religion, its system and people, to its demise." We reached the outskirts of Florence as I finished making my point.

The carriage halted at a rest stop, where we decided to make the final leg of the journey on foot. On the way, I told him, "I can secure you a position in the Medici printing press if you would like. There will be much work for us to do casting the Arabic type and you will be able to learn a craft that does not go against your vows. It might even impart some practical experience and skill to your Jesuit devotion."

"My place is not among the Jesuits!" he said with a faint smile, hiding the sorrow of a life wasted.

However, Siraj kept turning the idea over in his mind and, as we got closer to the river where the shade of the cypress trees poured over the old bridge, he agreed. Sunset was imminent. I invited Siraj to the Tavern of the Three Cypresses. The night was young, and the taverns were still welcoming the depressed and beleaguered. However, he declined, saying he was tired and preferred to have a drink at my place.

My little room with all its simplicity seemed to capture Siraj's attention as he looked over what few possessions I owned. Sculpting tools, printing equipment, and some old manuscripts I still held onto, not to mention the small knickknacks that travellers pick up along their way, fearing that they might not return to that place again: stones and handicrafts and bits and bobs that have no value except in the eye of the collector. I opened the letters I had received when Siraj noticed some shells of various sizes that I had arranged in the shape of a cross above the wardrobe. He asked me, "Have you become a Jesuit, Robert?"

I smiled as I began to explain the story of those shells, which I'd taken from the Monastery of the Divine Incarnation. However, the letter from Professor Jacob roused me from the quiet sleepiness that had begun to seep into my body after such a long journey and several sips of wine. Siraj noticed how my mood had turned. In a flash, I thought that everything had evaporated in an instant, but I composed myself once more as Siraj asked me, "What's going on?"

"The French have learned about the manuscripts," I said. "I have to act immediately! I'll tell you everything later," as I quickly dashed out in the same clothes I had travelled in, having found no time to change.

I walked immediately to the home of Alessandro, who welcomed me and asked, "When did you get back?"

"Moments ago. But something grave occurred while I was gone. I must visit the workshop where David the African worked. The duke promised me that four months ago, but he has forgotten, and I have not found a way to remind him. It has now become critical I go. How can I reach the duke?"

Alessandro invited me in. "He was summoned to Pisa to discuss the matter of withdrawing Tuscany from the wars of the Holy Roman Empire with the grand duke. I can write what you want to the head of the workshop, but tell me, what's going on?"

"Do you remember when I asked the duke about David the African, and how he may have hidden a large trove of manuscripts? It was a large library with perhaps more than 40 or 50 boxes of Oriental manuscripts—a vast treasure in the possession of David and the lady of Aragon—but they hid it, most likely somewhere in France, before arriving in Tuscany. No one knew that but me, but now somehow someone in France has learned of it as well. And they are on the hunt for this unparalleled wealth of knowledge."

Alessandro was bubbling over with questions, but he said, "We will sort this out later, but you must now prepare to go to Siena tomorrow. The workshop is there."

I left Alessandro's place and made my way to Arcetri. I couldn't bear not visiting Margherita, regardless of how late it was. When I arrived, I found her with Vincenzo in their courtyard. They were in front of the three houses where they had erected several miniature models of conical wooden towers, each of varying heights. Dangling from the tips of the cones were weighted masses, catching my attention as they swung at different velocities. As Vincenzo recorded some observations, Margherita was holding one of the masses when she noticed me turning toward them near the cypress tree that witnessed our first kiss. She dropped the weight and came running toward me, embracing me and saying, "You've been gone so long. I was worried about you."

The ball kept swinging in a strange fluctuating circle that was confusing Vincenzo, who had been watching the motion of the ball in amazement for some time before finally saying, "Galileo's mathematics did not describe this strange motion of the pendulum! We will need to experiment in daylight as well." We all began to ponder the dancing movement of the different models as I told them of the latest developments from top to bottom. "I was previously in a battle only with myself, but now I'm in a race against time." I told them I would depart the next day for Siena.

I noticed a light shudder work its way over Margherita, as if to say, "I don't want experiments, I want you!" I tried to reassure her that great things still awaited me here in Florence. I stayed with them until midnight, and when I was about to take my leave, I asked about her recent poems. She handed me a sheaf of papers, organized with great care. At that moment, I was unable to read them but when I returned, Siraj looked them over with delight.

"So you're in love with a poet?"

Chapter 30

Hasan arrived in Florence after hiding the library, likely somewhere in France, though he brought with him some manuscripts that he later sold to the Medici Library. He managed to stay in contact with Al-Hajari in the convent, and it may have been she who suggested they send a report to Holland about the Al-Razi text, hoping that the news would travel to her sister or to Yusuf, letting them know where the manuscript was. At least that's what I postulated as I made my way to the workshop about 30 miles south of Florence where Hasan had worked, or rather David the African.

Alessandro gave me a letter to hand to the head of the workshop to allay any surprise aroused by my unannounced visit. He initially thought I was an inspector sent by the duke and, when I showed him Alessandro's letter, he apologised and moved me to a small room for receiving guests. It wasn't too far from the wing where he lived, which was located on the upper floor of the main building.

The journey to this town outside of Florence required more than half a day, and so I had to wait till the following morning. The next morning, I accomplished little beyond wandering around the workshop itself and some of its annexes. It consisted of a main building three storeys high with a building in the back for the workers. There was also a storage room for worn fabric, used carpets, wood, and other raw materials.

The workshop differed little from my father's in Truro, where work began by hauling the raw material to the ground floor. There, it was separated and cleaned before being moved to a lower floor where most of the main work was done. Afterward, the sheets of paper would be raised to the upper level by a system of pulleys and levers, where it was finally scraped and dried before being cut, bound, and shipped to distributors across various Italian cities.

I met the head of the mill in his office that afternoon, and he apologized for how busy he had been that morning. His apology covered the entire litany of tasks and errands he had to see to. I hesitated to interrupt to tell him I wasn't there to file a report to the duke about the workshop, because I feared doing so would make him less talkative when it came to the African. For that reason, I told him I understood his situation and that I was here only to discuss the African.

He asked why I was so interested in the man, given that it had been ten years since he passed away. I told him that several years ago, before his passing, he had sold the duke some Oriental manuscripts, but that he had hidden a much larger stash. The duke had assigned me to find out more on behalf of the Medici Library. From that point on, the head launched into a long monologue. His ability to recall the smallest details about David the African, his craftsmanship, and his own doubts about his real story amazed me.

I only interrupted him from time to time to confirm some of the Italian words that I had not heard before, as well as to speed things up, because I was planning to return to Florence the same day. He gave me David the African's file, but there was nothing important in it save for his work contract and the shipments he dispatched and distributed during his repeated visits to Florence. There were also some other documents related to his employment that led to his promotion to the position of head foreman before he succumbed to the plague.

"I met the African in Florence after the Bohemian Revolt deteriorated into an all-out war between the Catholics and the Protestants. Two of my mill workers were forced to join the war effort as part of the Tuscan ducal contribution in support of the Catholic armies. I spent months looking for someone to cover for them, especially to sort and separate out cloth, which requires a certain level of expertise that is quite hard to come by. I asked the wool-makers and mill guild to supply me with workers, and, after a number of weeks, I was told about an African servant who had been liberated by his mistress after she entered into a Florentine nunnery."

As we spoke, one of the workshop workers entered and told him a shipment of used cloth, meant to arrive that day, would be delayed two more. The head seized the opportunity to talk at length with the worker about what they had to do and to ask him a number of questions, as if to display the extent of his punctiliousness. Then he turned to back to me, saying:

"I met the African in Florence and began to probe his knowledge. He told me that he had learned papermaking from his masters when they were in France, and he swiftly displayed the extent of his knowledge, from citing the varieties and qualities of paper to how to burnish and refine it. Although he didn't show me any documentation proving he was French or a freeman, he came to me via the guild, so I turned a blind eye to these minor omissions. Surely there was more to his story, and it seemed as if he were hiding something, especially after he concocted an unconvincing story when I discovered he was visiting a young woman living in the Monastero delle Murate in Florence. He called her the lady of Aragon, though she wasn't the daughter of a French baron as he had claimed in the beginning. However, I didn't concern myself much with all these details, as long as he was productive at his job in the workshop."

Then, pulling out an ancient file from a side drawer, he said, "I don't know what you want to know exactly. I lost such a good man when he died from the plague that was sweeping through Tuscany at that time. David was the most skilled and clever of all my workers. Thanks to him, I was able to introduce the technique of imprinting watermarks into the paper we produced. He also brought me two contracts to supply the convent and the Medici Library print house with paper."

"Did he leave anything behind before his passing?"

"There were some documents and papers among other things, and his last will and testament stipulated that they be sent, along with some money, to his former mistress in the convent. During the plague, however, it was extremely difficult to get any information. I didn't even know he had died until some weeks later, and I wasn't certain until I looked over the official records. Because of the trying conditions back then, the workshop stopped producing paper for more than a year, and I had to figure out a way to get by and assist my workers in doing the same, especially as prices soared and the restrictions on movement tightened. I wasn't able to correspond with this young woman at the nunnery until several months after his passing.

When matters began to gradually get better, I took his things and went looking for the nun. They told me that she had left the convent, and I tried to locate her address, but quickly got nowhere with that. In the end, the mother superior took the money and box from me, and I remember her saying that Sister Maria had promised to write to the convent once she settled down somewhere. They will send the box to her when she does. That was my last connection to this story."

I left the workshop and headed back to Florence the same day, managing to return just before dark. When I arrived, Siraj told me that a petite lady had asked for me and left a slip of paper with the name Sister Luisa inked on it. I read, "I've been looking for you for more than a week. You must visit me at the convent as soon as you get back." I told Siraj we would go together, because I was going to introduce him to Alessandro and the Viviani family.

Early the next morning, I found myself knocking on that small inset door once again, this time accompanied by Siraj, who was still feeling ill at ease. At the end of the day, when we had gotten back to the house, he said, "There is so much more to life than religion." At that moment, I feared atheism had taken hold of him, as it had begun to delicately slip into the minds of youth in Europe. I immediately asked, "Isn't religion life itself?"

The elderly lady led us into the cylindrical auditorium. The sun was not shining that day, and so I couldn't show Siraj those heavenly shadows up above, illuminated signs of the existence of God. He smiled, but his face changed a little when we learned from Luisa that I would enter to see the mother superior alone. Luisa apologized gracefully, saying, "Only because we are talking about a former nun, and the mother superior does not want to expose her secrets to anyone other than those close to her."

When I went in, there was a small wooden box on her table and she began to speak: "Your description of Sister Maria is what made us trust you, but unfortunately you are not one of her blood relatives. The fact that her sister served as your caretaker does not necessarily mean you are a relative, especially since she never met you and does not know you at all. We did, however, find this box among the things left behind by the previous mother superior. It seems to have belonged to David the African, who sent them to the convent, but they arrived after the lady of Aragon had already departed. What will reassure me that you are the right person to take possession of this box?"

"I don't know what will reassure you, Reverend Mother. I met her cousin Yusuf in a Spanish prison. I saw the guards whip him for five days straight. I never heard him scream once. He kept his head raised to the sky, lamenting this injustice to the Lord in whom he so firmly believed. Yet the Spaniards chose to view him solely as an infidel. I promised him that I would reunite him with his family. All I know is that his wife was like a mother to me, and she passed away a long time ago. My love for this family has purified me. What need for lying do I have, Mother?"

Luisa looked over at the mother superior with tears welling in the corners of her eyes. "He carries within him Maria's sincerity, Mother."

The mother superior handed the box over to me. "Maria departed for Venice when she left the convent. She didn't say exactly where she was going after that, but it's likely she headed to the Orient, because she had always talked about volunteering for a mission there. She had promised us that she would write once she settled down, but we lost all contact and news of her after she left. The box is now yours. However, if you find anything out about her, we would appreciate it if you sent her our regards and greetings."

I took my leave and, when I was outside the convent, I told Siraj, "I don't need the workshop head's gossip. I have learned all I needed from Luisa and the mother superior." And off we headed to the Viviani house.

Chapter 31

No one in Florence could have been happier than Margherita the moment she saw me in the entryway of the house. I took a seat and began to rummage through the box that once belonged to David the African. She saw Siraj and smiled diffidently. I told her who he was, and where we had just come from, while explaining all that had happened at the paper mill and convent.

She sat in front of me, intently watching my face and my preoccupation with the box, which held some money and the African's possessions along with various slips of paper and letters.

I took out a piece of paper written in Aljamiado:

"*The mother superior warned me against practicing medicine yesterday. She won't be able to protect me now that the order has come from the magistrate's office in the city. Despite the fact she herself witnessed how I healed everyone with my own hands. What do I do in Florence now that my uncle Hasan has passed away and Luisa has travelled and has been away for so long? What could have befallen her in these plague-filled days?*"

Then I took another slip of paper. A piece of news was written on it, similar to the news about the printing of the *Al-Hawi* text, but this time about another book. I pulled out another torn piece of paper excised from a manuscript of the *Al-Hawi*, marginalia flowing up and down the edge, this time in Arabic:

"*O reader of these words, I am a lost daughter of God. I am a lone* stranger. *After so many years wandering, this convent has provided me refuge, but it has only increased my loneliness and pain. My uncle Hasan was all that was left in this world, but he has succumbed to the plague and has asked me to go to the land of the Muslims. Who is there for me? O Lord, may you succour me through your beloved Prophet Mohammed."*

Then I opened another letter. It had been sent from Hasan, the servant.

My dear lady,

This time, there is no hope at all for your uncle. Nothing breaks my heart more than the thought that you will be all alone. The quarantine is entering its third month, and my condition is worsening. Before I lose the ability to do so, I am writing this letter to you. I have tried many times, as you know, to return to France to retrieve the boxes, but such a journey is impossible for me on my own. Furthermore, we would need a travel pass to cross the French border lest we be exposed and returned once again to Spain. I am wasting away and am barely able to swallow any food. I made a promise to Yusuf that I would look after you and take care of you, but such is not to be. Do not remain at the nunnery after I pass away. Your place is among the Muslims, not the Christians.

Go to the land of the Arabs. If you can't, then register for one of the missions to the Orient as a doctor or nun. I have instructed the workshop head to send what I am owed along with a box containing my prized possessions, among which is a ring that your father Ahmad gifted to me and three beads from a misbaha that was blessed by the black stone and the Prophet Mohammed's tomb and his companions Abu Bakr and Omar. There is also a piece of Egyptian cloth embroidered with prayers for protection, the Throne Verse, and six other short surahs.

As for the trove of manuscripts, I have hidden it among the rocks along the route leading out of Florence in the direction of Padua. You will find a map to it with this letter. It is best that you hire a carriage and take someone you trust with you to help. Don't wait too long, because there is no place for you here in this land. There will be much more for you in the land of your ancestors and forefathers, inshahallah. If you make it there, find someone you can trust to recover the remaining boxes that we left behind in Nice. It is the legacy of the Arabs, and they are the most rightful owners of it. God be with you.

Your uncle,

Hasan

I opened another letter and began to read:

My dear uncle,

I write this letter to you as pain weighs down on my heart. You are all that remains of my family. If you are still alive and reading this letter, I pray that your heart is not heavy with concern for me. For I have a Lord who protects me. I will take your advice of going to the Orient because, day after day, the nunnery only increases my sadness and depression. Were it not for the companionship of Sister Luisa, I would not be able to bear it at all. However, she has departed the convent, and I don't know when she will return. I went to where you guided me, and I found the box as you described and brought it back with me. Yesterday, I informed the mother superior of my desire to head to the Levant, but she was not receptive to the idea.

I tried to persuade her that proselytizing among women was more fruitful than among men, for they tend to be more easily influenced, and I could accompany one of the delegations as a doctor.

She insisted that even for a man it was not easy, and how much harder it would be for an unmarried woman. Receiving authorisation would require so many layers of approval. However, after seeing my insistence, she told me that all she could do was write to one of the priests she knew working in the French consulate in Aleppo, but that I would carry no official title, and I alone would be responsible for my decision to go. I gave her my agreement and, after that, all there was left to do was decide the date of my travel, which was set for after the deadly plague had passed. My dear uncle, I shall remember for as long as I live that you were devoted to my care and service. May God keep you if you are alive and bless if you are deceased.

Hind bint Ahmad Al-Hajari

I read a few more of the papers, two of which revealed that they had tried to set up a wool workshop to help them survive but were unable to do so. I also read another letter from Hasan telling Hind that he had finally convinced one of the news periodicals to publish a few words about the *Al-Hawi* text and to mention his name and hers in it. After I finished, I told Margherita, "I must go to Venice."

Siraj kept quiet the whole time and asked to leave once he realised his presence was unwanted. Margherita then began to bemoan her fear for our love's future, saying she felt as if she were standing on the precipice of a bottomless valley, like the one I had nearly fallen into near Nice. The difference was that, this time, we fell in together. After calming down a little, I said my goodbyes, promising, "My father the Morisco will witness our wedding. I swear that to you."

Siraj kept quiet as we made our way to Alessandro's. However, when we crossed the Ponte Vecchio, he apologized for having overheard everything I'd said to Margherita. "Why do you want this treasure? You have a secure job and everyone is crawling over themselves for your talents. And above all that, you have a girl who is the envy of the world."

"What I have never said to you, Siraj, is that when you came to take me from prison that day, I had been born again locked behind those walls. This love will have no meaning if I stop here. The secret of the Morisco is what gives my love its value."

Chapter 32

I came down with a cold while making my way to Venice and eventually it worsened into a fever so severe that I had to prolong my journey by a number of days. At the way stations along the route, I tried to treat myself with whatever I could find: cabbage leaves, the powder of clover flower, and honey, but nothing worked.

This cold thwarted any hope I had of moving about the town during the first days after my arrival. However, it did not stop me from taking note of the electrified atmosphere in Venice—the city was a powder keg waiting to explode. In reality, there was no explosion, but the city's denizens were in a froth over the current state and policies of the Council of Ten and Ducal Council, enough to make you think something dangerous was about to occur. It seemed as if everyone wanted to rule the city.

When I entered Venice, the city was fixated on the upcoming elections to the Council of Ten that were to begin soon. There was a sharp division in the Council between the elder ranks and the younger leadership, which cast its pall over the whole city. The elders had succeeded in imposing legislation that would prevent Jewish doctors from treating Christians while the younger members staunchly opposed such a measure.

Likewise, there was a fault line between the two sides regarding legislation that prevented men from embracing asceticism and imposed on some that they marry two wives—all of which was to confront the extreme lack of men due to the ongoing religious wars in central Europe. The elders supported the legislation, but once again the younger members stood in opposition.

On balance, those younger members saw it necessary to prepare for Ottoman revenge in response to the rumours that Venice supported the knights of Malta, who had attacked a ship full of pilgrims returning from Mecca to northern Africa. The elders who administered the duchy disagreed. In their view, the Ottomans would surely realise that it was a mere rumour, spread to sow chaos between the Venetians and Turks. And, in any case, the Ottoman fleet was not prepared to wage any new war at the moment.

There were also other disputes within the Council that made it the object of derision for so many. Such was the case with a new law making it a criminal act for the middle classes—owners of businesses and small landholders—to imitate the upper class in terms of dress, building style, and aristocratic customs. And so any new visitor to Venice ought not be surprised to see ducal guards stopping them and issuing a subpoena on the charge of using an opulent carriage.

Maybe that was what prompted some of the priests to stand decisively with three Jewish doctors who had levied a case against the council's legislation and who were able to gain popular support and empathy thanks to those monks, a support that was palpable as I wandered about the city. The only thing that could spoil my mood in Venice was the realisation that England would need 100 years to reach anywhere near the beauty, cleanliness, and greatness of Venice.

Several days after my arrival, I was able to deduce that Hind Al-Hajari had deposited eight Arabic manuscripts in the Biblioteca Marciana, but I could not be certain of this just yet. First of all, the eight manuscripts were not any that my father Yusuf had mentioned in prison. And second, the name in the library records referred not to a woman, but an Arab man from among the Christian community in Aleppo named

Naimat Allah Al-Khouri Al-Halabi. He was the one who had deposited the manuscripts in the library—the only ones they had.

My aunt Hind mentioned in her letter to Hasan that she had dug up the box he had hidden on the road outside Florence. What could have possibly been in the box other than manuscripts? Perhaps she needed to sell them? I had to find out more about Naimat Allah Al-Khouri, but who would I ask?

And so I wandered all over the city and its canals, searching for any trace or sign that could lead me to Al-Hajari. I visited the engraver I had met in Florence, but instead of helping me, he offered me a job in his workshop saying, "I'll pay you handsomely."

Navigation had come to a near-standstill in the Venetian port over rumours of the death of the Muslim pilgrims. So I spent the following days trying to locate Álvaro in the inns where sailors tended to stay. I didn't find him, but one of them stopped me after hearing me ask some women about Álvaro in one hovel or another.

His clothing tipped me off that he was an Orthodox monk He wore a black caftan-like garment with white sleeves, a brimless crimson *skufia* on his head. His thick beard, just beginning to turn grey in the middle, lent him a certain air of dignity. He asked me about Álvaro and how I knew him. I tried to spare myself the burden of a long explanation and said, "It's a long story." He said, "Álvaro wouldn't be here in Venice at this time, especially with the crisis between the Venetians and Turks."

I took my leave of him, trying to get away, before running back and politely asking, "May I ask you one question, Sir? Are you Greek?" He shook his head, then added slowly to compensate for my broken Italian, "I'm from Aleppo. A Christian from Aleppo." I asked him immediately in Arabic, "Do you know Naimat Allah Al-Khouri?"

He couldn't resist smiling at how well I pronounced the Arabic letters. "You seem to be a stranger here like me, but your knowledge of the archbishop of the Maronite church in Aleppo piques my curiosity. Why are you asking about him?"

I introduced myself and denied knowing the archbishop directly. He met my response with silence, as if awaiting more. I told him that I was a collector of Arabic manuscripts and had found the name Al-Khouri in the ledgers of the library of San Marco here in Venice dated 12 years ago.

"But Father Naimat Allah has never visited Venice, at least not since I've known him these last 20 years, and he has never shown an interest in Arabic manuscripts. I know him better than anyone. We serve in two churches directly opposite each other back in Aleppo."

"Then why would his name be in the deposit records of the library?"

"I don't know! But the man has never left Syria at all!"

I left the monk after learning his name, Yusuf Al-Musawwir, or "Joseph the Painter." He was from an Orthodox religious family that produced Byzantine icons, which was how his family came by the name, stemming from an occupation that had been passed down through the generations. I also learned where he was staying and that he was waiting for the Venetian port to resume operations so he could return to Aleppo. All this made me even more certain that it was Hind who had deposited those manuscripts. All there was left to do was figure out the relationship between Naimat Allah Al-Khouri and Hind. But how?

I went back to Father Al-Musawwir two days later, when he hosted me at the inn where he had been staying. It was filled with numerous panes of coloured glass held in wooden frames to protect them from shattering. Likewise, there were also tools and dyes and gypsum mould-makers. The man had purchased all this and was waiting for things to clear up, so he could take them with him back home. He told me how he made a living from this ancient ecclesiastical art and that even Catholic churches in the Orient came knocking at his door, which he said with some pride, given the traditional contempt between Orthodoxy and Catholicism. However, his art and excellence hovered above such confessional small-mindedness.

I asked if he knew a nun by the name of Maria of Aragon. When he denied ever hearing that name before, I said, "Her Arabic name is Hind Al-Hajari. Have you heard of it?"

Dumbstruck, he immediately said, "Are you sure that you've never visited Aleppo or Syria before? Or could it be that Hind Al-Hakeema's reputation as a physician has reached all the way to Europe?"

Trying to conceal my sheer delight, I said, "Hind bint Ahmad Al-Hajari?"

He noticed the electric look in my eyes and said, "Yes, she is the doctor of Aleppo. She and her husband are well known within the Mevlevi order in town, but she is not a nun. She is a Muslim among the people of goodness and virtue. Dozens of sick and afflicted from all sects go to see her and her husband in their home daily. She had not yet returned from the hajj when I departed Aleppo. But what makes you ask after her? Is it connected in some way to these manuscripts? In that case, you need a copyist and not a doctor."

Choked up by excitement, I stumbled over my words. "I must

travel with you, Father. I must see Hind. I have very important information that concerns her. I beg of you, please help me. I can't tell you everything now, but certainly you will know as soon as I meet her. I've been searching for her for five years!"

The father thought it over long and hard. Setting aside medical treatment as the motivation for my questions, he looked for another reason for all the eagerness that he saw in me. He said, "She also works as an astrologist, reading the fortune of those who turn to her by calculating the stars, though I don't know where she learned to do so. Is that why you are searching for her, Robert? She is actually hit or miss in that science. Her renown is in medicine and Sufism, not fortune-telling," he said as he stared at me.

"Not at all, Sir," I said. "I know things about her that even she does not know. But I can't tell you anything until I meet her."

"You will need a *firman* from Istanbul bearing the *tughra* of the Sultan in order to enter Ottoman lands, but it could take weeks, and your embassy must apply for it in your name."

"I don't need that. I will travel on my own and do not need any protection. I'm not going there for business purposes or to visit the holy sites in Palestine."

He thought that was best, as I would avoid having to pay bribes and fees to the *aghas* or being waylaid at inspection stations, at town gates and ports, to say nothing of the tribal sheikhs who took it upon themselves to protect some areas. It seemed strange to me that a person would need a stamped piece of paper in order to enter a country. Who could claim that he possessed an entire country for himself? Even the warring royal families in Europe didn't do that!

Chapter 33

Father Yusuf Al-Musawwir told me to come back in two days' time to attend a meeting organised by the priests who empathised with the plight of the three Jewish doctors, where Yusuf hoped to gather some news about the reopening of the port. Till then, he would think about my request to travel with him.

The meeting was to rally public opinion against the Council of Ten's prohibition against Jewish doctors treating Christians. When I attended, I was baffled by the citizens' ardour in debating the politics of the city and its consequences. One of them distributed bowls of steaming *ribollita* soup to all present, repeating "It's soup of the peasants and farmers. These wealthy men will never understand your pains."

Yusuf told me that, with council elections coming up in two days, the meeting was less a real recognition of equality among the Christian and Jewish populations and more a way to hatch plans to bring down opponents and support allies.

He asked about my own denomination, and I told him that I was Protestant by birth and that I had embraced Catholicism for a time, but now I didn't know what I was.

He chuckled. "Europeans usually have an antipathy to those who are different from themselves. They even look down on us Orientals despite the fact that we are coreligionists. Maronites can talk for days about the discrimination they face in Rome. There is even a college there to teach them Catholicism!"

"I was just there less than a month ago and didn't notice such a thing!"

"What was a Protestant doing in Rome, and in a Catholic college no less?"

"I was instructing Maronite monks in how to use an Arabic printing press."

The father looked at me quizzically and began to ask about the workings of this press and how to build and operate one. Then he said, "I think you could offer us Orthodox some valuable assistance in Aleppo."

After some reflection, he said, "I've thought about you coming with me to Aleppo, and I think that it's possible, provided you request a *firman* from the Sublime Porte, mentioning me and the archbishop in your letter. The bishop enjoys a certain esteem among the pashas of Aleppo and those with influence in Istanbul. Be sure to note the address of the English consul in Aleppo so that the authorisation will arrive there. You will travel with me as a workman to help me set up my equipment and cut glass. What do you think?"

I agreed immediately. "We will write the request together."

"You must prepare for the journey soon. This talk of killing Muslim pilgrims is mere gossip and navigation will open up at any moment."

Discussion of this supposed massacre had come up during the meeting, and the majority considered it a sign of the current council's ineptitude for believing the rumour and shutting down all movement of ships and trade.

Voting took place over two days, and the new council's first decision was to restore navigation in the ports. Father Yusuf Al-Musawwir transferred his goods onto the ship that would take us to Iskanderun. I stayed with him the whole time, helping him lug it all. He asked me to buy some presents to distribute on our way to facilitate our travels. Watches, magnifying glasses, glass beads and silverware would all make fine gifts for Ottoman officials.

The day before we were to depart, a great uproar bubbled up at the port as raisin merchants began tossing out crates of raisins and currants and emptying them into the sea after their storage had become prohibitively expensive and impractical following the disaster in London several weeks before, when Parliament signed legislation banning merchants from importing currants and raisins.

That legislative decision represented a crisis of confidence, as things had reached a dangerous new low between Parliament and the king. A military confrontation between the two sides could flare up at any moment. Father Yusuf heard me say, "May the fish of Venice gorge themselves on the raisins of the English!" He asked me the reason for the dispute and where I stood on the matter.

"Foreign trade is the causal reason. Parliament views our trade interests as aligned with the New World, Ottomans, and India more than with Catholic Europe. And the king sees the opposite."

The father kept looking at me, waiting for an answer to the remainder of his question, and when he saw that I was going to ignore it, he repeated, "Do your sympathies reside with Parliament in rejection of absolute rule?"

"The dispute between Parliament and the king extends all the way to how a woman should style her hair, the size of hats they can wear, and even how much hair can be let down before transgressing the limits of modesty. Can you believe it, Father?" I asked, as the father knotted his Persian shawl over his loose-fitting trousers. "And I love watching it all more than anything else!"

I made a request for an Ottoman travel pass at the English embassy in Venice before departing to Aleppo. I thought of Álvaro again as we saw sailors and crewmen standing in line at the registration offices in the port. The closure of the port had led to many of them losing their employment and now, with the return of operations, their jobs returned as well. As the ship sailed out of port, I said to Father Yusuf, "Álvaro was looking for sailors when I met him in Genoa."

Father Al-Musawwir asked me again why I was looking for Álvaro.

"I have a profitable venture for him," I said. "And he wants his own ship."

"What's the venture?"

"Coffee. Exporting coffee to England. We would be able to extract so many products from it."

Before departing, I had left a number of messages for Álvaro at the sailor hostels where I thought he might stay in the hope they would reach him. I wrote quite a few letters to others as well.

I wasn't sure how long I would need to spend in Aleppo and wasn't supposed to spend longer than needed to meet my Aunt Al-Hajari and find out where the manuscripts were. However, just in case, I added Father Al-Musawwir's address to the letters I wrote to Margherita and my father in England, as well as to Jacob and Father Mersenne.

During our long journey, I spoke with Father Al-Musawwir about sculpting and embellishment and the ways he was able to repeat motifs over and over in the artworks he created. I was trying to crack the code of what could make the printed book more in line with the aesthetic tastes of the Orientals. However, he dissuaded me. "It's best if you focus on that coffee venture of yours. The printing press will need 100 years more before it makes inroads to the hearts of Levantine people."

Father Yusuf hoped to establish an Arabic printing press in Aleppo. This had been an old Orthodox dream, but he said he was unsure how successful it would actually be or its overall utility. Printed material had made its way to the region for years, but only via the Catholics in Rome, who had begun to distribute it though none of it was in Arabic.

A week later, we called into port in Ottoman Smyrna to drop off some travellers and to let others board. I wandered around the city, but Father Yusuf advised me to not go further than the Latin Quarter, because I did not yet have a travel authorisation. In fact, that quarter was enough for a person to discover that Smyrna was a part of Europe, given how all commerce was managed by Greeks and Europeans. You scarcely came across anyone in Turkish garb except for a few shoppers coming from the mountainous hinterlands.

However, at times you would come across a European in local dress, crowned in a large Ottoman turban, as was the case with Hajj Karim Halifax, an English merchant who boarded the ship with us in Smyrna. He was already acquainted with Father Yusuf, since they both lived in Aleppo and, according to Father Yusuf, Mr Halifax had a shop in the large khan, deep in the heart of old Aleppo, and had changed his name to Karim after announcing his conversion to Islam some years back. In reality, I didn't understand what motivated his conversion, but the father told me he was quite involved in the sale of antiquities, acting as the main supplier to England's nobility for precious objects from the Orient and other ancient artefacts.

I grew closer to Hajj Karim when he found out I was an English citizen. He gently chided me when he saw all the gifts I had bought to distribute along our way, and he blamed Father Yusuf for this advice, saying, "It's easier to don the Turk's clothes and avoid paying bribes, rather than buying all these trifles. And if one must, then let the gifts be wine! The Janissaries prefer brandy over money by far!"

He spoke to me at length about the character of the Arabs and Turks, and it soon became clear that he preferred dealing with Turks. "Yes, Arabs are by their nature more poetic and loving toward strangers, but, once they become civilised, the Turks have a certain flexibility and receptivity to difference. Arabs, on the other hand, are more severe in their religion, while Turks content themselves with the mere appearance of it rather than any deep devotion. Moreover, the Turks prefer listening and experiencing life over reading the books that fill only Arab homes. That's why you will find Arabs philosophising and waxing poetic about literature and never hotly engaging in discussions of politics, unless they are complaining about their Turkish rulers!"

Hajj Karim also differentiated between "civilised" Arabs and those of the desert. He once had a bad experience with Bedouin that nearly left him dead. He proposed that I join him on his journey to look for the ancient kingdom of Palmyra as he searched for the enormous treasures that European explorers had long talked about. He was a man full of tales and regaled me with the story of a French band of looters who were killed by some Bedouin tribes many years ago.

Hajj Karim thought that the French thieves had not taken sufficient precautions and the map they used was imprecise. He claimed, however, that he possessed an accurate map and had been trying for some time to prepare for this dangerous journey and was now looking for a few hardy assistants. I politely declined, excusing myself by saying that I was not intending to stay long in Aleppo.

When we reached Iskanderun, Karim did not get off with us, but continued on to Tripoli, claiming that the air in Iskanderun was noxious and its climate wholly unsuitable due to its numerous swamps, in addition to the fact that the road to Aleppo was full of risks. Father Yusuf informed me that Karim was wealthy enough to bear the additional costs for the longer journey from Tripoli to Aleppo. However, Yusuf said, "The Iskanderun route and its weather, even with its miserableness, are not as bad as Hajj Karim makes it out to be."

Part 7

Longing in Aleppo

There was shouting and tears to welcome her while Sheikh Ibrahim prostrated himself, kissing the ground of Aleppo and thanking Allah for a safe return home. She stood there somewhat bashfully, showing nothing of herself, although she briefly lifted her veil to greet the naqib and thank the prominent citizens of Aleppo for welcoming her back.

Chapter 34

Between the sparse tree cover to the east and the towering hills off to the west, the expansive plain of Tuman spread out like the wing of an angel fallen from heaven. The caravanserai was located in the furthest southern reach of the plain, the edges of which were bordered by several humbly constructed sepulchres, finally ending in a well-trodden trail leading northward to Aleppo. A traveller along this route would not feel an inkling of homesickness or loneliness as he would assuredly come across small tombs and gravesites telling the tales of those who had come before and passed on as they made their way to the holy sites.

One night, during an ecstatic gathering of Sufis, Father Yusuf and I paid our respects by circumambulating a saint's shrine. He muttered the words of a *qasida* composed by the great poet and saint Ibn Al-Farid: "Between the battlefield of lovers' hearts and glances / This love I feel is no good if it leaves me ashamed." I asked Father Yusuf about this Ibn Al-Farid as we made our way back to the tent and to the mule drivers he'd hired in Iskanderun. "He's not a saint in the true sense of the word," he said, "but a Sufi holy man. His poetry of divine love is so delicate and refined it's even popular among us Christians."

It's impossible to describe Father Yusuf without mentioning the great reverence and decorum conferred upon him by his bushy beard, making his face appear larger than it was, and—juxtaposed with such a voluminous beard—his small stature and rotund belly left you at a loss for words. In any case though, one would likely have grown fond of him long before ever needing to weigh in on his appearance, and thus a person would instead find themselves extolling his lofty moral virtues and the gentleness and restraint he had surely acquired from fashioning icons and creating stained glass windows of unparalleled beauty.

Aethereal melodies wafted throughout the plains of Tuman, filling the still night air. We spent long poetic evenings accompanied by tea, tabors, and tinkling hymns as night lowered its veil over our tent, which reflected the soft glow of the fire until it eventually died out. Despite the fact that I understood Arabic, the father continued to translate most of the words that filled my ears in a layered polyphony of sound. "Listening requires greater sensitivity than merely reading," he would say. "It requires a delicate disposition to grasp the meaning."

Shortly after midnight, the only sound that remained was a faint weeping that filtered through the pitch blackness, coming from the camps of some Armenian pilgrims as they beseeched and implored God to not extinguish their fire until they reached Palestine, and to let their bodies be healed in the hills of Nazareth, on the rocks of the Mount of Olives, and to allow their souls be purified in the river Jordan. The father commented (with no small amount of dissatisfaction) on the growing number of Eastern Christians who were turning to the Latin rites of the Church of Rome, straying from their cherished Orthodoxy.

I could barely recall the last words he said that night as he talked of Aristotle's sojourn long ago in Aleppo. At daybreak, as the gates of the caravanserai opened once again, I said, "I felt an extraordinary serenity here in this plain last night. I slept as if swathed in the mantle of Christ or under the watchful eye of God the Father. What secrets does this place hold?" Derisively, Yusuf said, "The Franks never cease to rattle on like you have just now. They think the ground is theirs.

First of all, Christ never wore a mantle. Ever. And second, this is the Plain of Pilgrims from whence pilgrimage caravans depart, not just for Palestine but for the Hijaz as well!"

We entered the caravanserai to buy some provisions and gifts. Father Yusuf sought out his merchant friends and could hardly escape all their invitations to lunch, yet managed to content himself with leaving a prayer upon them. One offered to serve as my dragoman in Aleppo, but when I told him that he spoke Arabic ungrammatically, he chuckled saying, "The *khawaja* knows Arabic better than I do!" before confessing that he was an Armenian just trying to make a living.

Father Yusuf caught up on what had happened in Aleppo during his absence. As we left the caravanserai, he said, "The tax on livestock has been lifted, and the Sublime Porte has withdrawn the governor, judge, and mufti all at the same time. People have begun to fear for their money and interests because of the *agha* of the Janissaries. There is no one left now to repel his heavy hand except for the *defterdar* and *naqib al-ashraf*." I didn't understand anything he said, but he told me he would explain it all on the road.

Father Yusuf distributed some food to all the tents that were still pitched before we headed northward in the direction of Aleppo. Benedictions flowed after him: "May the Lord bless you, ya Hajj; May God keep and protect your parents, May God comfort you, Hajj Yusuf." I asked him about the honorific *hajj*, and he said, "The honorific isn't what's important. It's the prayer and blessing they give that creates a sort of reciprocal gratitude. It's as if you gave alms to yourself. That is what it means to be under the watchful eye of God, Robert."

The road from the caravanserai to Aleppo was in much better

condition than the road from Iskanderun. It was almost entirely paved with large flagstones, which meant that before noon we were already on the outskirts of the town. Off in the distance, Father Yusuf pointed at a wispy cloud, saying, "The bridge is directly below that cloud." Before we even caught sight of the bridge, the ochre-coloured minarets came into view. And by the time we reached it, the cloud had floated off.

A group of young boys was waiting in anticipation on the other side of Al-Hajj bridge. As soon as they saw us, they raced toward the Gate of Antioch, each one shouting, "I saw them first!" and "The gift is for me!" and "No, it's mine!" When we neared the square of the Churches in the new quarter, we found the Orthodox patriarch, Father Makarios, accompanied by the Maronite archbishop, Father Naimat Allah Al-Khouri, waiting to receive us along with a woman for whom everyone made way as she ran over to embrace Yusuf while the young boys eagerly opened the gifts she had distributed among them. At first, I thought this woman was Father Yusuf's wife, but I later learned that she was his older sister, and his absence had filled her with great anxiety after speculation ran rampant about why he had been delayed.

The city welcomed us before its inhabitants did—with its tidy streets and impressive architecture, conveying a sense of prosperity and people of high moral standing. Everyone greeted Father Yusuf. "It's like you know everyone here," I said, to which he responded, "You only say that because you are a stranger."

I entered Aleppo with the Morisco's secret, the spectre of Najma, and the love of Margherita on my mind. I had left everything I owned behind in Florence, except for a few things I would offer to my aunt. I don't think she ever imagined that I would show up so unexpectedly, and I tried not to think about how she might receive me. Would she laugh for a moment and then send me on my way, or would she break down in tears? I kept casting out a nagging thought that—because of all the trials in her life—she would show no emotion at all. As if she were a page stripped from the Book of Life and tossed into the Mediterranean, only to begin a new life elsewhere.

During the first few days, I was so enamoured of the place's beauty, I forgot why I had come to Aleppo. "Part of me belongs to Aleppo," I said to Father Yusuf when I asked him to go to the English consul. Father Yusuf didn't quite understand what I meant, but he repeated what he had said on the plains of Tuman, "The Franks think that the land is all for them!" Hind was not in Aleppo when we arrived, as she had still not yet returned from pilgrimage with her husband, despite three months passing since the Sultan's caravan had come back.

I asked Father Al-Musawwir why she was delayed. He said that she was a doctor and people probably had stopped her to treat their infirm, and this had likely held her up. In reality, I wasn't the only one waiting for her in Aleppo. Here, too, many sick and afflicted souls were awaiting her return. And so were the French, according to the English consul, a fact that caused me no end of anxiety as I exhausted various ways to learn when she would return.

I spent several days, as was my custom, drawing and sketching everything around me. The city was filled with endlessly fascinating objects, and I drew them all. Naimat Allah, Yusuf Al-Musawwir's son, accompanied me everywhere, taking me to many of the town's most picturesque locations. He was amazed by my ability to sketch something so quickly then finish it later from my memory and imagination. He remarked to his father once, while displaying my notebook full of paintings, "He makes 20 paintings in a single day!"

The young boy was a quick study, but spent most of his time helping his father in his workshop, where the pair fashioned icons for the churches in Aleppo and other cities that looked to Byzantine art as a symbol for their identity, particularly faced with the encroachment of Catholicism emanating from Rome.

In Aleppo, there is an intimate, yet seemingly haphazard harmony that merges into one perfect whole. Making your way through the streets and narrow alleyways, you feel as if the walls are clinging to you, spilling the secrets of what lies on the other side. In the beginning, my curiosity knew no bounds, and I wanted to peek inside, to see what took place within those Aleppo homes with their lofty windows girded with *mashrabiya* that obscured the view beyond. However, I curtailed my curiosity when I learned of the sanctity the residents of Aleppo attached to their homes, where plain exteriors belied the utmost care and attention to detail devoted to the interior setting.

Between its inhabitants and the stones used throughout the city, Aleppo was one long extended conversation that allowed me to catch only errant snatches from time to time. I must admit that, in the beginning, the multiplicity of names for stone used in building, decorating, and household use overwhelmed me. "Aleppo is a city that has no fear of fire!" said Father Yusuf, commenting on my observation. It was then that I thought that Aleppo certainly had to be the city where my father, Yusuf Al-Hajari—the "stony one"—had been born!

Around that time, a fiery star had lit up the noontime sky for several days. The *naqib al-ashraf* teasingly quoted a popular prophecy that was making the rounds among the population, saying, "Aleppo is far too dear to God for Him to burn it up." With its countless gates and night watchmen, I can attest that Aleppo is the Ottoman city closest to European hearts. It even possesses a private cemetery just for those who refused to return to Europe.

However, the English consul didn't share that view, and he kept urging me to see the Orient as nothing more than a place to get rich and return home. He kept repeating, "A city where you don't see a woman walking in the street in her radiant femininity is desolate and not worth living in!"

Chapter 35

The day after I arrived in Aleppo, I received an invitation to have lunch in the home of the Patriarch Makarios, to be held in honour of Father Yusuf Al-Musawwir. It was there where I learned that Hind had not yet arrived, nor had there been any news of her. The archbishop overheard me ask Yusuf about her and also heard Yusuf's answer. He asked, "Do you want to meet the doctor for a medical reason, Robert?"

"It's not exactly medical, my good sir. The matter hinges on whether you consider a question about a medical treatise to be a medical question or something else!" Then I brought up the fact that his name had been recorded in the Venetian library and asked him why.

"One of my Muslim trading acquaintances must have used my name to do his business there. But in a library? I find that strange," he said, as he asked Father Yusuf what prompted his own delay in returning to Aleppo.

The father began to recount everything that had occurred in Venice while I kept myself occupied by eyeing the carving on the wood furnishings in the patriarch's living room, along with the paintings of Saint George, the tapestries, and the verses from the Psalms that gave voice to otherwise mute walls. I inquired about the type of rock used to clad the windows, entryway, and fountain in the home's courtyard, as well as the *mashrabiya* high above it. Someone said that it was alabaster, which only made me think what an injustice that was to marble!

I called upon the English consul in the large caravanserai a week after I arrived, bringing along the young boy, Naimat Allah ibn Yusuf Al-Musawwir, to inquire about my authorisation to enter Ottoman territory. To get there, I had to cross a disorienting labyrinth of narrow alleys until I lost all sense of direction, before finally arriving at the consul's office. When he began to probe what had prompted my visit to the Orient I retorted, "Where is East and where is West exactly?"

The consul had heard about me from one of his contacts, who had told him about an Englishman who drew sketches of Aleppo and had managed to disguise himself to reach the *mihrab* of the Umayyad Mosque and sketch it from the interior, something no European had done before, based on what the consul had told me. For that reason, he was expecting my visit. Yet any interest he may have had in me quickly dissipated as soon as he learned I had not come via the Levant Company or by way of a personal acquaintance of his, or to engage in commercial trading. When I told him that I was waiting for Hajj Karim Halifax, he said calmly, "So let's wait for Hajj Karim then."

The consul asked me to describe Hajj Karim to verify my story of meeting him, but I declined, saying, "I don't like to describe people, but you can certainly confirm everything with Father Yusuf."

The consul began discoursing on what a European must and mustn't do while in Aleppo so that we might avoid colliding unnecessarily with the local inhabitants. Drunkenness and gambling were prohibited, and one must not break religious rules, or the Sabbath, or miss Christian prayers. "You must be careful to show your religiosity so that the Aleppans trust you. That's why Levantine companies always assign a priest for their English employees here," he said, as he continued to enumerate the many opportunities for trade and profit in Aleppo.

It was clear that his number one responsibility was to raise profits for the Levant Company and that, for him, religion served an exclusively economic function. The consul was nothing but a merchant himself and conducted business with other traders. That's why he kept asking me about commerce. The young boy with me interrupted him and said, "Robert came to meet Hind the physician."

"Hind Al-Hajari? She is nothing more than a physician who mixes medicine with astrology. Are you waiting for her as a doctor or as a fortune-teller? Even the French are asking after her. Has Europe lost all its fortune-tellers?"

"To tell the truth, I came on an adventure. I am a collector of manuscripts, but not just any manuscripts—rare ones. Have you ever heard of the Rosicrucians? Some warring princes in Europe are ready to pay their weight in gold for rare works on Gnosticism and Arabian magic. I'm looking specifically for a book entitled *The Wise Men of the Seven Stars,* and that's why I'm waiting for the doctor. Some years back, she deposited a book of the same title in Venice," I said, whispering in the consul's ear so that the young boy would not overhear, because he seemed to have a loose tongue.

The consul tried to divert my attention by talking about an upcoming hunting trip with Salukis that would allow me to meet some members of the English community. I thanked him and asked, "When can I move into the caravanserai?"

However, the consul declined to allow me to move into the living quarters at the great khan with the rest of the Englishmen. He kept saying that I had to wait for Hajj Halifax, to see if he would allow me to stay with him in his upper room, which meant I had to stay longer than anticipated in the home of Father Yusuf.

Leaving the consul, I said to the young boy, "You must now take me to the French consul."

Concern ate me up, knowing that the French too were waiting for the doctor. I wanted to find out for myself and went to see if I could get more information. However, I didn't stay long at Khan Obarak, where the French kept many of their shops, because the consul was not there, and I did not receive a warm welcome from the French who were. A kind of jealousy and uneasiness reigned between them and the English and Dutch. The French were far more politically in line with the Turks, and their community in Aleppo was much larger and more integrated than either the English or Dutch communities. However, that did not stop them from looking at me askance, as if I were a thief trying to steal information from anywhere I could.

The boy and I returned to his father's workshop, which abutted onto the main house. The gate to the house, however, was a hundred and fifty yards away, at the top of the Al-Hadiba footpath, near the Square of the Churches beside the Cathedral of the Forty Martyrs. Meanwhile the entrance to the workshop was on the other side, beyond the Jewish arcade and overlooking the intersection of Al-Faraj Street. It was a small, abandoned district covered in trash and teeming with feral cats. There were demands that its affiliation with the Armenian Catholic church end, given how it had been a source of contention among the four Christian denominations in Aleppo.

Someone coming from the centre of old Aleppo via Bab Al-Nasr would first pass through the square of the Churches and the entrance to Father Yusuf's house before turning to reach his workshop. As we approached the house from a distance, we found the boy's mother calling out to him to bring lunch over to his father. I have no idea how she knew we had arrived. When I asked the boy, he said, "My mother is inspired!"

I noticed that the food was more than enough for one or two people, or even three. The boy said, "I think my father has guests." And before we continued on our way, I found the mother handing me a sack, saying, "This is for the cats you meet along the way."

The situation was as the young boy said. As soon as we arrived, I found the father bookended by two Europeans. We all moved to the workshop's central *liwan* and set down the food. I told the father that my authorisation had not yet come and that the consul refused to give me any place in the khan. I also told him about the aggressive behaviour of the French. The father said, "I'll discuss your affairs with the consul. There are many rooms at the khan. He didn't offer you one simply because you hadn't come from someone he knew."

"I wasn't even asking him for charity!"

"It could just be that the timing was off. In all honesty, the Franks no longer feel as if they're in a strange land here, and that's why they dealt with you as a stranger rather than as someone like themselves. Even their youth are falling in love with young Aleppan Christians." He gestured toward the young man who was with him. Sadness and heartbreak were clearly etched on his face, as if his fate had been sealed and the father's words only increased his anguish. He was a Frenchman who had fallen in love with a local young lady, but her family had rejected his offer of marriage, and he had come to the father to seek some kind of solace.

The father introduced me to the guests. Then he turned toward the other man. "Robert is one of your brother Jacob's students."

"Peter? What a surprise!" I said. "The professor told me all about you, and how you were supplying him with Arabic manuscripts from time to time."

"Not since I converted to Orthodoxy. Our correspondence has become sporadic. Though now he wants me to consider a translation project of the Qur'an into Dutch and to look for manuscripts that could assist with that before returning to Holland. I'm still unconvinced by it all and don't ask me the reason!"

"Well, I know that no one has dared translate the Qur'an into a modern European language. There are only poor translations into Latin dating back to the time of the Toledo School of Translation. It would be an excellent project, Peter."

"Why doesn't Jacob translate it himself? I am busy enough with the messages sent by the Dutch and French asking me to conduct simultaneous experiments for them. The latest request came from my brother. He wanted me to verify the lines of longitude and latitude in order to adjust the dimensions of the Ottoman map of the world that a team of Dutch scientists had produced for the Sublime Porte. It will require much work in many Ottoman cities."

After we had finished our meal, I told Father Yusuf that the French consul had a guest with him from the court of Louis XIII, who was also waiting for doctor Hind. "I can't fathom what a courtier of the French monarch would want with an Arab Muslim doctor in Aleppo!"

Pouring some tea, he replied, "Peter is a friend of the French. He can suss them out. Our love-sick French friend here resorted to him to get in touch with me."

The father turned to the lovelorn young man. "The truth is, my son, the customs of Christians here are not like they are in Europe. In the end, we are Orientals and young women do not defy their parents. They will reject you simply because you might carry off their daughter and take her far from them. However, if your love is pure, then God will ease things for you. I'll talk to you more later to soothe your tender heart."

Our conversation continued for some time before Father Yusuf directed the discussion toward talk of the printing press, which, it seemed, had been an ongoing topic of discussion between him and Peter for some time. The father wanted to introduce the two of us so we could work together on setting up an Orthodox printing press, Father Makarios' long-held dream, and to beat the Maronites to the finish line, because they too had been scouting for someone who could help them establish a Catholic press in Aleppo.

I didn't want to disappoint him, but his request was far beyond the reason I had come to Aleppo. So without making any grandiose display of enthusiasm, I said, "The project requires a bit more contemplation. It's not at all an easy undertaking."

Over the following days, Father Yusuf withdrew from me, but continued to treat me well, hoping I would change my mind and help them with their plans. The matter grew more serious when, several days later, Father Makarios himself summoned me to his office to talk further about the project.

I had been inside the Roman church before and made several sketches of the altar and upper stained-glass windows, as well as the dome and arches that mimicked ancient Byzantine architecture, but I had never before gone into the patriarch's office. The office was accessible through a private door that opened onto a small back alley filled with sharbat kiosks, and the father told me to go in through there and not the main entrance. When I stepped inside, I was holding a bottle of *sharbat* that I had ordered from a small shop on the road.

The patriarch wasn't alone when I came in, making me hesitate a little before I said, "There isn't enough *sharbat* for three." The man excused himself. He was one of the officials in charge of the church's endowments, and he was there to update the patriarch on the current state of rents from the church's various real-estate holdings and other affairs related to the Orthodox church. A wooden sculpture in the father's office attracted my attention with its four square panels, which folded open to display panels engraved with leafy branches and blossoms, while in the centre the Virgin cradled the Christ child in her arms. I silently wished he would give it to me, even making me consider helping them with the printing press in exchange for this beautiful work of art.

The father spoke at length about his dream for a printing press, and how he had tried many times to bring one kitted with Greek typeset to Aleppo but had been unsuccessful, owing to the need for numerous technicians to operate it. In the whole East, there was only a single broken press located with the Maronites in Lebanon and another with the Jews in Smyrna. The patriarch had begun to think about a printing press equipped with Syriac letters, at least to begin with, and then he would work to acquire an Arabic press. He was even prepared to offer me three or four workmen as assistants.

The printing press would reside in the church and remain in the service of Christians only, thus skirting the Sultan's ban on printing books in Arabic for Muslims. He then began to tell me about the Maronites' attempts to bring a press to Aleppo and how he couldn't bear the thought of being beaten out. And, in any case, what need did they have for one?

Catholic books already flowed to them from Rome for free.

I tried to slip away by saying the issue wasn't as easy as he might expect and would be terribly expensive, especially since there were no workshops in Aleppo that could produce the material and tools needed for a press.

"Father," I said, "it's not quite that simple. There are intricate pieces and springs that can't be produced except by highly specific instruments able to mill and cast the iron. Even if we could procure all the letters, the plate holders, ink rollers, octagonal wheels, and paper-heating outlets, all these parts are produced at various specialised factories in Europe. We would have to bring an already assembled printing press from Venice. The ironmongers of Aleppo simply don't have a clue what a press is, let alone how to put one together correctly," I said, recalling my discussion with the ironsmith in Leiden I asked to reproduce the German moulds.

Truth be told, the whole issue rubbed me the wrong way. On the one hand, I didn't want to contribute to any competition between the Christians of Aleppo and, on the other, I had no intention of staying in Aleppo long-term. In light of such interest, I began to wonder why everyone thought a printing press wouldn't be successful in the Levant! I asked the father, "Why don't these consuls help you with this undertaking? It could be quite successful here!"

"The issue would become complicated and messy. There are specific agreements between the Sublime Porte and the European nations, and the Europeans cannot go about transgressing them," he said, as he waited for me to say something else, but I simply concluded that the issue needed much more thought. Not once in my life had I ever thought about a printing press solely for charitable purposes!

Chapter 36

I visited the English consul after leaving Father Makarios', hoping to learn anything at all about the intentions of the French. Father Yusuf had spoken to the consul. So, by the time I visited, he had already agreed to let me reside in Hajj Karim's room, but I would have to work out some kind of agreement with him once he returned.

The consul's shop consisted of three sections, separated by white marble arches, each supported by rounded columns that were decorated at the bottom with a black *ablaq* pattern and at the top with white paint, and a vein of pink alabaster no more than a thumb's width ran in between them, marking off the consul's shop from the other Englishmen's storehouses in the great khan.

A young man from York worked for the consul, as did an Armenian whose sole occupation appeared to be procuring silk, wool, and other fine cloth from Shiraz, Tabriz, and Mosul. When you entered the shop, you were first greeted by one of these two young men before finding the consul's office off in the back on the right-hand side. Father Yusuf let me in on his trick for knowing whether it was a good time to see the consul or not, which was by reading the two men's faces first! Sure enough, two smiling faces welcomed me that day, so I went in to see the consul and found him also in a cheerful mood, quite unlike on my last visit.

I told the consul that I planned to move into the khan the following day, but he was more interested in getting to the bottom of all he had heard about my expertise with printing presses, and how I was going to offer my services to the Orthodox Christians to set up their own.

It was almost as if I had committed some kind of crime in his eyes!

When I explained what had really transpired, he said, "It's good that you've kept out of this conflict. In any case, the strictness with which the Ottomans grant printing licenses to non-Muslims makes it an exorbitantly expensive business with no real return on investment, especially since the Arabs themselves, the majority here, won't buy them at all, given how printing in the language of the Qur'an isn't allowed."

He went on to say that, were it not for conducting business or engaging in exploration, homesickness and age wouldn't allow the likes of us to remain very long in the Orient, and we ought to take advantage of Ottoman concessions as much as we can, because who knows what kind of revolutions or tumult could occur in Istanbul and could affect the affairs of Europeans in these lands.

"The *agha* of the Janissary does little else besides keep an eye on the affairs of Europeans, and the taxes we pay are less than those paid by the local merchants. Gather up all the wealth you can, my boy, and return to England to live out the remainder of your days richer than the king." At this juncture in our meeting, it crossed my mind to tell him what had brought me here in the first place. Just thinking about the French visitor who was also waiting on the doctor's return was beginning to eat away at me.

I was just about to confide in him about the lost library of the Morisco when a clamour and racket rose up outside, making us quickly go out and take a look at what was going on. We could have passed through the door of the khan, heading out in the direction of the Gate of Antioch to reach Sinan Pasha Square to the south, but the consul suggested another, quicker route, located behind the caravanserai near the courtyard of the Umayyad Mosque and not far from the Sufi monastery of Aslan Al-Majdhub. For the first and only time since I'd arrived, I could see young women without the *khimar* covering their heads looking out from the upper windows, gazing up at that strange star.

Everyone was pointing heavenward to the blazing star, shining bright as the midday sun and creating pandemonium. Doubling people's anxiety was the popular belief that this star appeared only once every 3,000 years and that catastrophes would certainly follow in its wake. According to local superstition, if it appeared at a point above the moon, then there would be an earthquake. If it appeared below, then fire would surely break out.

People's religiosity increased over the following days, and mosques and churches heaved with worshippers. Many maintained that the worst was yet to come and the appearance of such a star was just another bad omen for a city already lacking a governor, a judge, and a mufti. Prices shot up, followed by a steady rise in petty larceny, while goods disappeared from the market as demand increased. Some people said that Al-Hajari's delay in returning was yet another portentous omen for the city.

At that time of the month, the moon was not visible, and so many people looked to Al-Sharif Al-Alami who was an instructor of mathematics, engineering, and astronomy at the Khusruwiyah madrasah. Al-Alami calculated the ascensions of the moon and this star over Aleppo, and he determined it was impossible that the two celestial bodies would meet. The *naqib al-ashraf* who was temporarily in charge of the city's affairs strongly supported this opinion. The consul confided in me that doing so was simply the path of least resistance for the *naqib*, who was already beginning to be worn down by the administration of a city consumed by other fears.

Demand for telescopes, which were sold in secret in the Venetian's shops, increased, as people wanted to get a better view of the star. Yet not everyone. There were some who were reluctant to use a telescope, given its infidel origins, while others gathered them up only to destroy them.

It perplexed me that Al-Sharif Al-Alami didn't speak out against this wanton destruction. He himself used other astronomical instruments with his students, so I paid him a visit in his laboratory next to the madrasah. When he saw me carrying a telescope, I hid it immediately, making him laugh and say, "Don't start asking me what makes a telescope different from an astrolabe!"

I had heard the name of Al-Sharif Al-Alami more than once as I made the rounds in Aleppo, given his prominent standing and influence in the natural sciences, particularly among the youth and students. After Father Yusuf's introduction, my relationship with him grew stronger, and I found him to be an enlightened man, well versed in the new solar model and equally aware of the trial of Galileo. So I began to visit him regularly, and he took equal pleasure in my company as I regaled him with the latest scientific movements in Europe.

Al-Alami had built a laboratory next to the Khusrawiyah and equipped it with the whole gamut of astronomical and engineering instruments of the time. He also had a small library filled with astronomical maps charting the mansions of the moon, alongside pedagogical aids used for calculating inheritances, for determining the exact hour, and for tracing the phases of the moon and the trajectory of the sun. Despite his openness to the new astronomical model, I was puzzled by the wariness he still exhibited toward us Europeans.

When I arrived at his laboratory, I said, "They're citing your opinion to justify the destruction of telescopes!"

"You can't see anything with them anyway," he retorted, "It's a trivial instrument." He showed me the *zij* table used to calculate the ascension of the moon and other charts for determining the new star's position in relation to the sun. "It is a very precise movement, nothing random about it at all. And it certainly won't wait for man's insufficient instruments to catch up."

"But the real value of these scientific instruments is the knowledge they offer us that our senses can't give us directly," I said, wondering why he ran this laboratory and invited students to it in the first place!

"Yes, insofar as these instruments draw us nearer to our Creator and lead us to discover His divine workings and the right times for prayer and the direction of the qibla and movement of the sun. Yet the telescope provides us nothing more than entertainment and only enriches those who produce it."

"The instrument helps us surpass the limits of our senses. How can you embrace the astrolabe and reject the telescope?"

"The astrolabe gives us precise numbers. Thanks to it, we no longer need to rely on our senses. All the telescope does is provide us with a magnified, but still blurred, image. We can't understand the universe through our senses because they are weak and misleading. Only with our intellect can we understand things. And thanks to mathematics, and to the instruments for measuring slope, we have sufficient knowledge."

Al-Alami kept playing with semantics. When I realized that he was rhetorically dancing around, I remembered Descartes undergoing the same mental gymnastics as he tried to find a foothold for the truths he held so dear.

"Al-Tusi once wrote that, if he knew the circumference of the moon's shadow during an eclipse, then he would be able to determine the size of the sun," I said. "In one of his thought experiments, he placed 60 observers one parasang away from a central point during a total eclipse. With their help, he could draw the circumference of the moon's shadow and thereby figure out the size of the sun. He hid within this thought experiment the fully fledged scientific method."

Al-Alami knew what I was driving at. "Sciences such as these are not in demand in Muslim lands, though a few governors or waqf administrators might allow them to be taught to students of sharia."

He then began to relate the travails he had faced with the former mufti. "Along with other ulama several years ago, I set up a wonderful broad-trunked tree of stone and brass that we called the "tree of usefulness" in the eastern courtyard of the great mosque. Each of its branches and leaves consisted of lines and charts and presented a mathematical principle. Students from all around would come to avail themselves of this mathematical learning that included time-keeping, calculations, and other useful knowledge. And so, for a while, we kept adding branches and leaves to this tree with each new observation we gleaned or each new experiment we ran with our students.

"However, the mufti was vexed that the youth were rushing to our scientific gatherings to the detriment of his own courses. He raised a complaint with the judge and managed to secure an order to remove it on the grounds that students were becoming distracted and diverting their attention away from the religious sciences. Three of our best instructors of engineering and the mechanics of time were subsequently transferred to Istanbul. I would have been imprisoned, had it not been for the *naqib* who intervened, allowing me to stay at the school on the condition that I no longer teach natural sciences except those solely in the service of religious knowledge."

After several days, he took me to see the *naqib al-ashraf*, having told him previously that I was a man of great scientific and mechanical knowledge. The naqib welcomed us warmly, and we began to discuss the use of instruments to confirm the position of this fiery star in relation to the moon, thus obviating the need to wait for Al-Hajari to return in order to set people's minds at ease with the knowledge and understanding that God had granted her.

The *naqib* informed us that he had sent someone to find out what had happened to Al-Hajari, and that she might be arriving within days. I asked him if there was any way that we could meet her before she entered Aleppo, saying that it would be best that she knew what was going on, so she could allay people's fears over this star.

The *naqib* didn't much care for the idea. Hoping to further press my case, I asked Al-Sharif why the *naqib* was not supportive of the suggestion. He pointed out that, first off, it was my idea, and I was a European Christian and quite a young one at that, and second, because the *naqib* did not want Sheikh Ibrahim Zini, the doctor's husband, to become puffed up.

Chapter 37

The days passed slower than an Eastern Orthodox mass. I tried to ingratiate myself with the *naqib,* first through my relationship with Al-Alami and then via Ahmad the dervish, who was the head of calligraphers in Aleppo, but the *naqib* continued to show no interest in me.

I had met Ahmad the dervish, a man in his mid-fifties, while at the English shops near the consul's residence. It was early morning, and he was searching around for lead and antimony. I had nothing going on at the moment, except counting the large stones in front of Hajj Karim Halifax's boarded-up shop and half-listening to the debate swirling among the English merchants, who were divided over the recent scuffle that had broken out in the streets of London between the king's army and Parliament. Overhearing the man ask for those two materials, I made a beeline to find out why he needed them.

"Why are you asking me?" he asked. "I don't even know who you are."

"I don't know you either, but I do know that those materials are used in making type for printing presses. Do they have any other use?"

"You speak Arabic well. I haven't seen you around Aleppo before."

"I'm English and arrived several weeks ago, accompanied by Father Yusuf Al-Musawwir, and I work with him from time to time. I'm awaiting the return of Hajj Karim Halifax, who promised I could work for him."

"Who do you know here in Aleppo?"

His question was perplexing. Did I need to know anyone? However, I said, "Thanks to Al-Musawwir, I've met the archbishop Al-Khouri and the patriarch Makarios, as well as Al-Sharif Al-Alami and the *naqib* and the Dutchman Peter Golius."

"As long as you know Peter, then you'll be having lunch at my house today. If you're otherwise unoccupied, would you like to help me out?"

I spent the day with him, and he introduced himself as the man who had changed the course of Arabic calligraphy 12 times! He went about his shopping and bought several templates, stacks of parchment, some ink and dyes, as well as a number of quills and engraving tools, and finally a small desk from one of the woodworkers. He did not, however, find the antimony and lead he was looking for. We went to his workshop not too far from the Khusrawiyah madrasah on the eastern side of the citadel.

As we passed by the great mosque, he asked me to wait for him with his purchases. He pointed up at the sundial affixed to the wall of the mosque's outer fence. As he pointed to the needle's shadow, he said, "When it reaches that degree there, then the time for prayer will have arrived."

As I waited for him, I wondered why they built so many towers for homing pigeons, but not a single one for a clock? I echoed the muezzin's words that I had heard so many times before. A tender, plaintive sound like the Sufi melodies I'd heard on the plain of Tuman. I felt as if there were some connection between death and the call to prayer, or so it seemed. As if that angelic melody transformed the *adhan* into some sort of anticipatory incantation for passing from this world into the next.

After he came out of the mosque, I told Ahmad that I had repeated the call to prayer. I said "*Ashadu anna Mohammadan rasul Allah. Does that make me a Muslim now?*"

He laughed. "In Islam, we don't differentiate between the prophets of God, and we respect all the monotheistic religions." Changing the subject, he said he still needed antimony and lead to craft personal seals for some customers. He asked afterward, "So what do you know about printing presses?"

"I know them as if I had invented them myself. I even trained Maronites in Rome on how to use one. Christians here, however, seem more interested in it than you Muslims, despite the fact that it reduces the cost of books and places them within everyone's reach. Yet I just haven't found anyone among the Muslims who really talks about it!"

"That's because calligraphy and copying manuscripts are part of our artistic tradition, and the demand for them both is great, certainly among the wealthy and learned of society. As for the printing press, we don't know whether it is an art or simply a craft no different from spinning yarn or producing swords. Penning something by hand, by contrast, is a precise art, experienced moment by moment in a manner no machine could ever understand or recreate. What use is a machine or speed when I enjoy the process so much more as I slowly put quill to parchment?"

"But that doesn't mean that printing is *haram* or that speed is a sin. We don't disobey God when we shorten time!"

"What is forbidden isn't printing itself, Robert, but applying the technique to the speech of Allah, which we sanctify. We protect it from becoming vulgarised and handled carelessly, copied hundreds of times and stacked up by the hands of non-Muslims."

At that moment, I felt a cold slap on my face as if I somehow had been rendered less human by the man who had just said they respected all monotheistic religions. However, something Father Gaddis had said about argumentation came to mind. I told the dervish, "But you all constantly use the name of God and verses from the Qur'an in seals, copying it over and over. Printing is no different from these seals, except that it's cut into individual letters and not whole words and sentences. Practically speaking, you all knew about printing even before us. The difference is that we love to learn from you, yet you Muslims have no interest in learning anything from us!"

"While you might be right, the subject is vast. I don't think you all come here truly to learn anything at all from us. Those of you I've met were always looking for something to ignite their imagination. In the end, you're all searching for adventures and stories. As for us, we're not going to get ahead of ourselves," he said before motioning to show we were nearing his workshop.

As we set things down, I said, "If you're thinking about an Arabic printing press, then I can help you. Reading for us in Europe has become a popular pastime and is no longer just the preserve of the elite. And thanks to the printing press, it has now become more profitable than copying by hand. Everyone will buy from you and not just the wealthy and well-off."

"Peter already said the very same thing. You must understand, Robert, the matter is complicated here. You would need to convince hundreds of people just to even raise the issue with the Sheikh of

Islam in Istanbul and, even if everyone agrees, the hand-copyist guild most certainly will not. Copying is their sole source of livelihood. There are thousands of them here and throughout Ottoman cities."

"Alright, so why exactly did the mention of Peter Golius earlier prompt you to ask for my assistance?"

"Peter is an old friend. He came to Aleppo following in the footsteps of his brother Jacob, whom I worked with when he was in Aleppo, as well as with the English priest Edward Pococke. I even hand copied manuscripts that they had ordered. And while they were both opportunists, they were also affable and kind. Pococke took a fig-tree cutting from me and planted it in a courtyard at Oxford University. In one of his letters, he told me that it had grown so large that he would take his afternoon break and read under its shade. He even told me it was the first fig tree planted in England. As for Jacob, to this day I still remember his tumble from atop a camel during one of our journeys into the desert. We laughed so hard despite his shouts and broken leg."

Now, having learned the secret of his limp, I said, "The left leg, right?"

"That's right. Do you know Jacob?"

That day, he spoke at length of memories he shared with Professor Golius. I brought up the doctor and how the *naqib* had sent someone to find out what had become of her. I also complained that the *naqib* was purposefully keeping me at arm's length, away from his inner circle. As the hour for the gates to shut drew near, and I was about to depart, he told me that he would take me personally to the *naqib* to inquire about Hind's arrival, although it turned out that she returned before he could make good on that promise.

Even now, I still hadn't met the Frenchman who was lying in wait for the doctor. All I had been able to ascertain was that he was a messenger from the Bibliothèque du Roi in Paris, dispatched to Aleppo in connection to some deal related to ancient Andalusian manuscripts now housed at the Bibliothèque, which caused me no small amount of fear and consternation. Could it be that the French had already reached the manuscripts and now needed to catalogue them all?

I was able to set aside my anxiety a little when Father Yusuf suddenly handed me letters from Jacob and Margherita, as well as from my father and Father Mersenne.

In his letter, Jacob mentioned that the French had made it to the Fort of Saint Andrew near Nice and turned it upside down but found nothing. Their information came via the French consul in Aleppo by way of the lady of Aragon's husband. As for their knowledge of the lady of Aragon and her treasure, Jacob also thought the husband was the source. He may have wanted to unburden his wife from stewing over these manuscripts, although he had not provided them with precise directions.

As for the letter from my father George, it was old, responding to the letter I had sent before going to Rome. He reiterated his apology and wrote that Najma had told him about her husband and her sister and the servant Hasan, and that they were perhaps in France, which is why he continued to ask about them among his acquaintances there. It was clear from my father's letter that he wanted to know what I would do if I eventually found Al-Hajari. Would I return home to them?

My father had also hastily penned an idea that came to his mind concerning seals used in the Levant and how perhaps it could be an avenue by which to introduce the idea of the printing press more generally. He wrote, "We could pursue a new method of printing by making metal copies of these seals and installing them on the tips of steel bars, which would automatically ink them with the press of a finger, while another lever strikes the seal onto the paper, thus reproducing the image."

My father provided a few sketches to clarify the idea and thought it could be successful in the Levant. "It's not just seals that we could strike mechanically. If they accept that, then next they will accept moveable type!"

Father Mersenne, for his part, thanked me for my kindness in informing him that I was going to the Holy Land. He told me that Father Gaddis had refused to deliver up the Savary printing press to the French, likely because of the enmity between France and Spain. He closed his letter by asking if I could bring back a rock or handful of soil from Bethlehem or Jerusalem.

As for Margherita, she wrote three letters to me, and I spent the remainder of my time reading her longing and anguish-filled poems, as well as her news from Florence and how things were progressing with the guide to Galileo's experiments.

Expansive like sunset's tint,

that colour-crammed bird

vanishes into the pallor of its ancient egg,

into the agonies of the shed shell.

It lies trodden under the feet of passers-by.

Tarry, you journeying bird,

carry me off in your claw.

A die relays you six wagers,

and you are a loser in all.

So roll not the stone:

In which lies your one chance of winning!

This poem of hers, which she titled *The Bird's Dice* was the one closest to my heart.

She told me that she had finally found someone to teach her how to play the violin and that Alessandro continuously asked when I was to return. As for Siraj, he turned down the offer to work in the print house and instead chose to harvest fruit in the fields of the Medici. She also wrote a few lines about a young Dane named Lukas Brahe who had come to Florence looking for me. I kept thinking about this young man who was none other than the student who had tried to gain access to the archives of the University of Leiden. But what did he want?

I began to write them all back. And within days of doing so, news of the arrival of Hind's caravan at the outskirts of town made it to my ears.

Chapter 38

I let myself be carried away with the throngs as they gathered at the bridge of Al-Hajj, south of the city, in anticipation of the doctor's imminent arrival. I stood near the Gate of Antioch looking on as a crowd of hundreds of labourers and handicapped awaited the caravan, led by the *naqib*, Father Makarios, and the French consul.

The English consul advised me to not join the masses because it was no concern of ours as Europeans. Maybe for him, but I had come all this way to Aleppo for this very moment! And, in any case, it was the Christians of Aleppo who zealously and jubilantly welcomed my Aragonese aunt, more so than the Muslims. So, I made my way over to the bridge to join in welcoming the convoy.

There was shouting and tears to welcome her while Sheikh Ibrahim prostrated himself, kissing the ground of Aleppo and thanking Allah for a safe return. She stood there somewhat bashfully, showing nothing of herself, though she briefly lifted her veil to greet the *naqib* and thank the prominent citizens of Aleppo for welcoming her back.

As I wandered around, aiming to spot my aunt, my eyes instead fell upon the French consul, who appeared to be trying (and failing) to snatch a private moment with Sheikh Ibrahim Zini. Amidst the tumult, I had trouble finding a place for myself among all those hoping to welcome her. Nobody knew who I was. For all they knew, I was just another adventuring English lad or perhaps a crazy man.

When I returned to the market, I met the consul, who asked sarcastically, "How did you find the welcome?" I gave a clipped response, "It was definitely a sight, Sir." He then quickly motioned for me to sit beside him. "We elicit no curiosity in them, Robert, while they pique ours deeply. These Arabs don't want to know a thing about us, while we know everything there is to know about them. What do you think is the reason for that?"

"What's the reason?"

"They must have something that we lack. Look how they destroy the inventions we bring them, even the ones that would ease their lives! While we, on the other hand, want to acquire even their long-forgotten ancient artefacts. They are so much simpler than we are."

"Isn't it because we are obsessed with classification? We classify peoples and countries as if God himself had ordained us for that very mission!"

"That's natural, Robert. Those who know more, classify more."

"What are you driving at, Sir?"

"Nothing at all. It's just that your comment about the gathering set me thinking. We do like to gaze at them as they go about their affairs. I've been in Aleppo for six years and still have not met a single Arab who has wanted to travel to England to experience it first-hand."

I left the consul thinking: Would we even welcome them if they came? The consul's questions continued to ring in my ears for days, especially when I found out that the doctor was treating Christians and Muslims for free, supporting herself off her husband's commercial dealings. I guessed this was what the consul had meant when he said that Levantines possessed something that we Europeans did not.

It was two whole days before I was able to see the doctor, and even then I had to double my efforts to get a chance, because the lines of the sick and afflicted waiting to see her were so long and I was uncomfortable asking someone to intercede on my behalf.

I finally met Sheikh Ibrahim to explain the reason for my visit: It concerned the health benefits of a certain remedy found in the *Al-Hawi* treatise by Al-Razi. He suggested I call on the doctor during her afternoon rest period. When I went in to see her, her clothing was quite similar to what nurses wore in Florence: a white tunic with a green head covering, paired with a heavier blouse of a greyish hue.

"It's rare that someone from the European community comes to visit me. You have your own doctors. Tell me, what's troubling you? What would you like to inquire about?" she asked, as I recalled the voice of my mother Najma placing me beside her during prayer time—those prayers for which my father George would reprimand her and to which she would reply in all simplicity, "I'm teaching him love, not prayer!"

I immediately placed between her hands Hasan's ring and the small painting I had taken from Baroness Despucci. She slowly reached for the ring and began to pore over the picture, then looked at me with eyes drooping from the passage of time. "Who are you, my boy?" These quivering words poured from her mouth, as if a great dam holding back a deluge of memories had suddenly collapsed, bursting forth with that simple question.

"I'm the child in the picture. I'm the son of your sister Najma. By adoption, I'm English, but by blood I am the son of Najma and Yusuf," I said, trying to staunch the haemorrhaging of her soul as best I could. "I've been looking for you for five years now, aunt."

She remained silent, gazing at the picture. Then she began to whimper, trying to suppress the sobs that filled her heart. In a faltering voice, she asked, "And where is Najma now?"

"My father Yusuf is in a prison in Spain, and I've been trying to free him. He was not fortunate enough to see my mother, who passed away in exile 15 years ago in England."

She readjusted herself in the chair, perhaps to conceal the emotions that were coursing through her. She then called someone to summon Sheikh Ibrahim who, as soon as he entered and saw the doctor slumped in her chair, cast his eyes toward me, the ring, and the small painting. He asked, "What is going on, dear?" She said, "It is a painting of my sister Najma. This young man says he is her son and Yusuf's." Having said that, she finally gave herself permission to weep.

The sheikh looked at me, trying to pierce through my eyes to see what lay beyond. "How did you come here? And why did you say that you had a question for her about Al-Razi?"

"Because I am a stranger who has been searching for his family for years. I knew that you two had informed the French about a valuable trove of Andalusian and Oriental manuscripts that my father Yusuf entrusted to you because it was his family's heritage. I have to reach those manuscripts before anyone else!"

The sheikh looked over to the doctor, who had fully surrendered to her tears, then said sharply, "You're just an Englishman running after wealth and nothing more. Why should we trust you?"

"I don't know! But do I really look like an Englishman? Fate tossed me into the same prison as Yusuf, and he asked for my help to reach his family. But Najma had already passed on, and he has no one else left but you. My blood is Arab, Sir. I want to free my father from prison. It has been 25 years, and he has gone from prison to prison and anguish to anguish."

I then turned to my aunt. "I've only known my true parentage for the last year. My father himself doesn't even know and thinks I was just another inmate."

I began to recount all that had happened to Najma and Yusuf and what Luisa had mentioned about the convent. Then I showed her the rest of Hasan's possessions and letters. When I finished, she said, "You open old wounds. Life didn't smile upon me until I finally reached Aleppo. What do you want now?"

My aunt kept trying to glean more information. The details I gave her about Baroness Despucci, Yusuf, Najma, and Luisa made her confidence in me grow until she finally embraced me. She broke down in tears when I told her about the news Hasan had sent to Holland, which could have established a connection between her and my mother, had the plague not hastened the demise of Erpenius, and had my adoptive father's communication with him concerning Najma continued. But for some reason it did not, and his search remained limited. And though he helped her by giving her shelter and safety, he made no effort to unite her with her family.

The sheikh dismissed the rest of the sick for the day so he could listen to the story and, by the afternoon, I was having lunch with the two of them.

"Why did you not return to the baron's family like my mother Najma had done?" I asked.

"Hasan kept saying that what happened only happened because of them. Later, we sent several bits of made-up news to France and Holland, hoping they would fall into the hands of someone who knew us. But in the end it was all for naught."

I told them what the French were up to, and how I intended to save Yusuf from prison. The sheikh said, "The French consul will visit us tomorrow evening. It seems that my previous discussion with him didn't lead them to the boxes."

"That could be so. They searched the entire citadel and found nothing. They are coming now to find out the exact location."

"There are dozens of boxes! How could they not find them?" Then after a short silence, he added, "In fact, I don't know the exact spot myself. All I told them was that the manuscripts were in the citadel."

Turning to the doctor, I said, "As I was on my way to Nice, I passed near the sprawling citadel that has now been abandoned. I have to know exactly how you hid all those boxes."

My aunt began to explain. "Hasan would go down to the bottom of the valley to bring back the rocks we used to build a wall. We stayed there two weeks, working only at night and under cover of darkness. Perhaps we should tell the French that the treasure is hidden in a blocked-off cave along the valley bluff."

"It would be best to keep their search far from the citadel," I said and asked them to keep the matter a secret.

"So what do we tell the consul?" Sheikh Ibrahim asked. "Do we turn down his meeting?"

"No. You must meet him, but at the same time you must lead him astray."

"The previous times I went to the consul myself and told him about the manuscripts, and I said that the Europeans were the most deserving of them because they truly appreciated the importance of the knowledge and science contained within those books."

"This time, it's the consul who is coming to you, perhaps with another man, likely a French officer or a manuscript thief. This time, both of them will be extremely keen to know the exact location."

I left Sheikh Zini's house after learning where the manuscripts were and after devising a plan to lead the French astray, just as my father Yusuf had done long ago.

I darted over to Father Yusuf Al-Musawwir's house and found him repairing one of the broken telescopes that his son Naimt Allah had found. I told him about my meeting with the doctor. And after gaining his total confidence, I revealed my Arab lineage. I said that I was going to travel to France but would return to Aleppo soon, this time with my father and the printing press in tow.

"Pray to the Virgin for my sake, Father."

The father praised me. "The Levant will remember you, Robert."

I then went to the consul to tell him about my impending travel and to settle any outstanding debts. I was surprised to discover Hajj Karim was with him, sipping wine, and I said, "But you're Muslim, Sir!"

"I'm Muslim in everything except for wine. I cannot live without it. If Muslims themselves sneak into Christian homes from time to time for a tipple, how much more leniency do I have, given I've only entered Islam in the last few years?" he asked, laughing.

I laughed with them. The consul had brought out the narghile and a backgammon board for his dear guest while the two young assistants moved the Hajj's belongings into the room and other helpers moved his goods into his storehouse.

"It seems that Hajj Karim has taken a liking to you, Robert, and he has no qualms about you staying in his room."

"I actually came for that very reason, Sir. I am departing for Europe in around two days' time."

"Did you find what you were looking for with Al-Hajari?" he asked, as if he were probing for something else.

"Not exactly. And for that reason, I must travel."

The two men began to ask my reasons, and so I pieced together bits of a story from my imagination. When I finished, Hajj Karim said, "If you're coming back to Aleppo, my offer to search for the treasures of the kingdom of Palmyra still stands. I repeat to you what I said previously: Your place is at the harbour of Tripoli and not Iskanderun. The ships depart from there daily to various Mediterranean ports. I still have my guide with me here. I can arrange everything with him if you'd like. You can consider all his expenses paid."

I warmly thanked the hajj and, the following day, I went to the home of Sheikh Zini to secretly observe the meeting with the French consul and the officer. Learning what I needed to, I said goodbye to my aunt who asked me to send her regards to Sister Luisa and the mother superior. Though I had the unfortunate duty of informing her that the reverend mother had passed away and her deputy had taken her place.

"I will eagerly await your return," she said, as she offered up prayers. "God has opened your heart, my dear Robert. May God save you for the sake of his beloved Prophet."

I didn't know Mohammed, but I do know God, and since God had opened my heart at last, I kissed my aunt's head and hand.

It was still dark as I left Aleppo, bidding farewell to its minarets and church steeples. As I neared the Mediterranean coastline, the names of all those I had left behind on both sides of those shores came rushing back, and the distance between *here* and *there* faded into nothing.

After a week, I made it to Tripoli and stayed at port for three days, unable to find direct passage to Nice or Genoa. And so I waited for a ship that would sail to Marseille. And, as luck would have it, I crossed paths with the French officer on board the ship. Both of us were making our way to Nice, but I was one step ahead of him because I knew him, and he still did not know me.

Part 8

Fate of the Morisco

I had come to the realisation that the Arabic press—the very thing that had gotten me wrapped up in all these adventures—was more than a simple press. It was a soul wanting to be reborn. And here I was, experiencing the profound effect such a border-crossing idea could have on a man. Even love, in all its majesty and glory, was nothing more than a simple prayer in the niche of this grand idea.

Chapter 39

La Lune pushed away from port, carrying with it pilgrims returning from Palestine. In the beginning, I was told it was a religious ship, and therefore I would have to wait for a commercial vessel to depart several days later. In the end, however, and after several attempts, I was able to persuade the operator that I was indeed on a journey in service to the word of the Lord, having come from the holy valley in northern Lebanon, where the Qadisha caves and Deir Qozhaya, with its monks whose miracles filled at last count more than 13 volumes, were located.

We crossed the Mediterranean on this rickety old French vessel that greatly resembled an Ottoman ship, except that the openings once used for cannons were now boarded up, and the rooms behind them now provided additional storage for goods and other cargo. Just below these slots were other openings where oarsmen used to toil, although they were no longer needed, which might explain why there were so few soldiers on board.

For just a moment, I thought that, were it not for the prayers reverberating throughout the entire ship, heading out to sea aboard *La Lune* would be nothing short of suicide. Time and faith had turned it into a holy church slipping through the water, and I couldn't deny the odd peace of mind and tranquillity I felt, similar to that night on the plains of Tuman. The only thing that could wrest me from such a peaceful state was the undercover French officer.

Together, he and I charted a course across the Mediterranean. I had a sneaking suspicion that he was watching me carefully, like the Mediterranean itself, which reminded me the whole time of the letters I had forgotten to deliver to Yusuf Al-Musawwir before my departure from Aleppo. The Mediterranean called me to toss them into its depths, whispering to me: I am the tomb of all tales.

I will send them myself from Marseille, I confided to the sea, as I held tightly onto my leather satchel where I kept writings and other papers. The sea kept looking back at me with a sly calmness, asking, "Is there any other task you've neglected?"

I spied the French officer a number of times on board. Once, I tried to see whether he recognised me or not. I drew close as he tried to take a late afternoon nap in one of the deck chairs near the stern of the ship. Hailing him, I asked "Was this your first visit to the Levant?" He looked at me and, with the same calmness as the sea, he said, "Are you speaking to me?"

I apologised for the disturbance, and he said, "It's fine," then returned to his silence. I remained nearby, looking across the ship as it sliced through the waters in pursuit of the sun before it dipped below the horizon. The officer's stature and bearing did nothing to make one dislike him. He was well-dressed, with a neatly trimmed, triangular beard that was in style with the Paris literati of the time, and which made the chin look as if it were being hoisted up by a narrow black sail, while his moustache, upturned at the edges, appeared pointed and sharp. And with his blue silken shirt, its black buttons and golden collar, it was impossible to feel anything other than respect for him, even if he were the enemy. I thought, *It's a pity he's a Frenchman.*

When he noticed that I had not left, he turned toward me and asked, "Are you English?"

"Yes. I spent six months in Deir Qozhaya."

"Did you not visit other places during your stay?

"I was planning to go to Palestine to bring back some of its soil and stones for my mother, but I was unable to do so. I thought I might ask if you had perhaps been there."

"Take her back some rocks from Marseille. She won't know the difference!" he said, relaxing his head and closing his eyes once more.

"Are you pulling my leg, Sir?"

"I've never met a religious Englishman in my whole life. However, if you want, I think those ladies over there were in Palestine," he said, gesturing to some women gathered in a tight circle around a priest who was reading to them the stories of Saint James the Great, as some softly wept at the horror of that saint's tribulations.

I didn't move from my spot and, when he noticed, he told me that it was his first trip to the Levant and that he'd been on a special mission to Aleppo. I cried out, "How did you manage to convince the operator that you were on a religious journey?"

I backed off my question, knowing that his bearing was sufficient to persuade the Devil himself that he was trustworthy. "How did you find the Orient?" I asked. "I myself enjoyed great respect among the Maronites. They respect foreigners and enjoy their company, although it is rare that they ask about their homelands."

The French officer adjusted his position and extended his hand to shake mine, introducing himself as a courtier in the palace of Louis XIII. I introduced myself as a printing press technician in a printing shop in Leiden. Then he said, "Christianity preceded Islam in the Orient, and yet the population nonetheless views us as strangers. The East does not belong exclusively to its inhabitants. We too have a stake in it, given how we have spread throughout it so deeply. The Turks understand that point very well, having come as outsiders from central Asia, while we were the first to have religious claims in this land. Yet the Mohammedans refuse to understand, and they still look at us as if we were nothing more than crusading invaders.

I lent my full attention to the man, despite overhearing the priest begin to recite a prayer in the distance. The officer added, looking at his pocket watch, "Our challenge with the East is this: Since Islam arrived after Christianity, it has a clear-cut position toward our creed. We on the other hand must exert enormous effort to tease out the faults and failings of Islam. There is simply nothing about Islam in either the New or Old Testament. And so consequently, we stumble around in our relationship with the peoples of this region. We simply don't know how to situate ourselves in relation to them.

"Beyond that, Levantine Christians are more similar to their Muslim neighbours in customs and traditions. They sit on the ground, they spend lavishly on marriage, their clothing is billowy and flowing, and their women cover up and keep hidden from guests. They even have their own sepulchres, and, like the Muslims, they rely on oral traditions rather than the great theological writings we possess. It's no surprise then that Islam is far more enticing to the Christian than Christianity is to Muslims because Christianity already forms part of their history. There is no shock when a Muslim reads our holy book, unlike us when we read theirs. A large part of our ancient history is present in their Qur'an, albeit with some differences. So, in the end, we must be absorbed into the East and not the opposite, because they will never be absorbed by us at all. The Mediterranean was once a single entity, but today its peoples are growing further and further apart."

As darkness fell, I took my leave of him. As we disembarked at the port, I bid farewell as two guards received him and escorted him to one of the offices at the harbour. I crossed paths with him one last time, though from a distance, one early morning as his team searched along the valley of Saint Andrew for the trail descending to the bluff, according to the directions the doctor had given them. I didn't quite know how to describe my feelings toward him at that moment, because what he was searching for was already in my possession as I left the area near the citadel. Earth is God's alone and, anyway, as I recalled our discussion earlier on the ship, I wondered: What is *East* and *West* if not a manifestation of our own crisis with directions?

In the port, I met some of those ladies who had visited the sacred sites and was able to take from them a handful of soil from Palestine, which I sent to Father Mersenne, along with a short letter I ended by saying, "The Lord was born in Palestine for a purpose." I also posted some letters to Jacob, my father George, and Margherita.

Marseille was buzzing with news about Cardinal Richelieu falling ill and dying after being ravaged by a number of diseases. Many people thought he was the reason behind Catholic France's decision to join the Protestants in their wars against Spain. I, on the other hand, was more consumed by buying what I needed in order to extract the Morisco's secret and by searching for a carriage and coachman for that very purpose.

After five days of strenuous travel, we made it to the ancient citadel, which was said to have withstood the bombardment by Hayreddin Barbarossa during the days when the French monarch relied wholly on Suleiman the Magnificent in his wars against the European kings.

The citadel was located at the end of the valley of Saint Andrew near the shores of the Mediterranean, about two or three miles outside Nice. I told the coachman what we were going to do, and he displayed his willingness to stay with me till we reached Genoa. Everything I asked of him, he executed without question. Though as we hoisted the final box and loaded it into the carriage, he briefly remarked, "What an incredible hiding place!"

Hasan had selected a spot hidden in a distant corner behind the citadel, surrounded by a thicket of trees near the valley bluff. There he built a square wall connected to the citadel itself. It was made of stone in the Moorish manner for protecting valuables. The wall was so thick that you had to remove more than a palm's span of mud and stone just to reach the boxes. To further camouflage the place, Hasan filled in the walled area with bits of bones and rocks, in addition to placing ancient tree trunks all around to prevent anyone from easily accessing it.

Dawn in its splendour was just about to break as we removed the final box. And despite our sheer fatigue, we dashed off immediately to Genoa without making a stop in Nice. Another week of travel lay ahead of us, and we had to leave French territory as quickly as possible.

In Genoa, my relationship with the coachman grew even stronger, when I told him what I planned to do with the boxes, especially after persuading the old Jew Antonio to allow us to keep them in his bookshop in exchange for a small sum.

For the next three weeks, I kept returning to the port of Genoa looking for Álvaro, who was supposed to have arrived there by mid-autumn. When money started to run low, the coachman and I spent some time transporting cargo. One day, I asked him, "There is nothing forcing you to stay with me, and you know I have no money. What makes you so sure that I'm not tricking you or that things might not go as hoped?"

He began to say that he didn't know, but then offered, "The Catalan revolution was strongly supported by the cardinal, but now that he is dead it is destined to fail, and Spain will surely take its revenge. And throughout the ages, Marseille has always been a theatre of conflict. So, maybe I just wanted to save myself and had nothing to lose in Marseille!"

I took his anxiety into consideration when he asked me, "And what if this man doesn't show up? Will you stay in Genoa forever?"

"We will stay until the beginning of winter. If he doesn't come by then, we will go to Florence. I've left him messages in Venice, but I don't know if they reached him."

As October dwindled away, Álvaro finally made it to Genoa, where I met him in the seafarers' hostel. I told him that this time around my presence was no coincidence, and that I had been looking all over for him. From the looks of him, no one would have the impression that he was doing well, and it seemed that he had to find a bigger pipe to obscure a new scar on his upper lip.

I said, "You do not appear well, my man."

He nodded. "I've got to go. I have enough troubles as it is." But then he followed up with, "Unless, that is, you're looking for some work out at sea."

I asked him to give me some of his time to show him something. He agreed, and I took him to the Jew's shop where the coachman was waiting. I showed him the boxes and said, "This is worth more than 15,000 gold lira, and I have a buyer—Duke Lorenzo de' Medici. I've got a carriage, horses, and a coachman. I lack nothing except for a captain. Will you join me in exchange for getting your own ship?

He eyed me seriously, his head filling with ideas. We all sat together and talked things over, including the coachman, who over the course of all these trials had become my partner more than just a hired hand. Two days later, we were all departing Genoa, heading overland for Florence.

Chapter 40

I parted ways with Álvaro and the coachman at the baptistry of San Giovanni, leaving them behind to watch the festivities of the Virgin Mary's feast in honour of her saving the city from the plague. On that solemn occasion, they removed a church bell from a pool of water to baptise dozens of children in it. Notably, the bell itself had been stolen by corsairs along the Barbary coast many years ago and was only recently recovered. Throughout the city, streets were brightly festooned, and shops overflowed with Florentine biscuits topped with phrases praising the Virgin.

While the convoy of revellers headed northward, my path would take me south to the foothills. And so I left the two men with the carriage as I went by foot to find Margherita, like a pilgrim making his way to Galilee. I was profoundly content, and my good humour nearly lifted me above the clouds. I had come to the realisation that the Arabic press—the very thing that had gotten me wrapped up in all these adventures—was more than a simple press. It was a soul wanting to be reborn. And here I was experiencing the profound effect such a border-crossing idea could have on a man. Even love, in all its majesty and glory, was nothing but a simple prayer in the niche of this grand idea.

I came upon Margherita celebrating the Day of the Virgin, surrounded by friends and relatives, far from the din and clamour of the city. She glided in between the cakes and cups of wine, the dancing feet and band of musicians, and sidled up against my chest as she buried her face in my shoulder. Encircled by the strained smiles of young Florentine men who themselves were dreaming of Margherita,

I kissed her and said, "I've returned with the manuscripts and left them outside Florence, so I could come directly to you!"

Grabbing my hands, she exclaimed, "Had you not returned, I was well on my way to entering the convent!" She led me away, gesturing for Vincenzo to follow us to the "gateway to the new century," the name Vincenzo had given to his home laboratory. There, the two of them displayed the 16 octavo sheets that would form their guide to experiments for amateurs. It all reminded me of Margherita's letters to me in Aleppo. She had a knack for leaping effortlessly from deeply profound emotion to the highest peaks of logic and rationality all in a single bound. For her, there was no difference between pouring out tears and calculating a mathematical operation! Or maybe it was, in fact, the opposite. The gulf was so wide between the two poles that she was forced to rationalise both by treating them as one in the same.

I asked them about Lukas the Dane in order to find out more about what he wanted. Margherita replied that he had asked to accompany me to the Levant without indicating why. His purpose didn't seem to be related to trade, but rather to an ancient book on Arabic magic.

"He asked what prompted you to go to Rome. Maybe he suspected that you were looking for the same thing he was, and that's why he wanted to follow you!" Vincenzo added before I said that I must see Alessandro at once and meet the duke.

They told me that the duke was in Pisa and would not return before the end of the new year. The decision to withdraw Tuscany from the wars in the northern lands was still under discussion. Vincenzo read what was on my mind and said, "You can meet up with them there. You have to complete your mission and free your father from prison. We will be here waiting for you." He looked at Margherita, who added, "Within my heart there is an entire life waiting for you."

Álvaro and the coachman arrived just as night fell, and we took our leave, heading next to Alessandro's. As soon as he saw the boxes, he said, "We will leave at once for Pisa. There will be no end to the duke's excitement when he sees this trove! Now, even the supreme pontiff himself will be forced to pay us a visit, and Florence will be no less grand than Rome." As we made our way to the library to unload the boxes, he continued to talk about the nearing end of the wars in the north. Though nothing had yet been decided, it did seem they would sit down at the discussion table. "An end to war would be quite beneficial for ducal affairs here in Tuscany," he said as he pointed to the boxes, adding, "You'll have to catalogue these, Robert."

"We won't leave all of them here. I need to hold onto some of them to take to Spain. It is likely that we'll need them there," I said to everyone's surprise.

While the boxes sat in the Jewish man's bookshop, I rummaged through them and prepared a list, determining what I would keep for myself and what I would sell to the duke. I showed the list to Alessandro, saying, "I will take a quarter of the boxes with me, but will return with them, and later we will agree what to do with them." Unloading the boxes in the library, we finished up and headed out to find Siraj.

The hour was late when we arrived at Siraj's place and woke him up. The very first words from his mouth were, "How could you sketch Father Gaddis' seal?!" He had searched through my things and discovered the drawing. He couldn't forgive me for this deceitful act and was himself incredibly remorseful for stealing it in the first place. He asked if I was intending to forge it. I couldn't say for sure why I had drawn the seal before giving it back to Father Gaddis' messenger, but perhaps it had something to do with Álvaro. It was my meeting with him that first planted the idea of returning to San Sebastián in my mind. Though maybe it wasn't the first. Baroness Despucci had also mentioned something like it when I had met her.

Siraj was unsure whether he should join us on our journey back to his homeland, Spain, and hesitated before eventually agreeing. Our plan wasn't just to liberate the Morisco, but it also involved something else that Siraj feared even more.

We departed Florence for Pisa in the same carriage we had taken from Marseille. It was much lighter this time, and it was just a matter of days before we entered to see the duke in his family's palazzo, where he was elated to learn that the Medici Library had received hundreds of Arabic and Persian manuscripts.

The duke promised me 14,000 lira, but in light of how truly huge of a sum that was, he needed a week to receive authorisation from the grand duke and the family council. Yet I went back to the duke the next day, after Álvaro suggested we barter for one of the ships anchored in the harbour of Pisa. The duke thought it was a good idea, but still had to receive approval from his cousin, the ruler of the duchy.

In the end, we received a ship and 3,000 lira. In my possession, there were still 200 manuscripts, all selected with the utmost care. Perhaps I wanted the Morisco to hold onto something of his family's heritage. Now, all that was left was to prepare to go to Spain.

Álvaro suggested that the vessel should continue to fly the Medici flag to ensure our safety in Spanish ports, owing to the strong relations between Tuscany and Spain at the time. We lingered a bit longer in Pisa while the ship was kitted out with supplies, which also gave us more time to select the seamen who would sail with us.

Choosing sailors was no simple matter. The code of behaviour on the high seas was dominated by mischief, impudence, and nosing around in the affairs of others. How else would a sailor act, imprisoned as he was in a confined space for weeks on end, all for the sake of a few handfuls of coins to be frittered away in the taverns of cities in which fate had thrown him ashore!

We had to come up with a story to keep the meddlesome sailors out of our business. At first, Álvaro didn't agree, but in the end Siraj's suggestion won him over. We would say that our boxes held the remains of Spanish soldiers who had lost their lives in the wars of the Holy Roman Empire, and that Siraj was the monk appointed to escort them back. And it turned out that this ruse summoned forth that high-minded and noble spirit that sailors were normally forced to bury beneath the rubble of their hard and miserable existences. And so this journey for Álvaro was the safest of any he'd had to date.

Siraj chose two among them to include in the execution of our plan. The first was a middle-aged man we found begging in the alleyways of the port. Siraj apologised to Álvaro, saying, "I found him breathing as saints do." At first, the middle-aged man refused to join us, because he hated the sea. "A sailor doesn't break his oar, but he might drop it and run off," he said, as if to justify his refusal. However, he quickly changed his tune when we told him that he would not have to do deck work, but instead would be required to watch over the soldiers' "remains" being repatriated to Spain.

As for the second one, he was a young lad whose mother was trying to gain Álvaro's sympathy as we were just about to ship out. She begged him to take her son, but Álvaro pushed back, saying that he didn't even have the mouth of a sailor! But the boy's mother convinced him that her son was strong and could curse up a storm and swear even by the "fish of the Nile." He would manage to take care of himself. "War took his father and brothers," she said, "and all I have left is him, and they will take him away too soon enough!" The young boy didn't stop crying at his impending separation from his mother, who was going to be all alone, but Siraj tried to cheer him up and managed to convince Álvaro that he would watch over him.

Álvaro had never been as happy as he was on the day we pushed out to sea. He had become an admiral, and we were now obligated to call him Cap'n Álvaro. Our ship soon joined up with a Spanish merchant convoy, ensuring the voyage would be safe from Barbary pirates, though I joked, "What do you have to fear? You're circumcised!"

Chapter 41

I could rhapsodise for days about the moment of departure from port. Watching the world shrink before me always gave me a sense of being in control. It was as if everything gradually reverted to that moment of creation, when nothing in the world existed except for me. This feeling of omnipotence would dissipate, however, each time I reached a new port of call. As the world slowly filtered back into view, it filled me with the fear of things ending and complexity enveloping me once again. That is what I had in mind when I suggested "the end" to Father Savila as a fifth Jesuit principle, whereby you summon all your energy for salvation as you feel the end approaching.

The world seems so small and simple—at least until disappointments begin to pile up. As children, we think we can grasp it all in our hands, but soon enough we discover just how much larger it really is. Years ago, leaving Truro for Amsterdam, I thought I was going to change the world. But then I fell victim to terrible beatings by guards and inmates, and it seemed as if I was nothing more than a delicate, ephemeral bubble—and one with a very limited chance of survival.

Curiosity alone is not enough to understand this world. We must put into practice what the Morisco called the "attack and retreat," fully aware that we are separated from the world yet connected to it at the same time. Doing so requires first a personal conviction that we are contingent—accidental—like the soap bubble. And second, we must not have any expectations of this world we inhabit and which, sooner or later, we are all destined to depart. And so for me, one of the signs of true wisdom was having a multitude of safe harbours in which to rest my heart.

After coincidence united my path with Álvaro's in Genoa last year, and I learned of his wish to one day captain a ship of his own, I began to think about returning to San Sebastián, though it took an entire year before I could actually sort out my next steps. And during that time, I kept everything to myself, not wanting God to mock my plans, as the Spanish say. At first, I thought it might be easier if I did as Father Mersenne suggested and make a trade with the French or Spanish, but I backed away from that when I remembered I had already told the French about the printing press. There now stood before me no other choice than to find a more direct approach, even if it was riddled with risks. Is that not the "attack and retreat" about which the Morisco spoke? That you enter into the world through the least expected door?

The plan I discussed with Álvaro, Siraj, and the driver entailed delivering a large wheeled box full of manuscripts accompanied by a sealed letter from Father Gaddis, requesting the prison warden allow Yusuf to examine, separate out, and index all of the texts. Yusuf would then conceal himself inside the box to be surreptitiously transported back to a carriage waiting to whisk him away to our ship, which would be ready to lift anchor immediately. The kink in the plan, of course, was that the box would likely undergo inspection both upon entering and exiting the prison.

The coachman offered up an idea popular among ironmongers in Marseille, who fashioned transport carts by designing a large box made up of multiple smaller ones that could be separated and rearranged in myriad configurations to accommodate and fit goods of any size or shape. I asked, "Could we construct a secret hiding place in the box that nobody could detect?" He said, "Yes, that's certainly possible."

According to his plan, the hiding place would only be created once all the other boxes were assembled and would be located at the bottom or on the side according to the design of the box. It would be like a cabinet opening from the side and so, when the smaller boxes were assembled, the back and bottom parts would naturally create a void that would go unnoticed. To reach it, one would have to disassemble the boxes. By doing so, the empty space would itself instantly vanish. It was nothing more than a game of voids. We drew diagrams for the box and its various components, but didn't begin building it until we had arrived in the city.

Siraj insisted on scouting out conditions at the prison before putting the plan into motion and thought it best to give Yusuf notice beforehand. I told Siraj that the only one who could help would be the stationer, but he had been banned from visiting Yusuf. So we set that aside as a backup idea for the moment. Siraj seemed quite optimistic we could pull this off, especially since the prison warden would recognise him from when he came to transfer me from the prison, and therefore would likely be more trusting though I wondered if he would remember him at all.

From the outset, Siraj stipulated that he did not want to be alone inside the prison, and so the middle-aged man and boy were chosen to go with him—despite my pushback against the idea, because Siraj might be forced to confront the guards and would need burly sailors by his side, not a middle-aged man and young lad. However, Siraj was planning to avoid confrontation altogether. Neither one would raise anyone's suspicions, and so Siraj let them in on the plan.

Our arrival during the Christmas festivities proved to be a boon for our mission, given how the prison made efforts to brighten and lighten things up for the prisoners during those days—perhaps as a way of engendering positive feelings toward Catholicism in the hearts of the unrepentant and non-Christians. As for myself, I set to the task of carving Father Gaddis' seal and studying his handwriting, based on the letter he had sent me when in Rome.

We reached the port of San Sebastián in mid-January and immediately got down to constructing the box on the ship's deck. Over several days, we experimented and adjusted the dimensions, always checking how easy it would be to undo, reassemble, and transport. I thought back to those years long ago, when I had handed my own fate over to the crates of the printing press, hoping to make it back to my country, but in the end to no avail. Would this plan now work and save my father Yusuf?

The day after we sailed into port, I met the stationer on the ship's deck. We learned that, just within the last few months, they had begun to allow him to visit Yusuf again, roughly coinciding with when Father Gaddis had recovered his seal. Perhaps out of gratitude, he had asked the warden to ease up on Yusuf and restore some privileges that had been previously cut off.

We also learned from him that tensions at the prison were high, following a prisoner revolt some months back. Twenty inmates had been executed, and the prison itself had become overcrowded, as the warden's burdens grew greater and greater. All the grand reforms he instituted ended up in total failure. I asked the stationer to go visit Yusuf and divulge what we were planning, but to not reveal that I was his son. He agreed at once and with an air of melancholy remarked that they had been delaying his liberation for more than ten years.

A week passed before he managed to visit the prison and let Yusuf in on the scheme. When he returned, he told us how conditions in prison had deteriorated. Yusuf suggested that we fill the box with a great number of manuscripts so that the work would require several days, allowing for the plan to be executed on one of them. Yusuf also mentioned that one of the guards could help on the condition that he escape with us, too. After the recent executions that had taken the life of the Saltman and nineteen others, Yusuf had begun to feel lonely and despondent.

Yusuf determined the plot would go into action over a period of three days. If they were unable to extricate him on the first and second days, then conditions on the third would definitely be favourable, because the warden would be off-site and occupied in the middle of town, dealing with another execution. The coachman suggested we use two different carriages so that the boxes didn't return in the same carriage they had arrived in. So we hired another carriage that would transport the boxes back to the coachman's carriage, which would be waiting along the escape route.

We executed the plan on the day Yusuf decided. The hired carriage was sent, driven by two of Álvaro's sailors. According to the plan, the boxes would be delivered along with Father Gaddis' letter one day prior to the arrival of the monks, and thus the boxes would remain with the warden. The crew had been trained to ensure the warden would notice the large box was actually separated into four boxes, which would be far too small for an adult man. I confirmed to Siraj that the warden wouldn't touch the boxes, but he indicated that keeping them with him would reassure him.

The following day, accompanied by the middle-aged man and lad, Siraj arrived and happily discovered that the warden still knew who he was and immediately offered them a large room connected to his office. Yusuf was summoned and, as soon as he arrived, he set about his work, whereupon he immediately realised that he was face to face once more with the manuscripts he had lost in the Pyrenees—a fact I forgot to ask the stationer to tell Yusuf. Stunned, he asked Siraj in the presence of the warden, "Where did you get these manuscripts?"

Siraj deftly answered, saying, "I am not authorised to inform you of their origin. And I don't believe the warden permits you to ask such questions. I can give you a reply once Father Gaddis agrees, but that will take days." Yusuf retreated into silence. Siraj told me what had transpired after returning to the ship, having been unable to execute the plan because the warden and a guard had been present the whole time. Siraj thought that Yusuf's silence was strange, and the confusion on his face was clear. Had the warden not been consumed with other things, he surely would have noticed immediately.

Chapter 42

"We shouldn't wait for the third day," I said. "Tomorrow, when you return to the prison, you will carry a letter from an anonymous sender. The letter will ask the warden to meet me at the stationer's shop in the early afternoon to discuss a conspiracy that will go down during the following day's execution. An attempt to smuggle out the prisoner." Siraj agreed and, as he went back to the prison on the second day, he passed the letter to the warden, claiming it was from an unknown person and had been handed to him as he made his way to prison that morning.

I managed to get the stationer to agree that, once the warden came to his shop, he would delay him there for as long as possible, in order to give Siraj and his team enough time to fully execute our plan. The merchant dithered, saying, "That could really put me in a tough spot later, and they will surely raise a complaint against me and could even arrest me!" To put those fears to rest, I offered that he escape with us, and we would compensate him for all his losses.

Upon his arrival the following day, Siraj immediately noticed that the guard from the previous day had been replaced. The warden left at the appointed time for the rendezvous with the unknown sender and was escorted by three of his personal guards, leaving two to remain outside his office. As soon as the coast was clear, he began to assemble the boxes to hide Yusuf. They waited a short time then made their exit, but not before swiping off the wall the painting of *Christ the Redeemer* and diagram by Archimedes, which I had asked Siraj to do because my heart was still so smitten by them.

The guard who was in cahoots with us spoke to one of the other guards, asking him to help bring out the box while telling the other to stay put, because the Morisco needed some more time to finish up his work and the monks couldn't wait any longer. Our guard then escorted them back to the carriage and over to two other guards, who were standing sentinel at the exit gate. He told them that, on orders of the warden, he was to accompany the monks onward. Along the way, the carriages were switched out, and then everyone made a mad dash to the ship.

The warden waited around in the merchant's shop for over an hour. As time eked by, and the anonymous person's delay wore on, doubt began to fill his mind and he raced back to the prison, but by then it was too late. Álvaro had hoisted the anchor and the ship had set sail out of the harbour the moment the stationer arrived.

As they made their way to the ship, Yusuf pestered Siraj for information about the source of the manuscripts, but he kept saying that Robert would tell him everything. So, as soon as his wobbly feet were able to stand on deck and his hands gripped the ship's railing as it pierced the sea toward distant horizons, he began to scrutinise all the faces congratulating him on his newfound freedom. He was searching for someone he knew, and the moment he saw me, he ran toward me, giving me an enormous hug as the ship burst into cheers.

"It's taken me a long time to get back to you," I said, as I showed him the painting of his wife and child. "And the secret was more complicated than I could have imagined." A flash of understanding swept across his face, and he asked, "Is the child a part of the tale?"

"Yes. He is your child."

He fell silent for what seemed an eternity as he pondered the portrait. Then, as he raised his head and gazed at me, he said, "This child is you. My gut was right. You aren't English."

"That's right, Father. I tried every possible way to reach you, but I couldn't. I ended up all the way in the Orient just to make my way back to you. And now, aunt Hind is impatiently waiting for you in Aleppo."

He embraced me again, this time for even longer, before we removed ourselves from the crowd and went off to a corner so I could tell him the rest of the tale. He didn't shed a tear, as crying would have been a far too inadequate expression of his pain and all that he had lost. His face, however, told a different story, especially as I related to him the death of my mother Najma and Hasan.

His sorrow was like a plaintive melody composed deep within a sailor's heart, one to which not even the planks of the ship were privy, though a melody nonetheless, and one capable of reminding him for a fleeting moment that feelings were more reliable than senses. It was as if something swelled within him, recreating a scene of somewhere he had been before, but in reality it was nothing more than deeply buried dreams as he faced his struggles alone. And yet through it all, at every twist and turn, those dreams managed to stay alive.

At least that is how my father Yusuf explained it as he described his life. "It's like there is a rope attached to the last beam I saw in the house we fled from forty years ago in Zaragoza, stretching all the way to the mast of this ship now. The rope became knotted up, one kink atop another, shortening the rope more and more until it seemed that life was just one great knotted jumble that suddenly untangled here on the deck of this ship. As if our house's beam was now here beside this mast and both were bitterly laughing at the gulf of intervening years between them."

Later, Siraj asked me, "Will your father return to Islam?"

"He never left it in the first place."

"So then you saved his religion."

"Who is to say? What I feel more is that I saved myself. But what about you? Do you still despise Arabs?"

"I don't think so. The moment I became free of Father Gaddis, I began to see Arabs with some sort of neutrality. That's why I'm here with you."

My father slipped away from us as sunset drew near, and he ensconced himself in an isolated corner of the ship, where he humbly stood praying his first Muslim prayers in many long years. He prostrated himself long enough that I began to be concerned. When he finished his prayers, he joined us on the captain's bridge.

The first thing my father Yusuf said was, "Allah takes precedence, then myself. The taste of prayer is sweeter when it's sincere."

Siraj asked, "So weren't the Spanish right to have doubts about you after all?"

"Perhaps yes, if they themselves bestowed the right to life," my father said. "The eternal problem of man is his ignorance of the divine realms. Who is able to hear the voice of God more clearly?"

Siraj fell silent before adding, "But the capacity to discern divine signs creates disparity among people."

"We hear the voice of God with our hearts and not our minds, and for that reason alone we mustn't measure this disparity with rational scales," my father said before falling silent once again. At that moment, I chimed in: "There is one thing left for us to do in Spain before we depart for Tuscany. We must recover the French printing press from the Monastery of the Divine Incarnation."

Siraj and I had conceived a plan, but it rested on us arriving at the monastery before news of my father's escape from prison had reached them. The plan would involve Siraj and I appearing before Father Gaddis to ask him for forgiveness and pardon. We would attempt to convince him that, without anyone to operate the printing press, they had no use for it and in fact returning it to the French in exchange for full compensation for its value along with Yusuf's release would be of far greater value to Spain.

However, Yusuf warned us of just how dangerous all this would be. "Gaddis is a man who takes every precaution. He left me imprisoned for 10 years just to be safe. It's best you forget the whole issue of the printing press."

"But I promised Father Yusuf Al-Musawwir in Aleppo."

"This can all be resolved another way without risking your lives."

Everyone agreed with Yusuf, especially Álvaro, who was uncomfortable with stopping in Bilbao because to do so would unnecessarily expose the ship and his dreams to danger. I agreed and gave up the idea. It would have been all too difficult.

Siraj and I still felt that it was not impossible, however. It would just take more time and planning—neither of which was available, especially as news of Yusuf's escape abetted by Siraj began to spread. And so we retraced our steps back to Florence.

Yet, for a time, my obsession with the printing press continued to rattle around in my head. I still hoped I would be able to recover it and bring it to Aleppo. How was I going to break the news to Father Yusuf Al-Musawwir?

I handed the rest of the money and manuscripts to my father. He refused to take any money, but he did select the manuscripts that were dearest to his heart and gave the remainder to me. When we arrived in Florence, we negotiated with Alessandro so I could hold onto this collection.

Mindful that Spain could still be looking for him, my father Yusuf Al-Hajari did not stay long in Florence. I was, however, able to keep my promise to Father Yusuf Al-Musawwir, and the very first set of Arabic letters we cast were for the press in Aleppo. I sent them with Yusuf to Aleppo, while I would bring the rest of the printing press myself later, so as not to raise any suspicion.

My father left for Aleppo before witnessing my marriage to Margherita, and we soon left Florence, returning to England as summer drew near. We stopped for two weeks in Leiden, then straightaway headed for Truro, manuscripts and Arabic type in tow. As summer faded into autumn, I received the first letter from Aleppo.

The letter was first sent to Florence and, from there, Vincenzo sent it on to me. It was from Father Yusuf Al-Musawwir and said:

Our dearest Robert bin Yusuf Al-Hajari

May God keep you safe wherever you may be, in the East or in the West. I write you this letter from Aleppo to let you know that we are awaiting you impatiently. Soldiers captured your father Yusuf just days after his arrival. Someone had informed the authorities that he had brought Arabic type to Aleppo, and he remained imprisoned for five months. However, they released him just a week ago after giving up on finding anything incriminating. Needless to say, the polarisation in Aleppo between those who support the printing press and those against it has only grown more fierce. Your aunt Hind and Sheikh Ibrahim Zini (who by the way was the one who placed the name of the archbishop Al-Khouri in the Library of Venice and brought your aunt Al-Hajari to us) have joined those in support of the printing press. We have even succeeded in persuading the naqib al-ashraf and Al-Sharif Al-Alami to our side, too. Conditions have now grown favourable for setting up a printing press here in Aleppo. Even the guild master of the calligraphers, Ahmad the dervish, is not opposed to it in principle. For now, the typeset is hidden in a safe place, so bring the remainder of the press to us when you can. The archbishop supports us, and it will be a joint Christian-Islamic printing press.

By the way, I found a message that I think belongs to you. It may have inadvertently fallen out while you stayed with us and was found by my son Naimat Allah. I pray that you forgive me for opening it, but I didn't understand anything in any case, because it appears to be written in Latin. I now return it back to you. I pray that the Lord bless and keep you.

We are waiting for you.

Love,

Yusuf Naimat Allah Al-Musawwir

Aleppo — 17 October 1643

When I opened the attached envelope, I found a bundle of papers inside from Father Mersenne to Galileo that had not yet been read. I had no idea how they made their way to Father Yusuf Al-Musawwir! I folded them up with the intention to return to Father Mersenne as I cast my eyes toward the painting that we had taken from the warden, and which now occupied the entire wall of my office in the printing shop of my father, George. Just then, Margherita entered, carrying with her some Arabic coffee. She asked me about the letter from Aleppo. I handed Father Mersenne's envelope to her. She opened it up to find numbered pages filled with diagrams of experiments accompanied by brief summaries below each one. Atop the first page, the father wrote a short phrase: "Ignorance is the enemy of mankind and experimentation is the mother of all knowledge." She looked back at me, wondering what it all meant. And, after taking a first sip of my coffee, I said to her, "I must get back to Aleppo!"

Christiaan James

Translator

Christiaan James is an American diplomat and literary translator. He holds a degree in Middle Eastern Studies from Harvard University and has lived and worked throughout the Middle East and North Africa, including Yemen, Tunisia, and Egypt. His first translation of Yemeni author Badr Ahmad's Five Days Untold was longlisted for the Republic of Consciousness prize in 2022.

Mohammed AlAjmi

Author

A writer and a poet from Oman, Mohammed AlAjmi is a researcher interested in the philosophy of science and artificial intelligence and has published works on consciousness, enlightenment, and the philosophy of criticism. He holds a bachelor's in Mathematics from Sultan Qaboos University (Oman) and Computer Science from the University of Southern Queensland (Australia), in addition to having studied the philosophy of digital sciences at the University of Tilburg (Netherlands). A founding member of the Omani Society of Writers's philosophy committee, he also helped establish the Rawaq Muscat literary salon. His first novel, The Secret of the Morisco, was longlisted for the Sheikh Zayed Book Award in 2022.